Ultimate Obsession

Milton Jones

22 August Press   **Charlottesville, Virginia**

Ultimate Obsession

If you see them, and you do not cry when you see them, you do not see them.

—*Milton Jones*

Part One

As I write these words, probably no more than a few thousand persons have read the poems of James Campbell. Even more than his being the first man of my adulthood, James Campbell was a true poet. And you never forget a true poet.

Never.

—Elizabeth Brewer

Chapter One

I first noticed him in philosophy class, arguing with the professor. No, not arguing, lecturing to the professor. He never argued. He spoke with an intellectual confidence that was as much a part of him as his sandy hair and piercing blue eyes. "The gaining of power is inborn in human beings," he said, "while the love of beauty can be killed." From this point, their discussion veered from Maimonides to Spinoza to Kant. His memory was astounding and I wondered was that the real definition of genius? Just a good memory?

My memory lacked genius, as my professors were quick to point out. "The feminine brain simply cannot retain facts," my organic chemistry professor liked to point out from his lectern before I dropped the class. "This is not an admonishment, just an observation," he added as if this acknowledgement turned him from a brut to a gentleman. In the autumn of 1948, I was one of a select few women attending the University of Virginia as an undergraduate who was not confined to nursing or education degrees. I was a history major with a minor in philosophy. Leaving Rouss Hall, I watched the colors of the Blue Ridge Mountains swing between the powerful green of summer and the wilting beauty of autumn. There was a peculiar kind of chill in the air which gave newness to things I'd seen before.

The path to my next class was narrow. Overhead the merging branches broke the afternoon sunlight. I hurried by a man—I never bothered to ask his name—who had been severely injured in the war, perhaps in France or during the battle of Midway in the Pacific. His face was damaged and his empty right sleeve waved in the wind like a limp flag. I hurried by, avoiding his eyes.

Nineteenth century German history. I took my seat in back,

beside the windows. My class load was heavy and thankfully this was my last class of the week. I was exhausted and overwhelmed, and it was only September. Professor Emmett Schmied was a small man of ritualistic precision. He was the personification, if not a caricature, of German control. Talking stopped when he entered the room. He opened his briefcase, pulled out a black roll book and placed it on the lectern. I had heard that he endured much harassment during the war, swastikas painted on his car, threats of violence, but today he calmly studied the class, recording the absentees. He returned the roll book to his briefcase and placed it with great care on the floor under the desk. He faced the class. "Last time we were talking about the activities of Prince Metternich during the year eighteen thirty-six," he said. I took notes the best I could. Professor Schmied considered Metternich a visionary realist, not a cynical and reactionary parasite of power.

My mind wandered. I thought about the injured man I had passed on the path. He couldn't be more than thirty. Was he married? How would it be as his wife? The war had caused so much suffering. Germany had suffered, too, of course. Reconciling philosophy class with history class went beyond my comprehension. A new understanding needed to emerge to balance the beauty of nineteenth century against the destructiveness of the twentieth.

As I gathered my books and purse, I was startled by the sandy-haired man from my philosophy class. His eyes were piercing to the point of being intimidating, until he smiled. His gap-toothed smile was awkward and childlike.

"Are you German or English?" he asked.

"What?" I stammered in my obviously southern drawl.

He offered his hand, "My name is James Campbell."

Hesitantly, I took his hand. "And I'm Elizabeth Brewer."

"Yes, I know your name."

"What?" I said again as I pulled back my hand.

His awkward grin reappeared. "Nothing is without thought."

The university formed an almost perfect rhomboid. One side

abutted Charlottesville, a charming old Virginia town, another side was next to farmland, and the other two sides gradually faded into a dense forest. We walked on the sidewalk along the old brick wall which separated the college from the town. James ran his fingers along the wall until a yellow mutt scampered in front of us and urinated on a fireplug.

"They're ugly, those things, I hate them." James said.

I was shocked. "You hate dogs?!"

"Not the dog," he said, "the hydrant. Its cap resembles a church." I chuckled lightly. He was by far the most irreverent man I had ever met. "Imagine this," he said. "The dog may be run over by a street cleaner. Now imagine the church as a dog. It might be killed by some kind of church-killing street cleaner."

"The hydrant has its function," I said, playfully.

His voice was soft, his tone conciliatory. "I didn't intend mockery. You are right. Sometimes my attitude is a little flippant. Really, I don't care very much about churches or religions. One religion is probably as good as another."

"Don't let my roommate hear you say that," I said.

James took me to Bonner's Diner. The diner was too quiet and too out of the way to be popular. The rough wooden floor was scarred, unvarnished and unwaxed. Only one of the five round, marble-top tables was occupied, by a couple talking quietly. The sign on the wall behind the glass counter read: TABLES FOR WHITES ONLY. The diner was cold and I sat down without removing my coat. James sat across from me.

"The owners were an elderly couple who live over their store," James said. "The husband cooks and the wife run the cash register. Their only children, two sons, were killed in the war."

I pulled my coat close around me. "That's so sad."

Mr. Bonner arrived to take our order. He had the large, low belly of elderly men. "How about a coke and a roll?" James asked.

"I'd rather have an orange drink," I said, "no roll, please." Mr. Bonner quickly returned with our drinks and a roll for James.

As I sipped my orange drink, James starred at me. "I don't like your name," he said. "Elizabeth Brewer. You don't look like an Elizabeth. It's too long. Never fits well. Who is Elizabeth? *What is she that all the swains commend her?* Beth. That's the name I would give you. That name is like Maud, but for the twentieth century. It's romantic and just a little docile and inefficient. Elizabeth Brewer sounds like a female gynecologist. Beth Brewer. No. That's like a monstrous imitation of Spencer, and I never liked Spencer anyway."

He repeated my new name as if he were repeating a sentimental poem. "Beth. Beth. Beth. So pretty." He touched my fingertips. His hands were soft, like a man of thought but no action. He was too young to be a veteran. Lucky. I doubt he would have survived combat and the way my brothers recounted the horrors of basic training, I doubt James would have survived that either. He reached into his pocket. "You don't mind if I smoke, do you?" He lit a cigarette before I could answer.

"No, of course not," I said, even though I hated cigarettes.

James smoked half the cigarette then crushed the rest in the ash tray. "Your face is thin and you have red hair," he said, appraising me as if I were an apricot at the market. "A woman with red hair and a fat face looks bad. But you have red hair and thin cheeks so you have a simple loveliness that many find appealing."

Was I blushing? I held my purse tight in my lap, anxious to leave, and at the same time afraid that if I left, I'd never see him again. "You sound like you've been drinking," I said.

He lit another cigarette and held it delicately, like Humphrey Bogart in *Key Largo*. "You have a pretty face. Clean. Pure. Sensuous. Pure sensuality is beautiful and you are a sensuous woman. The prettiness of a girl and the sensuous beauty of a woman. You don't dance, do you?"

No man had ever spoken to me like this. I felt light headed. "No," I said, "Not often."

"No, of course you don't dance. Dancing is a mechanical thing, and a truly sensuous person could never move himself in mechanical patterns. Beethoven was a very sensuous man and a horrible dancer. I once read that his music fell on him as if it had some kind of Platonic existence of its own and came on him like a horde of slaves out of that cave. Beethoven could neither avoid it nor understand it."

James spoke with a seriousness that frightened and intrigued me. I touched my cheek, wanting to hide my blush. "I've never thought of myself as a sensuous person. And except for not dancing, I have nothing at all in common with Beethoven."

James laughed. "Will you see me tonight?"

"Tonight?" I was confused. "We just met." I stood up from the table. "I can't, I have—."

"Do you want me to walk you home?"

I fastened my coat and put on my gloves. "You don't need to do that."

"Then I'll see you next week," he said. And just as unexpected as he had arrived into my life, he left. I watched as he walked out the diner, shutting the door behind him.

Chapter Two

The sky was darkening and it was growing colder. The cold wind penetrated my thin coat as I hurried home, thankful that tomorrow was Saturday. I shared an off-campus apartment with my roommate, Gloria Laxton. She looked like one of those rugged northern European peasant-women I'd seen in the newsreels, and just like those sad, displaced Polish refugees. Gloria was always talking about food and money. Her only redeeming quality, if one could consider it redeeming, was that she savored gossip more than anyone I knew. Most of the students ignored her even though she was a senior and maintained an A average with no apparent effort. Her major was mathematics—unusual for a girl in 1948.

I knew Gloria would be waiting for me with dinner prepared. She opened the door just as I was searching through my purse for my key.

"Tell me now, where have you been!?" she demanded. "Out playing? You know I've been worried sick over you."

I tossed my books on the sofa. "I'll talk later. I want to eat something and I want to get out of these clothes and take a hot bath."

"Well, dinner's ready, Elizabeth." She exchanged her harsh inquiry for sarcasm. "And it's been ready an hour, but you go ahead, throw down your books. Get your coat off. Get a hot bath. Don't worry about me. I don't have anything to do except warm things up for you." She led the way to the kitchen.

"Wonderful." I said, not taking the bait. "What's for dinner?"

"I'll surprise you," but Gloria was incapable of keeping a secret. She grinned coyly, as if I was a boy she liked. "No, I think I'll tell you now. How does meatloaf and baked apples sound?"

"Sounds pretty good." I tossed my coat on my bed and followed her to the kitchen. "Need any help?"

"No," Gloria said, "Not a thing." She whistled a happy tune as she opened the oven and checked the meatloaf. "Some say meatloaf is better warmed up a second time, but I say meatloaf is better fresh out of the oven."

I plopped heavily at the table. The baked apples were already on the table and smelled delicious. "I'm sorry I was late." I unfolded my napkin.

Gloria pulled the meatloaf out of the oven and placed it beside the baked apples. "Do you expect your family this weekend?"

"Mother would have written me if she planned to come up," I said.

Both Gloria and I had been reared by religious parents and it was my turn to say grace. "Heavenly Father, bless this food to the nourishment of our bodies and the enrichment of our lives. We ask this in Christ's name. Amen."

I handed Gloria my plate. "Now," Gloria said as she served the meatloaf and apples, "I want you to tell me why you were late."

"Do I have to have a reason?" I said as I enjoyed the apples. Gloria was an excellent cook.

"If alpha is a condition of beta, then beta implies alpha."

I took a bite of the meatloaf before answering, "You mean if Napoleon's defeat at Waterloo was dependent on his being born in 1750, then his being born in 1750 meant he must be defeated at Waterloo."

"I'll believe it if you tell me why you were late."

"But Napoleon was born in 1769."

"Elizabeth Brewer, I don't care when or why or how Napoleon was born, but I know when somebody's trying to get rid of something that smells."

I shrugged, "I'm too tired to play this game." I wanted to change the subject, "Do you have a seminar meeting tomorrow?"

"At eight-thirty." She served herself some apples and meatloaf. "Elizabeth," she said.

"Yes."

"I love you, Elizabeth. I love you like we were sisters," she hesitated, trying to find the words. "More! I love you more than my own sisters. You and my books are all I have. Do you know what I mean? We have been good friends for such a long, long time." She stared at me so intensely, as if she were studying every hair on my head, as if she were the summer sun burning my skin, as if I were the meatloaf and apples and she was starving.

I had to make her stop. "I met a fellow at school this afternoon. We went to Bonner's and I had an orange drink. That's why I was late."

She sat back in her chair, shoulders slumped. "A date? With a man?"

"No."

"Was he one of those Jake-of-quick-hands?"

"No, not at all. He asked me out but I turned him down."

"Why?" Gloria asked, almost tearfully, as if I had refused a vacation in Paris for both of us. "Tell me if I know him. What's his name? Tell me about him, Elizabeth."

"He is tall and he has light hair." I said, "And I would say he's fairly nice looking."

"And why did you turn him down when he wanted a date?"

"I simply had a feeling that it would be wrong. That's all. He seemed wrong for me." I finished my dinner and took my plate to the crowded sink. Gloria was a good cook but a terrible housekeeper. "I'll wash the dishes tonight." I grabbed an apron and filled the dishpan.

"What is wrong with him?" She asked, following me to the sink. She stood beside me as I cleaned.

"There's nothing wrong with him, Gloria, he's just not right for me."

"Tell me why not!" She insisted, almost begging.

I couldn't understand why this mattered to her. "Gloria, please, I don't know exactly. I don't want to talk about him anymore. You know how this kind of talk, your constant asking about my personal life, makes me uncomfortable."

She turned away from me, pretending apathy. "Will you go home for Thanksgiving?"

"I'm sure I will. What about you? If you don't go home, come with me; mommy and daddy always want to have you."

She leaned against me like a scolded puppy. "I would rather go with you, Elizabeth. I don't want to go home. My mother's people are coming down from Maryland. You know how Grandmother Fowler is. It won't be long before she'll have to move in with one of her children. Uncle Earl and his wife don't want her, and she used to fight with her other daughters like they stank of cat pee."

"If your grandmother does move in with your parents, what does that matter to you? You won't be going back to that house, will you? Certainly not if you choose graduate school."

"A single woman can never count on anything," she said wistfully.

I finished the dishes and gave her a hug. "Get your laundry together. In the morning I'll wash it. Do we have soap powder and bleach?"

Gloria checked the floor cabinet. "Enough. Did you know the price of soap powder was up two cents? Here's the old price marked out. It's funny I didn't see this when I bought it."

Chapter Three

I slept with the window opened two inches; the way my mother believed would assure strong lungs. My bedroom was cold in the morning when I woke. I shut off the alarm, closed the window and turned on the radiator. I pulled on my robe and hurried to the bathroom. Gloria had left her laundry beside her bedroom door, just as I had asked. After breakfast I gathered our wash and headed downstairs to the basement.

The washroom was clean, drab, and empty. Taut clotheslines were strung through eyebolts between the long walls. At the far end of the basement the door to the furnace room was padlocked. A deep laundry tub and a wringer-style washer were beside the stairs.

I separated four loads and started the first load in the laundry tub and then moved the wet bundle to the washer. I had just finished and was hanging up this first load to dry when our neighbor Mrs. White came downstairs searching for one of her children. She had five. "You seen Herman down here, Elizabeth?" she asked. Herman was her youngest.

I shook my head, "I haven't seen him."

"I'll tan that boy." Mrs. White sat heavily on the steps and watched me. I couldn't blame her. With five children, she seldom had a moment of peace. "You don't know her, but Mildred, that's my sister, she's four years younger than me, she's getting a divorce from her husband. His name was Alfred Turner. Maybe you heard me talking about him. He likes people to call him Alf." She snorted sarcastically, "Alf, what a silly name for a grown man. I told her that when she married him. I told her he was no good, but she wouldn't listen." She looked around and lowered her voice. "Alfred's a drinking man, you see, and now he's gone and deserted her and the kids and he's having himself one big time living with some woman in Hampton."

"That's terrible," I said. If I didn't get rid of Mrs. White soon, she'd tell me her life's story. "I'll send Herman to you if I see him."

"Thank you, Elizabeth, I'll tan that boy's behind when I find him. But do you know what that man had the nerve to ask my sister?"

"What?" I asked just to be polite. I wasn't really interested. Mrs. White's family was always in an uproar.

"He had nerve enough to ask her if she was taking good care of his children. Can you imagine that? And him living with that hussy in Hampton."

I started the next load of laundry, "Your sister's husband must send her money to support his family."

Mrs. White put her hands on her hips. "Believe me he'd better! But he wouldn't if he didn't have to, I say that now and I mean it! The only reason he gives Mildred a cent is because he knows she'd get herself a lawyer if he didn't support her and the kids."

I returned to hanging the wet clothes. I had to use the laundry stick to push a large air bubble out of one of Gloria's sheets.

"I never saw that man but he smelled of whiskey. When a young man takes to hard drinking, he's got something that's weakly inside him like he's crying after his momma. Mark my word, that's what he is going to be doing when he gets some age on him, too. He'll never be no good for himself or anybody else. God help my poor sister for being a fool enough to marry him." She leaned back on her arms, her legs stretched apart. Her stockings were rolled at her ankles and I could see the spider veins and black hair on her legs. My stomach churned. "Boys!" she exclaimed as if it were a curse, "Never have boys, Elizabeth. They're not worth half what it cost you."

"My mother used to say, 'I wouldn't take a million dollars for either of those boys, but I wouldn't give a nickel for another one'," I replied.

"Your mother is a smart woman," Mrs. White said. She stood wearily. "I'd better get to looking. If I don't find that boy, there's no telling what he might get himself into."

After she left, I hooked the drain nozzle to the edge of the sink and released the drain. I was happy to be alone.

As the laundry dried in the basement, I studied in the living room. Gloria returned from her seminar and dropped on the couch beside me. She listlessly unbuttoned her coat. "You don't look like you particularly enjoyed yourself today." I said.

"I could cuss. Endless, stupid talk. Everything about school is getting me down this year. I see you did the wash. Thanks."

"At least it's not raining," I said.

"I'm starving," she said. "And all we have to eat is leftover meatloaf. If we had the money, I'd throw it out. If and if then if. Money is just like mathematics, everything is sat on by a heavy-tailed-if."

I laughed. "Heavy-tailed-if! That's a funny saying. Gloria, you're just in as sour mood. We both know your morality wouldn't let you throwaway food."

"I can dream. One day maybe I will. I can see myself buying a twenty-five pound turkey and eating the breast meat then throwing all the rest away, just to know how it feels."

Rugby Road was narrow and very beautiful, with broad trees and old houses. Gloria and I walked arm in arm in the late autumn splendor to the grocery. Children skated, stretching their arms out wide to catch the breeze. Others rode bicycles and a group of boys were throwing tops. I loved to hear their laughter.

Silverstein's grocery was on Jackson Street. It had two tall windows upstairs where the owners—an elderly couple and their adult son, Benjamin—lived. A stunted tree stood in the grassless gap between the curb and the walk, one of its roots had broken the walk. The screen door bore a bread advertisement. The inner door was solid.

Inside, the store was too warm. The odors of sawdust, raw meat, smoke and vinegar were too strong. Strips of old flypaper, still full from the summer, hung down from a single long string. There was nothing particularly unusual about the store, yet I was always put off by a foreign and ancient quality, as if this ought to be in a primitive part of western Asia. I walked slowly behind Gloria as she took a single cart. Two boys and one girl were bumping one another and drinking soft drinks.

"I mean that!" I heard from outside. I glanced and saw a group of white men talking. One of the white men was pointing a chewed cigar at an old black man who expressionlessly looked back as if he had not heard him. Another white man, whose gnarled face resembled boat wood attacked by tunneling saltwater worms, put his hands under his long coat and lifted his loose pants. He said, "I voted for Strom Thurmond last year. Will again in fifty-two, God don't take me. You talking about old man Tyson a while back; I knew old man Tyson's daddy. His name was Jack. I remember like it was yesterday the day Jack Tyson shot that nigger girl in her foot 'cause she spat on him. That nigger girl never walked right again after that. She won't but about ten year old. He was one mean rotten old man, Jack Tyson, likely the meanest man I ever knew, and his son's just like him, you know that's so."

The man with the cigar was rubbing the base of his neck, his cigar moving nervously in his mouth. "Yessir, Mr. Cooper." he said. "I went with the Democrats again. Always have. I voted for Harry Truman, but if Thurmond wants to run again, he'll take my vote"

Gloria was breaking stem remnants from string beans, examining each bean pod individually. A young blonde woman with her arms crossed over her purse was at the counter waiting for Mr. Silverstein to bag her groceries. Mr. Silverstein said something to her and she took her bag of groceries and went out. Mr. Silverstein nibbled on a white cracker. I could not remember seeing Mr. Silverstein when he was not eating either crackers or bread. He ate with concentration, as if he deliberated before putting each cracker into his mouth, as if he could take no pleasure in the eating. His age must have been sixty, but his skin was smooth and soft. He was bald and so round-shouldered and bent that his neck projected almost perpendicularly from his body.

Mrs. Silverstein, a semi-invalid, sat motionless in a chair by the door. She seemed much older than her husband. Her hair was gray and always pulled to a tight knot in back. The Silverstein's son, Benjamin, sat on a stool, pricing cans. Benjamin looked like his father, but unlike his father he never smiled or said a word to Gloria or me.

Gloria asked me to get some yams. "About five pounds. I'm thinking of yam cobbler tonight."

"Do you realize how much sugar that means?"

"You think I shouldn't be eating yam desserts?"

"Neither of us."

"Go on. Get them now and when these are gone I won't want any more for a long time."

I did as Gloria wished and picked out five good size yams.

Mrs. Silverstein began making a loud clicking noise. "Are you girls going to buy something?"

"Yes, ma'am," I said as I put the bag of yams on the scale. Benjamin marked the bag as I waited for Gloria.

"Buy some tomatoes today. Look at the tomatoes," said Mrs. Silverstein. Gloria frowned when she picked up one of the tomatoes. I knew she would not buy anything not on her list. Mrs. Silverstein looked back to the door.

The man chewing on the cigar pointed at Mr. Silverstein. "White without and black within, a nigger in a white man's skin."

Mr. Silverstein ignored the taunts and greeted us warmly, "Hello, Miss Brewer. Good Afternoon, Miss Laxton." He handed his son an order that had just come in. "Have this order together by three-thirty."

Mrs. Silverstein waddled over and snatched the order out of Benjamin's hand. "Let me read that order! Who's is this?"

"Mrs. Cobb," Mr. Silverstein said.

Mrs. Silverstein grunted as she read the list and grunted even louder when she had finished. "A whole chicken. They don't have money, and they're too good for wings and necks, I suppose. That's why the Gentiles don't keep their money; they're always feeding their stomach with rich food. And we're supposed to pay for it, I guess. We run a charity? There's charity at the Salvation Army. "

"They'll pay," said Mr. Silverstein, laboriously.

His wife grunted again. "When?"

Her husband ignored her. He took the paper from her and gave it to Benjamin and finished our order.

Chapter Four

The white clouds on the horizon reminded me of the mountains. The sky was like blue vellum this Sunday afternoon as Gloria and I walked slowly home from church. We took the short way over the campus. I was happy to walk. "Let's go see Ameele," I said.

"Who?"

"Ameele Clark," I said. Other than Gloria, Ameele was closer to me than anyone at the college. Ameele had many friends, most of whom I knew no more than casually. Her major was art and she had labored self-consciously as an artist. The only thing in life she treated seriously was her art. She lived according to her own order.

When we arrived and Gloria met Ameele there was immediate mutual dislike. Ameele's family had long been wealthy whereas Gloria counted every penny. Ameele's home was a material reflection of herself. Lush and colorful. The walls from the wainscoting to the high ceiling were hung with many paintings. She invited us into her studio where the light was good through a picture window. The walls were eclectically decorated with a crucifix, a shelf holding a fat, sitting Buddha, to whose protruding navel Ameele had tied a blue ribbon with a bow, and a miniature cow's bell, and two Picassos prints: *The Lovers* and *Girl before a Mirror*.

Ameele was elegant and had an intelligent face, like Vivien Leigh in *Fire Over England*. Her hair was dark and hung down her back. Her eyes seemed to cut through objects and people. She spoke little as she showed us her latest works. Color, more than subject or design, was a fascination for her. She spent many hours studying variations of color. She loved bright, strong color, with complex gradations merging into lines of darkness.

Several of her paintings had been shown and sold. She did not need money, of course, which added to Gloria's irritation. Ameele's painting of a church graveyard looked familiar, like something I had seen around town. She traced the yellow of her painting to the point where it tapered into obscurity about a dark red. "My father sent another case of Sauterne," she said. "I opened the bottle just this morning." Sauterne was Ameele's only alcohol and she drank a great deal of it. She offered to share. Gloria, as expected, refused and opted for a glass of water instead. Ameele was seldom reluctant to discuss art. "How do you like my newest paintings?" she asked.

"I like this one more than some others you've done," I said as I sipped the Sauterne. "I prefer it because it's simpler than the others and much more definite."

The painting was not at all an accurate representation. The church was proportionally much too large and it was distorted out of shape, as if the power of the colors altered the structure. The trees looked like objects of a colorful dream. The only person, a man standing beside a gravestone, was a thing of colors without life. This did not surprise me at all. Ameele seldom painted people.

"This is a new direction for me," Ameele said. "I want to be more objective. I went to the churchyard about twenty times, and each time I made a sketch and studied the colors and shadows. Every time it was different, but something about the place itself does not change, something that's inside and that was what I want to paint."

Gloria drained her glass of water, "That's all unbearably lucid," she said dryly.

Ameele laughed.

"Isn't there a contradiction?" I asked. "Or is it my imagination? Something about your explanation seems either missing or wrong."

"Have another glass of wine and won't notice the contradiction, Elizabeth," Ameele said. She glanced at Gloria, "you can have some, too."

"I don't drink alcohol," Gloria sulked. "All of this," she waved at the multitude of paintings, "is like something out of Kant that you can read fifty times and not understand." And to me she added, "I want to go home."

Ameele rebuffed Gloria as if she were an irritating gnat. "Theory. Every artist must follow a theory. But an artistic theory is not a scientific theory: it's much closer to a political theory. Mine is that I want a blending of my memories of the colors and shapes, not of the colors and shapes themselves. Some artists use photographs."

"What would you call that, something like sacrilege or idol-worship?" I asked.

Ameele laughed and I blushed. "An interesting idea."

"You're patronizing me, Ameele."

"If I am, ignore me. No, not sacrilege. Calling a photograph an idol gives it too much significance. I compare an artist's using photographs to a doctor's using a textbook in the operating room." Ameele removed her apron and hung it on a hook. "No comparison is perfect." she said. "I've got to clean my hands. You'll stay for dinner, won't you?"

We sat at the small table in the kitchen and ate canned soup and brown bread. Ameele did not like the bland taste of white bread. "How well do you know Ma Bradder?" she asked.

"Hardly at all," I answered. All I knew was that Ma Bradder lived in the great dilapidated hilltop house whose gables were visible above the trees from our apartment. She wore shabby clothing and wandered aimlessly about the campus, silently moving her lips.

"You've never talked with Ma Bradder?"

"No," I said and looked at Gloria, who was still eating. She shook her head.

"I'm surprised," Ameele said. "I would think you'd find her interesting. I don't care about her, but her old house is grotesque and wonderfully ridiculous. I've decided to paint it."

"Have you now."

"Yes, inside and outside, I see a quality. It's like something alive, something that wants to be petted, touched. But people don't want to touch it."

"Like an old child in an orphanage." Gloria grumbled as she ate.

"Yes, exactly," Ameele enthused. "I expect to be working in or about the house for at least two months, probably three. I don't know if I can stand Ma Bradder that long."

"Or an idiot," Gloria added. I should have hushed her but she went on. "I remembered when I was about twelve to fifteen the sister of a friend of mine was an idiot. She was able to speak intelligibly so her mother made little effort to isolate her from the other children. It was terrible. They took turns taunting her and slapping her ears. She was so homely and so without defense and so pathetic that she was almost beautiful."

"That's lovely," Ameele said, which seemed to startle Gloria. I doubt that anyone had had ever told Gloria she was lovely before.

Gloria put down her fork and engaged with Ameele. "Tell me more about Ma Bradder," she said. I was glad to see that she was warming up to Ameele.

Ameele was happy to have an audience. "The interior of the house is even more fascinating than the exterior. Marvelous old furniture. The parlor is my favorite room. I want you two to see it. There's a mantle over a closed tile fireplace, the most fascinating colors and design. And an enormous carved mirror over the mantle. The fireplace, the mantle and the mirror are the purest merging of color and shape I've ever seen, totally without any symbolism. Think about the churchyard, every inch has hidden symbolism. If I go to complete abstraction, I lose touch with reality, but if I use a tangible subject, I retain some symbolism. But with this painting, if I can do it correctly, I can break the dilemma, then, I'm sure it'll be one of the best things I've done yet."

"Heavy-tailed if," Gloria snorted, "but what of Ma Bradder? How does she live?"

"Of that entire house she actually lives in only two rooms, and they're filled with stacks of newspapers, broken dishes, all sorts of junk. You've seen her hunting through trash cans. She collects writing paper for her imaginary children. I have no idea who they are. The old woman's still living in the Depression."

"She must be close to eighty," I said.

"I don't know how old she is. Maybe she's eighty. She's strong as a bulldog, and she's half crazy. She had hold of my shoulder as soon as she opened the door. She pulled me into the house, literally. When she told me to sit, that's what I did."

Gloria and I laughed, and we talked about Ma Bradder until Ameele drifted back to art.

"The dust and the colors. Imagine: The dust over the colors and the colors forcing themselves through the dust. Imagine how much power was necessary. That power has a quality of its own, at least partially apart from the colors. And that power was always the same."

I was not uninterested in the concepts she was trying to tell me, which at the time seemed neither obscurantist nor tangible, but approaching both extremes simultaneously. More than Ameele's words were her insistence, which I resented, that we listen to her talk about art when we wanted to discuss Ma Bradder. I interrupted. "Why don't you paint Ma Bradder's portrait?"

Ameele scowled. "I want to want to paint her, but good portraiture is difficult and she is a mysterious woman. I don't know her well enough to capture her mystery."

"Maybe I can help."

Chapter Five

I was not able to sleep that night. At midnight I left my room and sat alone in the heavy leather chair in the living room. I was profoundly unhappy. I could very clearly see Ma Bradder and Mrs. White and Mrs. Silverstein as if they were in the room with me. Each was old and each was sitting as I was sitting. I was terrified of becoming old. I prayed to God to that I wouldn't become like these women. I was only twenty-two years old, but something within me was changing. Aloneness went through me like cold embarrassment, like being naked before my brothers.

There was a cloud of moonlight in the room. The water pipe noises seemed organic, as if they were alive. I was occasionally startled by a truck on the street. I held my robe around me tightly. I pushed myself away from the thoughts of the three women. I began to think about my own more immediate future. I did not want to teach. I knew I could never be a good teacher. I had no impossible problems, and would grow into whatever might happen.

I returned to bed and lay with the sheet and blankets pulled to my throat. The window was open but the fresh air didn't clear my head. Irrational anxiety flowed through my body. I was not able to sleep. I thought of the women in my life. My mother, Gloria, Ameele. Perhaps I was drawn to Ameele because, like Gloria, she seemed only incidentally a woman. Even Ameele's name was masculine, French, the spelling altered. My body drew away from the mere chance of being touched by a man. Was something wrong with me? How many women have asked themselves that question?

Then, quite vividly, I remembered James Campbell. I felt at once very calm and safe, but anticipatory. I remembered every word he had said to me and every gesture he had made. He had called me a sensuous woman. The idea was foreign to me, but at that moment I did feel sensuous. I was quiet and tired, and I finally felt myself falling asleep.

Chapter Six

Tuesday afternoon I was carrying my notebook and the first volume of the Memoirs of Prince Metternich, thinking about how to attract James' attention. When I saw James, I smiled shyly. I was sure I had offended him.

He immediately walked over, as if he were expecting me. "Will you walk with me, Beth?" he asked. I nodded and we went again to Bonner's Diner. I was nervous and barely spoke. As usual, the shop was very quiet. James ordered a coke for himself and an orange drink for me.

"I'm sorry about Friday," I said. "I behaved like an infant."

James looked into my eyes but made no assuring motion. Oddly, I found this comforting, as if I understood his silence. "Tell me about yourself," he said. "Tell me about your family."

I spoke with unease. "My family," I stammered. "Well, I'd call them ordinary or average. They aren't special except to me, of course. I have two older brothers, Tom and Lewis. My mother's first baby, a girl, died at eighteen months. My home, we have a few acres, about three acres, south of Petersburg. It's just a garden; you couldn't call it a farm. I'm sure you'd like our house. Daddy's a carpenter, the old-fashioned kind of workman who does a job right or he doesn't do it all. He learned the trade from his father, and granddaddy was the same kind of man. The two of them built our house. That was before I was born. Daddy would rather die I think than sell that house. He told me they carved a message behind the mantle, saying that the men who build this house are better men than those who will tear it down."

I took a breath, surprised that I had talked so much. I was usually the listener, not the talker.

"Your parents sound like good people. I want to see them."

"I'm sure you can meet them at Thanksgiving or Christmas if

you wish."

"I want to see them now, through your description." James' studied my face. His piercing blue eyes seemed to remove my will.

"You want me to describe them?" I asked.

"Do this, Beth. Try to see your father the way he was when you were a child, and tell me about him then."

I lowered my eyes. "Daddy is an honest man. He is religious, too, but when you know him, you understand that he was an honest man who was also a religious man."

James said, "He's honest from within, not because he has a theory of honesty."

I talked freely, "I remember when I was a little girl, I must have been about eight, I had a friend named Peter. He told me his father was going to make a kite for him. I had never wanted a kite, but if Peter was going to have one, I wanted one, too. So I asked Daddy, and Daddy said he would make the kite when he had the free time. Peter's father never made his kite, but the next Saturday Daddy asked if I still wanted mine. We made it in the morning and flew it that afternoon. I'll never forget that kite. It was five sided, about as tall as I was, and it had two long tails." I glanced up at James to make sure he was still listening. "Children remember that sort of thing. It makes yes and no mean something real. That's how Daddy is, if he says he will do a thing, it means he knows he can do it. And he always does it."

"Do you think you're like your father?" James asked.

"I probably am."

"You say that casually?"

"Uncertain, not casual." I sipped my orange drink. "I know my feelings about honesty have come from my father. And my mother, too. I used to be terribly naive. I expected everyone to be like my parents. Here at the college there's so much deception and self-deception. I accept that some people lie for gain, but the lying for nothing, that's still hard for me to understand." I looked away. I wished there was a window to stare out. "My vision of honesty isn't as clear as it used to be. Daddy has a much clearer idea of honesty than I do now. He's clear and certain about everything he does. Hundreds of times I've seen him work, always the same way. Before he does anything he studies the job, you should see him. He gets a totally calm look. He knows exactly what he is doing before he begins. And his work is always perfect."

James rubbed his fingertip on the lip of the soda bottle and the glass hummed. "I do like you, Beth," he said. I blushed. I didn't know what to say. I'd never known a man like James before, so mysterious yet brilliant. "Tell me," he said, "do you remember Tom Hyde?"

"No," I answered truthfully.

"Tom Hyde was a thief. Thoreau mentions him. When Tom Hyde was about to be hanged, the hangman asked if he had any last words. Tom said, 'Tell the tailors to remember to make a knot in their thread before they take the first stitch.' No praying, no begging. Just an everyday truth. Thoreau liked that. So do I. As Thoreau says, any low truth is better than any high-sounding untruth. The same thought was in Blake and Hemingway. But neither of them sees it like Thoreau."

"I've never read any of them."

"Each was a good writer but real honesty is the most uncommon quality in the world; it's a kind of genius that governs the head from the solar plexus. The way you tell me about him, I think your father must have that kind of honesty."

I brushed aside the compliment. "You're making my father too much of a saint."

"Not a saint, but maybe too much of a hero," James said. He abruptly added, "Are you going to let me walk you home this time?"

We did not talk as he walked me home. I was happy with James but I did not trust him. I wondered how much he had said about honesty was sincere and how much was flattery. I was not able to follow his thoughts and I was unsure if the reasons were my own insufficiency or James' confused thinking. He had qualities that were both appealing and odd. We walked in silence until he said, "You told me about your father, but you didn't tell me about your mother."

"Mom is the talker in the family. Not like Dad, he's quiet. Mom was a mountain girl and she never gets tired of telling old stories, especially about children playing pranks on farmers and schoolteachers."

As we neared my apartment I found it harder to think of things to say, but I wanted to remain with him, not to go upstairs, and a nervous quiet stirred between us.

"You love the mountains, don't you, Beth?"

"Very much," I said.

"I have always liked the psalm which begins, 'I will lift up mine eyes unto the hills, from whence commeth my strength.' The mountains have strangeness, like a brother who hates you."

What an odd thing to say. It made me wonder about James' background. "I think I ought to know what you're talking about, but I don't," I said.

"I look at the mountains and they are as if no one who ever lived is buried there," he said. "As if the dead never lived. There is a power in the mountains, maybe it's in everything natural, but I think it's strongest in the mountains. The power seems to smother even the thought of man. It's a strange contradiction, that the mountains can give one man strength as they destroy the memory of another."

James came to the stairs with me, but he did not go up. "I want to see you Saturday evening," he said. "I know a place."

"All right."

"Wear something casual. I'll come for you at seven- thirty. I have an automobile." He didn't kiss me and I lingered at the stairs for several moments after he'd left.

Gloria was sitting on the couch looking through a graduate school catalogue when I came in. She put the catalogue aside. "You found yourself a boyfriend, I see."

"No, we're just friends."

"Friends? You're beaming like a nympho, Elizabeth," she said. I scoffed at her insinuation as I took off my coat and threw it across a chair. "Come here, Elizabeth, I'm not about to let you get off so easy. You're going to sit right here and tell me exactly what's going on between you and your boyfriend." Gloria moved the school catalogue aside and patted the couch. I didn't sit. Instead, I went into the kitchen.

"Elizabeth," she called as she followed me into the kitchen.

"Let's have supper first," I said. I immediately regretted my words. Gloria had already prepared dinner. "Gloria, why do you insist on making things so difficult for me? You know I'd never tell you what you want most to hear. And don't be so sure I'm hiding anything now. I'm not."

"I believe you, Elizabeth," she replied with a sly grin.

During dinner I told her about my conversation with James. She responded with predictable criticism. "Doesn't this all seem like queer stuff, Elizabeth? If his mind's on baseball or cars, at least he fits the common mold, so you can see what he's up to. But not this one. He's talking about honesty. That means he's not honest. You take my advice and drop him before you get used to having him around."

I shook my head. "I think I like him."

"You think you do?"

"I haven't known him long enough to be sure."

"Saturday night you'll find out, but don't you let him talk you into anything. Don't think because the water's smooth you can't drown."

I was frightened and confused. When a man and a woman are young and beginning a relationship, a physical presence between them obscures many things. For some women this physical presence is as spiritual as it is exciting. I wanted to enjoy the physical between us and to be secure in the spiritual. James had told me I was a sensuous woman. Increasingly I was sensitive to my own sensuousness.

But sensuousness had a price in the autumn of 1948. Alice Frost lived in our apartment building, too, I reminded myself. Alice appeared older than her thirty years on this earth. She had the sick and frightened appearance of a woman who knows severe gynecologic suffering. Alice had two infant sons and a four year old daughter. Alice's last pregnancy had been difficult, and after the birth she almost died of internal bleeding. Her husband would not allow her to use, nor would he use, any contraceptive. Gloria and I were in the basement doing the wash and Alice was taking diapers off the lines. "I understand from Gloria you have a new boyfriend, Elizabeth," Alice teased.

I gave Gloria an angry look. Gloria shrugged. "I just mentioned it to Alice, nobody else," she said.

Alice folded the diapers and stacked them neatly in an aluminum-framed folding carrier. "Don't you be in the hurry I was to say yes, Elizabeth, look at this." She patted her protruding abdomen. "Is this what you want to look like when you're my age? Don't get yourself stuck like me in a cold basement folding diapers and spending your every penny on doctor bills."

I stared at her belly in horror. "Oh no! Alice, you're not pregnant again, are you?" I asked.

She shook her head. "Rather be dead than have another pregnancy, Elizabeth, but I sure look the part, don't I." Alice's lips quivered weakly. "That husband I got, he thinks he's not a real man if he can't get me pregnant every year. He hates me now. I know he does, but I don't want another baby. I just can't. It's tearing me apart. Jesus knows, if it was him dripping blood every time he sat on the stool, he'd think something different."

I struggled to find something to say as I unknotted a sheet in the wash. "How was your new baby?"

"Terrible," Alice said. "He cries all night. Poor thing, his bowels won't move like they should. I hate giving him so many enemas, but God help me I don't know what else I can do."

After Alice had carried her wash upstairs Gloria whispered to me, "Something else about Alice I haven't mentioned." Gloria glanced at the stairs to make sure no one was entering the basement before she spoke. "Alice doesn't want the news to spread. Not even her husband knows. She's having a hysterectomy."

I was shocked. "She told you that but she hasn't told her husband?"

"She's afraid to tell him. The truth was she wants the operation so she'll be sure she won't have any more children. But she's afraid her husband will desert her if she's not a whole woman."

I reeled at this news. I knew nothing about contraception and little about sex.

Saturday arrived and I was getting ready for my evening with James. I was taking a bath. Our bathroom was always warmer than other rooms and the bath window looked down on the lane between the rows of buildings. I was finishing my bath when Gloria knocked at the door. "Elizabeth, you need me to iron anything?"

"No. Can you tell me the time?"

"It's after five. Almost five-thirty. Dinner's almost ready."

I got out of the tub, pulled the rubber plug and hung the chain over the faucet. I dried and put on my robe and slippers. Gloria called to me from the kitchen as I opened the bathroom door. "I want you to sit down and eat now before you get dressed, Elizabeth."

I mocked her lightly, "Yes, mother."

"Stop that, Elizabeth, I am not your mother!"

"I know you're not, Gloria, but do you? You run around here after me doing things for me like the mother of a sixteen-year-old going out on her first big date."

She ran her fingers through my curls. "You didn't wash your hair, I see. I know, not enough time. But if you'd done what I told you and not helped me with the laundry, you would have had more than enough time."

I laughed. "Gloria, you DO sound exactly like my mother."

"I bet you didn't think to put any scent in your bath water." She sniffed at my neck. "No, you didn't."

I was too anxious to eat more than very little, but Gloria ate far too much butter and potato and gravy. She was chewing a large piece of fatty beef when she started in on me about James, "This new fellow of yours is going to be different from the others, Elizabeth. I know. I can feel it."

"You must have gifts I never recognized."

"I know you, Elizabeth. It's no gift. I can feel it here." She dropped her hand to her breast. "One way or another he's going to be a bad sort, and it scares me, Elizabeth. It really does. I told you before, but I'll say it again, if you use your head you won't get mixed up with him."

"I haven't known James long enough. I've heard that when a woman meets the man she is destined to marry, she knows immediately. If it does mean anything, I don't feel that way that about James."

Gloria's face had a delighted grin. "Know when you'll be sure about James, after marriage, when you're buying a new dress and you find yourself wondering how the buttons or the zipper could be managed by larger fingers."

"Gloria, I can't believe your vulgarity."

Gloria closed her eyes in mock bashfulness, "Well, la-do-da."

"Is that the sweaty odor of jealousy I smell, Gloria?"

"Someday you'll be the one going to get a hysterectomy, and tell me, Elizabeth, what will your lover think of you then?"

Panic spread through my body. I thought about the plight of Alice Frost with too many babies and the surgery that was her only way out.

Gloria must have seen the panic in my face. She softened her tone and wrapped her arms around me. "I should bite my tongue off," she said. "Don't think about it, Elizabeth. You know how sometimes I say such stupid things. I just love you so much. I wish we could be together forever."

Later, as I was dressing in my best skirt and blouse, I began wondering about the evening with James. Once more I was unable to free myself from the mute dread of being like Alice Frost. I knew nothing about James. His talk of honesty puzzled me because I knew that between a man and woman honesty can be an area whose lines are constantly changing with a word or a touch. I would never shop for clothing as Gloria had suggested, but, then again, I could not imagine myself intimate with James. I told myself, I wanted to go out tonight and have a good time.

In the kitchen Gloria banged on the wall. "You better light a match, Elizabeth. It's past seven already." I hurried to the living room and waited with Gloria. "Elizabeth, I'm sorry," Gloria said. "The words just popped out of my mouth. I love you. Maybe I don't sound like I do. But I really do love you. If I thought my dumb talk would make anything bad happen to you, I wouldn't want to live another day."

"I'm sorry, too, it was cruel off me to say you were jealous."

"You're not still upset, are you?"

"I'm not. Not so much as I was."

Gloria smiled playfully. "Listen to me, Elizabeth. When he comes, I want you to let me go to the door. You go to your room. Men like to be kept waiting, at least at first. They say they don't but that's—."

"Childish," I said, finishing her sentence, "that's what it is, Gloria."

She pouted affectedly, "Please, Elizabeth. Do this for me, and I'll buy you a new brassiere."

I laughed, "That's certainly an interesting offer. It's against any good sense I may have, but I'll let you, if you promise you won't scare him away."

Gloria leapt like an eager child when we heard the door. She took my hand. "Hurry! Elizabeth, hurry!" She pushed me to my bedroom. "You stay put and let me talk with him awhile, then you can come out."

I hid behind my door, feeling very foolish. I went to the bed and sat on the edge, and was able to convince myself that my hair was messy so I took my comb from my purse. My heart beat quickly as I listened.

"Hello."

"I'm trying to find Elizabeth Brewer's apartment."

"This was it. Won't you come in? Please, sit down. Here. On the sofa."

"I suppose you must know who I am."

"Of course. My name's Gloria. I live here, too." She began showing James around. "This is the kitchen, this is my bedroom, and—

." I could hear her coming closer. "—and that's Elizabeth's room." I popped out and everyone laughed, even James. He took my hands. His hands were cold.

James' automobile was a black coupe with no back seat. He drove slowly through town, passing the park. He turned onto the highway. His automobile had a heater and I was soon warm. The childishness of my hiding in my room came back to me. I was wonderfully innocent with James, like the cool air of a summer storm in a warm evening. I listened to the beat of the wheels over the breaks between the sections of concrete.

Neither James nor I had spoken in the car until James asked me, "Are you too warm, Beth?" He seemed nervous or shy, I couldn't tell.

"I like it." I told him, smiling. Again he drove silently.

Then he said, "When I saw you tonight, I thought you were very pretty." I did not know what to say but the wonderful innocence remained. I was unable to think of myself with him as a woman with a man.

"I feel happy tonight," I said.

"Thank you, Beth."

Joy was in the sound of James' voice. I enjoyed the moment as such a moment must be enjoyed, quietly, as the automobile moved through the darkness. I said, "You haven't told me where we are going."

"Have you been to the Barn Playhouse?"

"No, but I've seen posters."

"The name fits. That's all it really is, a barn remade into a playhouse. Some students organized it two years ago as an experimental theater. I've been involved with it since the beginning of last year. You didn't hear about our being charged with obscenity last year?"

"No," I answered as James drove past a dimly lit farm. I could hear the cows moaning, settling down for the night. Suddenly I remembered that James had told me to dress casual, yet I had worn my best blouse and skirt. My mother would be upset if I ruined them.

James said "That's how well known we are. Harold Midggett—you don't remember him?—a Salvador Dali mustache—Anyway, he talked the group into putting on a little thing about a nun. The sheriff's office threatened to close us permanently if we didn't get it off. He was going to use some fire violation."

"You didn't close."

"No. We negotiated. The sheriff won, and we took it off. We generally do four plays a year, that leaves lots of empty time. Tonight we'll have two, both pretty short."

"Are you an amateur actor?"

"One time last year I had a small part. Once was enough. I sounded like a high school kid reading a paper in class. I wrote two short plays last year that the group put on. And tonight we are going to see two plays. I wrote one. The other is a comedy. Mine is not a comedy."

"You don't write comedy?"

"Comedy is too intellectual, it's too much a matter of definitions, you define yourself then you define everything else. If you sand off a certain veneer, you find that the comedy writer is really a lexicographer. To be aware of the definitions without letting them grow on you, that's the need; at least that's what I think is needed."

"That's interesting," I said, hoping that I sounded intelligent.

"This play of mine isn't really a play, it's only a question. I haven't tried to kiss you."

I was confused by James' unconnected words. "I know." I said.

James said, "I care about you, Beth, and I don't want us to be closer until you understand what I am. I will not pretend with you. Maybe after you see the play, you will think I am insane. Oh, I know that's an exaggeration. But you have to know first. I am the most alone kind of man, the man who is poor and wants to create serious art. I use the wrong word. Wants. It's a compulsion, not a desire, and I am going to follow it. If it were only a desire, maybe I could take a professorship and teach Romantic poetry or something."

"I don't know how I could ever think you insane." I said.

"You still don't know enough about me, Beth. I can't explain in a few simple words. I have an enormous need to respect myself ethically and a compulsive need to create serious art, and I can't allow anyone or anything to stop me. In a very real way I am a true puritan, but not toward sexual morality. I hate sexual puritanism."

I was puzzled by James' use of the word insane. Nothing else was truly foreign to me. I did not understand the fascination for art, but I knew of it through Ameele, and, of course, I had known the need for ethical self-respect from my childhood with my parents.

James turned onto a dark and narrow clay road. "Are you frightened out here alone, Beth?"

"Not very. But if something should happen to the car, a breakdown or something, how far would we have to walk?"

"It's two and a half miles, almost exactly, from the highway to the playhouse. But people do live up here, and they're good people, most of them. I have spoken with many of the people who live up here. Each of these old roads is a world in itself, with a kind of people you can't find anyplace else."

At the limit of the headlights a small animal ran across the road, and James slowed the car. James turned onto a roadway barely wide enough for a single automobile, and I was startled and relieved by the sudden glare of lights. He pulled into the small lot, above which were crossed two cords of naked white bulbs. The lot was crowded by about twenty-five cars.

"Are we late?" I asked as we got out of the car.

"These things may not begin on time, but they're never early." James opened the door for me. The air was very cold. The coldness seemed almost visible under the lights. The ground was hard clay. James took my arm.

"It really is a barn," I said as we walked.

"You're surprised, Beth?"

"I didn't disbelieve you, but, yes, I am a little."

"I don't mind," James said. "In fact I'm glad. I don't think I want to be trusted absolutely. That's Mr. Oliver's truck. He owns this place. He's a good old man, but strange—maybe he'd have to be to let us use his property. That old man has more life than most people at school, but after the trouble with the play about the nun, he's now got a quick eye for the sheriff."

"You don't expect any trouble, do you?"

"I don't know. Not with the comedy. Anyway, don't worry."

We went inside and James deposited a bill in a slotted locked box. It was warm and smells were thick, a mixture of coal and smoke and the lingering odors of animals and grain, not completely unpleasant. The full audience sat on crude benches. The bare stage was a simple platform supported by an uncovered wooden skeleton. Wallboards as tall as a man flanked the platform on both sides. The red glow of the coal stove opposite the door and the simple stage lights merged unevenly, producing moving shadows which made the interior seem much smaller that it was.

We found two seats and took off our coats.

The comedy began abruptly. It was an absurd mockery of politics, constructed about a can of fruit in which the principal character, a silly young woman, discovers a cockroach.

During the break before the second play, James, among others, went out for a cigarette. Alone, I felt I belonged here, and I felt I belonged, almost inevitably, as by an unchangeable destiny, with James.

When James returned, we talked of the comedy, and he told me things about members of the group. He talked about Delia, the actress who played the lead, and about Charles and Treavor, two young actors who seemed to prefer the company of each other over the attention from their female fans. I had never heard of such a thing.

Then the second play began.

Chapter Seven
THE PLAY

(Young man wearing dark sunglasses, holding a cane.)

My name is Michael. I am blind. You can see I am blind and old. Look how dry and old my skin is. I cannot see you standing there by the door with your hands in your pockets. No, you and color, even space apart from my own motion are empty ideas to me, and I know I do not know them. I want nothing. Desire is alone in my darkness, without an act.

(Pulls off the sunglasses, throws away the cane.)

You simple fool! I'm not blind. Nor am I old. I am young. I know I'm not blind because today on the street, on my own street not more than a hundred feet from this spot, I saw an old man. What? What is your question? I will answer you. No, I did not kill him. But wait! Don't take me for a moralist. I lie. I lied to you. Remember that. Would I lie if I were a moralist? I will answer you. No, there was no policeman. You have no right to attack me. You see, he had a certain beauty. Yes, it was a kind of glow, and that was why I did not kill him.

(Michael's wife, Anne, appears. She's playfully pulling him)

ANNE

Come to bed, Michael. Be with me now.

MICHAEL

I can't

ANNE

(Seductively)

Why?

MICHAEL

Reasons. I have no dream with it. I am too weak for the dream or too strong to dream with you.

ANNE
(Moves behind him, her arms about his waist)
Not weak. Strong.
(Faces him, her arms still about him)
We are married. I want my rights of marriage.

MICHAEL
Lawfully married. Wed. Husband and lawful wife. My love, it's an ancient law that's in you, and I move my hands with love from your shoulders up your slender throat and higher to your face that's lawfully lifted to me. My love. My thumbs could crush your eyes and love you. I would love you blind, eyeless, sightless. My love. Love is weak and with that loving weakness I could press the power of my hands into your loving eyes.

ANNE
I'm frightened, Michael.
MICHAEL
Love and viciousness, first a trembling of weakness, then all cruelty.

ANNE
Please.
MICHAEL
(Removing his hands from her face)
I won't harm you, Anne. I see no image in our bed.

ANNE
Look at my face. You have seen my body. Can you say I am not beautiful? Have I lost my beauty for you?
MICHAEL
You are a beautiful woman.
ANNE
Do you love me?

MICHAEL

I would die for you, Anne. I love you.

ANNE

My eyes love you. My body loves you. I want a child. Come with me now. I want to be a woman with my husband's child.

MICHAEL

No child.

ANNE

Mine. My child, Michael. I am a woman, and I do not fear it. Let me and I will be as full hearted as any woman who ever gave her milk and her sleepless nights to her child.

MICHAEL

I won't.

ANNE

My love will cover the pain with soothing cream. My love will break the bones of sorrow. The touch of love will make every labor a rich man's dream.

MICHAEL

I love too deeply for love.

ANNE

Pity me, Michael. Love me and pity me in my need. I need the child. I need to feel within my dull womb that life that through me eats the food I eat, that is yet is not me. And you. As if my hand had its own living soul, that I might hold it and caress it and kiss it and both give my love and receive it back.

MICHAEL

I love too much for love. Wanting. Words. Theories. Theories are thought, but pain is left to feed on nothing. Nothing is its best food. Better nothing than milk of your dry breasts or the mouth to suck them. Better than a heart to beat upon your own heart, Anne. Nothing. No milk, no heart, no mouth, no child.

(Two young girls appear, one wearing a grotesque mask, chanting and dancing about Michael)

Pretty Girl
My heart, my heart beats
>   a merry tune to life,
>   O father not-to-be.

Both Girls
I beat, I beat in beauty.

Pretty Girl
My compact gay, my looking glass.

Homely Girl
My mirror cold, my looking glass.

Pretty Girl
I'm gay in glassy rain
>   O father not-to-be.

Homely Girl
I'm gay in glassy rain,
>   O father not-to-be.

Pretty Girl
I climb a tree.

Homely Girl
I skip a rope.

Both Girls
O father not-to-be,
>   A single heart of not-to-be,
>   A single self for all us three.
>   To be a not-to-be's to be
>   the same for one or two or three.

(Anne runs off stage, in tears. Old Michael appears. Young Michael leaves. Old Michael talks to audience.)

OLD MICHAEL

I was a poet then. Before. I mean before my wife died. And before. Before we were married. When I knew so many women, beautiful women, as many as I wanted. I don't seem to remember how long ago. Years. Many years. When I was a young man. Those days I wrote my poems with a heart that seemed oppressed by the gravity of a feather. Trite. But those were my best days. And they left me something. I still have something. I can still create. Listen to me, a poem:

When I was young, the years ago,
When tea buds rose, love lifting dew,
And Spanish moss from cypress hung
And mocked- that I was never young,
She was pure and pure she rose
'Gainst godhood in my hands she rose
So long ago, when I was young
And Spanish moss from cypress hung.

The words do have their rhyme. Your eyes tell me you know, my friend. That this is no poem. No more than the beginning of poetry. No more than virginity's passion is rhyme. Less. Much less. An old man's memories of a young man's dreams. You know I am too old for the struggle, too old, too weak. Age and unrelenting pain have dried up my strength to endure the hacks of the blades which cut a man into a poet.

(Cleaning woman enters, pursued by two boys)
CLEANING WOMAN
Git 'way! Git 'way!
FIRST BOY
Git 'way! Git 'way!
SECOND BOY
Want my money? Come on home with me Lilly. I'll give you a dime to clean out the toilet bowl.
CLEANING WOMAN
Boy! Git home you'self! I'll cut off you head an' feed you blood to my dog.
BOYS TOGETHER
(Singing)

She's the Lilly of the Valley
And she is black as hell
She's got a white lover
And his name was Dunstan Tell
(Boys run away, laughing.)
CLEANING WOMAN
I ain't jus' som' ol' dog what 'em boys can do with jus' what they please. My daddy was a black man. Ain't no white man on my mamma. An' I do swear by Jesus that sits by the right han' ah God's father almighty, Baby Girl. I tell you soon you know words, I say if I ever know that you let sam' white man use you, I'll cut out your heart and feed it to my dog.
(Old Michael addresses Cleaning Woman)
OLD MICHAEL
Anything bothering you, Lilly.
CLEANING WOMAN
Not a thing, boy. How's your mamma?
MICHAEL
Mother's fine.
CLEANING WOMAN
That's good to hear. Your mamma's a good woman, boy. You ought to know that thing an' be glad as you can be. There ain't many good folks left these days.
OLD MICHAEL
I'll tell mother. She knows about your baby being sick. Want me to tell her something?
CLEANING WOMAN
You tell your mamma my baby girl's just as strong as she can be.
OLD MICHAEL
Lilly, can I ask you something?
CLEANING WOMAN
Sure, boy.
OLD MICHAEL
I heard some of the boys talking. Is it true a colored baby's

born white?

CLEANING WOMAN

(Laughs)

That sure is the truth. It's like the Lord couldn't make up his mind. Sometime they sure do start out white as snow.

OLD MICHAEL

I figured they were just talking.

CLEANING WOMAN

No, boy.

(Cleaning woman leaves)

OLD MICHAEL

(Old Michael alone, talking to audience)

I am no god, conceived without the things of time.

I am not alone, loving myself alone or feeling nothing.

I do not move the universe by my moodless laws. It does not concern me. I need not dream of it. Nor will I allow, silently without struggle. I damn him and curse him that names me a microbe to a distant eye.

(Soldier Enters)

SOLDIER

Mike. Come over here. Want a drink?

(Old Michael refuses)

Suit yourself. Say, Mike, how about letting me hold a five to payday? You know me.

(Old Michael gives the money)

You're a friend. Sure you don't want a drink?

OLD MICHAEL

No thanks.

SOLDIER

Come to town with me tonight. This country's got some wild girls. Goddamm. They'll do anything you want for a couple of bucks.

OLD MICHAEL

No. You know I'm married.

SOLDIER

So, I'm married too. Who gives a damn? They say the army

travels on its stomach, yeah, maybe. What's Top call it? A three leg march? But you want to wake up stiff every morning humping to the latrine, that's your business. Thanks for the five.

OLD MICHAEL
(Old Michael, alone)

Anne. Anne. Too much. Too much. I knew you would die. And of my living. A word does steal a deed, but what's a poet? What but to know a tongue of words, poetry in its obedient words while deeds pass undone, impossible as a timeless verb. Like tightgutted Byron murdering with emptiness, murdering beauty for beauty and love for love. Beauty, perfection among the pleasures. Words. Words like cut ferns have covered every hole in this life over which I have walked. Reason. Useless, hated reason. Lilly's children's children play and skip rope and eat and throw oatmeal on the floor, and they will copulate and generate others to know their beauty which is strange to me. They will mock me. Can any man call it right that any man will lose altogether what he most loves? My child, she mocks me too, unconceived in Anne's dead womb. What else? Ambivalence, the name of the blades which make a poet? Ambivalence? The poem was the dream, and the dream was the unmoving mover of all life. If not reason, what? Hatred? Hatred for life? That which was a coward's murder. And if I kill, do I not destroy the ambivalence which was the overflowing fountain of dreams. To kill a child for poetry—or for poetry not to kill, which is more absurd? I am weak, weak beyond criterion of weakness conceived by any man before. There can be nothing for me.

ANNE
(Anne, as a Spirit)

Michael. You have been weak, and you have killed me, whom you loved. I cannot love you again, but I return to you this one time to warn you. Listen with your heart. Go now to a holy garden, for the days of dreams have passed. Look to a heaven. Or, if you cannot, die from art into idea. I know now these are the same for you. Fall, or from your heart you will die.

OLD MICHAEL

(Old Michael, alone)

My name is Michael. I am blind and old. You can see I am blind. Look how dry and old my skin is.

END OF PLAY

Chapter Eight

The audience left and James emptied the coal ash from the stove. He returned with black smudges on his hands. After he cleaned up, he introduced me to the seven players. Principally, I talked with the young actress named Delia. She portrayed Anne, the wife in James' play. She praised James and his play and condemned the audience for not appreciating his creation.

"They're all addicted to sentimental motion pictures," she said with an overwrought actress's flourish. "They are incapable of appreciating great theater." I found her manner distracting. She was unable to take her eyes from James. I waited while the seven players reveled in their performance and planned for the next performance. Their dramatic enthusiasm was comical. In contrast, James seemed mundane and prosaic about the entire evening.

We stayed behind after the audience and actors had left. The silence was intoxicating. James sat on the stage. "Come here by me, Beth." I did as he asked. He was as a director upon the stage. "See the nakedness of the theater when they are gone? The benches and the coal stove and I." He paused taking it all in. "And I sit on this stage. This was the best part of the performance, after everything is over, and I'm here alone."

"You love it, don't you?"

"I possess it. I don't feel possessive for many things, but I feel it for this place. Maybe that is love, a primitive kind of love, at least." We fell into a silence together until he asked, "Are you tired?"

"Not at all," I answered. "I'm glad you brought me here."

James turned off the lights and we walked out into the open night. Millions of stars appeared. "I'm afraid of the sky of stars, Beth," he said.

This surprised me because he didn't seem to be afraid of anything, "Like looking into God's eyes," I said.

"There is a sense of mystery, but nothing so vulgar as religion," he countered. "It's the mystery of an automobile motor if you are not a mechanic. You can see the sky of stars when there is no artificial light, no moon either, and the air is cold and dry. A sky full of stars has power, as if it will crush you and you know you can't escape. There is no kindness in the stars."

I thought back on the play, "Delia almost worships you, you know."

"Delia worships her own dream, and if I'm in it, she imagines she worships me or loves me. There's never been anything between Delia and me."

"Does your play have a title?"

"The Death of Beauty."

I felt a chill. The night wind moved the trees before moving through me. I rubbed my arms, wishing I could ask James for his coat to keep me warm. I had foolishly dressed to impress rather that dressing sensibly. "Yes, I can see why you would choose that title. Michael's beauty dies. He loses his wife and his hope."

"It's more complex than a loss of hope. It's more universal and more specific. Michael is totally aware that beauty and goodness are opposites," James said this as if he were talking about gravity or similar phenomena. His confidence drew me in; he was my prophet and I his apostle. "Michael was born a gentle lover of beauty and humanity. He loves both. Unlike much of the modern world, Michael is capable of distinguishing between beauty and hedonistic vulgarity."

I considered this. "What does Michael mean when tells the old man 'I was a poet then'?"

"The poet is the truest representative of humanity. Ambivalence is to the poet what conflict is to the general world. Without ambivalence, poetry and other kinds of creative art are not possible. Art is always a falling and a fight against the end. The opposition between beauty and goodness is ambivalence, but Michael is so deeply sensitive to them both that he cannot endure the conflict, and it weakens him too greatly for him to be a poet."

"The play begins again," I said. "Michael repeats what he said at the beginning. I thought this was to show his madness."

"The question is moot. Whether he is mad because he repeats or repeats because he is mad. Madness and repetition, especially of something important, must be almost identical. We like to say that war is madness, but if the alternative is repetition, words become meaningless. Do you remember what Anne tells Michael at the end? He says something like, 'the days of dreams have passed. Look to the heavens or die from art into ideas.'"

"I remember."

"Anne was offering him the practical solution. Become an intellectual. The artist and the intellectual are as different as a man who is awakened while he is dreaming differs from a man who awakens naturally and doesn't remember his dream. She was telling him to adjust. That's why artists hate intellectuals."

"I think I understand," I said.

He took my arm. His fingers curled into my flesh, almost hurting me but not quite. "Do you, Beth? You must know by now that I am Michael. Love is too flat a word for what beauty means to me. Worship isn't a strong enough word to describe it. Beauty is the source of my strength. When I am tired or sick, I go to beauty. I begin where Michael ends, when he goes insane." He released my arm. "You still don't see, do you?"

His intensity frightened me. I rubbed my arm. "I must not."

"I absorb people, Beth." He was like a ravenous wolf as he spoke, hungering for something I could not give. "You may not be aware of this yet, but you will be. It is my choice. I am allowing myself to absorb everything. Everything, do you understand. Michael knows the questions. He knows they will destroy him. I begin at those questions."

"Are you serious?"

"I am totally serious."

"You are warning me to be afraid of you."

"Does it sound pretentious?"

"Fear has its appeal," I said more coyly than I should have. His eyes were black in the night. His pale skin took an unearthly hue. He stood as if at attention, like a soldier ready for battle. Tense. He was always so tense. It was like talking to an earthquake or hurricane. Like talking to a tornado. Frightening and fascinating.

"Beth, what I want you to know is that I cannot allow myself to be guilty for you. You must understand before you allow yourself to be with me emotionally. I'm not a happy wandering lyricist or a religious versifier you see in the back pages of church publications. I have given myself totally to art, do you understand. If you care for me, you also will be vulnerable to all that art demands."

I pondered James' words as we left the theater. I was afraid but I realized I was not afraid of James. I feared for myself. I feared my willingness to enjoy my fear. "Why me?" I asked as we drove back to campus. "Why did you speak to me in the class?"

"I need a woman."

I felt close to tears but I wouldn't let James to know how this casualness had hurt me. I turned my head away from him. The car rumbled over the clay roads.

"Is there a reason you should feel degraded?" he asked. "That I want a woman cannot surprise you. When I approached you, I knew your name and that you were intelligent."

When a man you care about says that he wants you because you are a woman, it is a strange awakening. We drove in silence the rest of the way to my apartment. James walked upstairs with me to my door. He held my hands.

"Thank you for the evening," I said.

"Good night, Beth." he said.

I watched him as he returned to his car and drove away.

Later, as I lay in bed unsleeping, remembering this day, my joy was strong, yet muffled and suppressed. I mulled the words *I am a woman with James*, and I wanted them to be true. I cannot say why, but the very complexity of James seemed to justify my adoration of him. His complexity seemed at once very sexual and confusing emotion. It drew me to him. It gave me an almost metaphysical love for him. But it also kept me from him. If James had approached me sexually tonight, I would have rejected him, I was certain. I knew also that in the future it would be different.

Chapter Nine

Thunder woke me. It was past sunrise but my clock said three-thirty. I had forgotten to wind it the night before. Rain was coming in the window so I quickly put on my robe and hurried to close it. I twisted the knob to turn on the radiator and put on my slippers.

Gloria was in the kitchen, meticulously applying liquid polish to her white shoes, the ones she wore to church. "So you finally got it in your head to get out of bed," she said. "Will you go to church with me, Elizabeth?"

"I don't know. What's the time? My clock went down last night."

Gloria looked at her watch. "Quarter to ten. Eat breakfast if you're hungry and get ready."

"Did you call the Johnsons?"

"I called Margret," Gloria said. "She'll pick us up at ten-thirty."

"I don't think I'll go with you."

Gloria placed the shoe on a flattened paper bag to dry and pushed the felt-tipped rod into the bottle, tightening the cap.

She headed to her bedroom. "Come in here, Elizabeth," she said. "I want to talk to you." I begrudgingly followed. "Sit down," she said. I sat on Gloria's bed and pulled my legs loosely under me.

Gloria's bedroom told more about Gloria than she ever could. The dresser, the chest of drawers, and the pair of oval tables on either side of the bed were all bulky, made of heavy wood, elaborately carved and painted a dull ivory. On every flat surface were porcelain and glass figurines of angels and other religious trifles. A surprisingly deep yet soft chair, the back draped by a large white doily, was by the window beside a pink and white floor lamp with a flowery shade.

"Well?" I asked.

"Listen, Elizabeth, I want you to come to church with me. I'll make your breakfast while you are dressing."

"I don't want to go, Gloria!" I was tired of repeating myself. I started for the door. "I'll get my own breakfast."

She reached out. "Don't go, Elizabeth. You can wait to eat. I don't mind going to church alone." She pulled me back to her bed. "You must have been awfully quiet when you came in last night. I never heard you. You must have enjoyed yourself."

"I don't know what time I came in. I suppose it was late."

"If you didn't know how late it was—and it was late—you must have had a good time."

"James is with a theatrical group at the school, and he wrote a play."

"Imagine that!" Gloria exclaimed. "That is something really special. Was it at the college?"

"No, it wasn't at the school. The group refurbished an old barn. But it was clean. There was a good crowd."

"Was the play any good?"

"I think so, especially for an amateur playwright like James. I thought it was very brave."

"Didn't you used to know a boy who wrote poems?" she asked.

"You're thinking about Wilber," I said. "He wrote sarcastic humor for the school paper."

"I remember Wilber. You dated him two years ago. Now your James writes plays. Tell me about this play your new boyfriend wrote."

"It was a little difficult to follow," I explained. "A man who may be insane was remembering the past. He had a wife who wanted a baby. The baby was born deformed, so he didn't want it. That's what happens but the play was actually about his inability to reconcile goodness and beauty. His wife dies. That's apparently why he goes insane, although James would disagree with my assessment."

"So, I see." Gloria said. "That's a reason to go insane. Listen, I didn't tell you my news. I talked with Alice last night after you left. She's been seeing a gynecologist in Richmond and now he's agreed to do the operation. He didn't want to do it, I understand. Alice talked him into it."

"What operation?"

"A hysterectomy."

"I thought she was pregnant," I said. Gloria only shrugged.

Chapter Ten

Ameele always brought a folder of sketches with her when we met for morning coffee in the Fine Arts Building. She spread them across the table, ten or twelve sketches of the interior and the exterior of Ma Bradder's old house. "Elizabeth, come with me to Ma Bradder's this afternoon."

The thought of ever seeing that old house and old woman made me queasy, "I never want to go to that house again."

"You've been there before?"

"Just passing by."

Ameele looked skeptical. "Then why are you afraid to meet me there?"

"It depresses me."

"You're being ridiculous. So the house is old, so what? You can't let yourself be dictated to by mere things. It's awful enough having people tell you what to do." Ameele separated one of the sketches from the others and held it in the sunlight streaming in from the bay windows. "This is my favorite, Elizabeth. The piano and the fireplace. You can't tell anything about the colors from this sketch but even without the colors the images are striking. A piano that nobody plays and a fireplace that never has a fire." She lowered the canvass, "but without the bathos," she added. "The difference between the two can be seen in the intricate yet natural design of the fireplace contrasted against the elaborate yet artificial carved legs of the piano."

I studied the sketches. "Yes, I see, the designs are not the same."

"Elizabeth, sometimes you can be so hellishly suffocating," she scoffed. "But I forgive you." She put away her sketches. "I have a secret I haven't told you. I've finished the painting that came from this sketch. The piano is white, or it would be white except for the dust, which is gray and red. I do want you to come to the house this afternoon to see the painting."

I was balancing Ameele's request against my almost superstitious dread. "Is it a good painting?"

"I honestly believe this was my best work yet."

My curiosity overwhelmed my dread. "I'll be there at three-thirty."

I borrowed Gloria's bicycle and pedaled to Old Ivy Road, passing the new Birdwood golf course. Through the trees I could see the attic windows of Ma Bradder's house. I could see the green pantile roof and the castellated towers. I turned right and sailed down Ragged Mountain Lane until I came to the end.

There it was, at the end of the street. I had only once before come to the old house, exploring with a friend three years earlier when I was a freshman. The house was as grotesque and pathetic as I remembered it. The white paint was blistered and peeled with great bare areas as brown as the wooden shingles. The veranda was the length of the house and overlooked an enigmatic garden. The garden had been skillfully planned, if not by a professional landscaper then by someone of means who had loved and understood plants. A continuous low wall of smooth stones surrounded the garden and shaped it into a complex and delicate network of paths and beds. Now all was obscured by weeds and bushes. I visualized how this garden and this house had once been before age and neglect, and I very much wanted to leave.

Ameele's car was parked behind the back porch, which was broad and covered. The porch screen was ripped and sewn with brown cord. The holes stuffed with cotton. I knocked several times, no answer. I picked up a small stone and threw it at the upstairs window. Ameele finally came to the door wearing her artist's smock and holding her sketch pad. She opened the door. "I was beginning to doubt you'd come," she said.

The kitchen was smaller than I would expect in such a large old home, and oppressively hot. It had a pungently sweet odor, both musty and choking. The room was cluttered with an electric cooking stove, a top-coil refrigerator, a table and four chairs, an over-sized potbelly stove burning wood, a wooden firebox, and a great rattan rocking chair. A stack of magazines beside the chair and a stack of newspapers in the corner completed the disarray.

Ameele was watching me impatiently as I scanned the room. She opened one of the two interior doors and motioned silently for me to follow her. "She sleeps in here," Ameele whispered as if we might come upon a ghost. I peeked into the room, which served as both a pantry and as Ma Bradder's bedroom. The bed was narrow. A chest-of-drawers was the only other furnishing. "This part of the house isn't worth seeing, Elizabeth. I want you to see the parlor."

The second inner door opened into an enormous dining room. The only furnishings were a tall, slender crystal cabinet and a massive, ornate dining table. Over the table and totally dominating the room hung a great chandelier of delicate swan-neck arms and almost numberless elongated crystal droplets. Opposite the kitchen doors were French doors and, to the side, another wooden door, which led into a hall and upstairs.

"Fantastic, isn't it?" said Ameele, looking up at the chandelier.

"It's beautiful," I agreed.

"At least its cooler in here. The kitchen is too hot to think."

Ameele opened the French doors and I saw Ma Bradder sitting by the windows over the veranda. She was as old and gray as I had imagined. Ameele wrapped her arm around my waist and introduced us.

"I hope I'm not disturbing you by coming here, Mrs. Bradder," I said. "Did Ameele tell you I would be here today?"

Ma Bradder looked up at me and smiled. She took my hand. Her grip was surprisingly strong. "Ameele? Yes. I have two visitors today."

"I told her you would be here," Ameele said.

"You have a lovely home, Mrs. Bradder."

She nodded and dust flew about her as if she were an antique piece of furniture. "It's a very old house. I don't recall just now what year it was built. Were you a friend of my husband?"

I glanced at Ameele before answering. "No, I never knew Mr. Bradder."

"My husband died in nineteen and twenty-seven. You're so young. I'm a silly old woman. You're not nearly old enough to have known my Alexander. My husband's father built this house. Alexander was the oldest of the boys, you know. Alexander Martin Bradder. Martin was his mother's maiden name. Lovely she was, up to the time she died. How old was she then? I believe she must have been about sixty. That's too young to die, don't you think." She let go of my hand. "I don't believe I know your name, my dear."

"Elizabeth Brewer."

"Elizabeth. Pretty name. Ameele has been coming to my house for a long time. She's an artist. Did you know that?"

"I know."

The room was full and rich, but ridiculous, as if it had been planned to mock its own richness. A pair of slate palates hung opposite the fireplace flanking a very large brass Persian table, intricately engraved, a central design surrounded by bearded kings. A Persian rug partially covered the floor. The furnishings were highly eclectic. But the upholstery was uniform, a deep red velvet. The piano and the fireplace were as Ameele had described them.

"This is from another world." I said.

She moved to the fireplace and beckoned me to follow. "Here is the center of everything in the room. Let your eyes relax. Disconnect them from your brain, and see just with your heart. Nature will do everything for you if you let it."

I did as Ameele told me. The effect was strange. Ameele returned to Ma Bradder. She sat beside Ma Bradder and folded back the sheet of her sketch pad. She began to draw.

"Elizabeth and Ameele," Ma Bradder said. "You both have pretty names. They are different, but they are both pretty. And you are both pretty girls."

"Thank you, Mrs. Bradder." I said.

"The children call me Ma. Will you call me Ma too? You don't mind calling me Ma, do you, Ameele?" she said as she looked at me.

"I don't mind," Ameele answered.

"I'll call you Ma if you wish," I said.

"Now! You call me Ma right now!" she snapped.

"Ma," I obeyed, "from now on I'll only call you Ma."

She relaxed. "Good. Good. I like that." She gazed out the window, clutching the arms of her chair. "Did you see my garden, Elizabeth?"

"I saw it. I think it must have once been beautiful."

"I used to work in my garden every day. Now I don't. I only remember. I have my trees. I love my trees."

"Did you design the garden yourself, Ma?"

"It was Sarah's garden. Sarah was my cousin and my husband's first wife. Sarah created the garden."

Ameele spoke up, "I didn't know you were your husband's second wife."

"Yes. Sarah was Alexander's first wife. It was so long ago. Sarah was a lovely girl. She was twenty-three when she died. She was so smart and had such a fine voice for singing. But she was sickly. It was with her first child that she died. The child was a stillborn girl. I was with them, Sarah and Alexander. She was holding his hand. She said to me, 'Mary'—That's my given name, Mary—'Alexander will be alone when I am dead. He will be needing a good woman to take good care of him. You know the Lord says it's not good that a man should be alone.' I remember pushing back her hair from her forehead as she lay on her deathbed. That's when she asked me. 'I want you to promise me you will take good care of Alexander,' that's what she said. I told her I would do anything she wanted. Then Sarah said to Alexander, 'Promise me you will marry Mary and love her because I love you and I love Mary'. And so he promised to marry me. But I was only seventeen and I didn't know what she meant. I didn't know at all."

"He promised?"

"Yes. He promised to marry me."

"But why did you go on with the marriage?"

"Our families took us as promised. Alexander never said a word about not marrying me. Sarah died that same day. "

Ameele asked. "Was this Sarah's furniture?"

"Nothing in this house ever belonged to Sarah. Not a thing. Alexander was a strange man that way. He didn't care if I lived in Sarah's house, but he didn't want me to have any of her furniture. He sold everything before we were married."

Ma Bradder struggled to get up from her chair. I helped her and she put her arm about me. "Let's you and me go to the kitchen where we can talk."

She was like a child, the way she sounded, as if she were trying to keep secrets from Ameele.

Ameele said, "I don't plan to be here much longer. Don't leave if you want to ride with me."

"I have a bike." I told her as I followed Ma into the kitchen.

Ma Bradder inserted the rod into the notch of the potbelly stove and lifted the iron plate. She pushed a few short pieces of firewood into the stove and replaced the cover. "I swear no place on this earth gets as hot as one of these old things. Sit down, my dear. Sit here. I'll make us some good hot tea, and we'll be so comfortable. I love my sugar. Do you drink your tea with sugar? Sit down, my dear."

I thought I might pass out from the heat as I took a seat in the rattan rocker. "I use a little sugar," I said.

Ma Bradder filled the kettle and put it on the stove. "I always loved my sweets. Honey is better. Bread and honey. I could drink honey like it was thick water. 'Course, I used to drink honey water too. But fact was I never liked honey in my tea. Some people do. My sister's girl likes honey and tea."

Ma Bradder talked almost incessantly about her likes and dislikes, about her day by day life, about her gathering paper for children of poverty, about her friends at school, how helpful they were, how some of the boys cut wood for her, how the school administrators were kind.

I listened and smiled. When she tired I said, "May I ask you something?"

"Anything you want to know."

"Do you have children of your own?"

"I had two. Mary Ellen and Susan. Two girls, and they're both dead. They've been gone for years."

"I'm sorry to hear that," I said.

Ma Bradder stared silently at the kettle on the stove, only moving when it came to a boil. The tea pot was brown and glazed, and her cups matched the pot. "Ameele likes tea, doesn't she?"

"Yes."

"Good. Good. I'll make enough tea for the three of us. I do try to say what's true. You believe I do try, don't you, Elizabeth."

"Yes, of course."

"I tell lies. I told your friend that none of the furniture belonged to Sarah. That's a little lie. Upstairs, there's a clock and a table that were hers. So I do tell lies. Nobody can ever be sure what I say is the truth. I didn't used to be like this. I used always to tell the truth. But now that I'm old I don't seem to care as much as I once did. What makes us old people tell lies. Do you know, dear?"

I shook my head, "that's just a little lie."

"You wouldn't think it, but I used to be quiet a snob. I used to fancy myself quiet a lady. I wore beautiful clothes in those times. Not to say Alexander was rich when I married him. The things I did with him. Mercy me! Now, why don't you fetch Ameele, and we can all sit here at the table and have our tea."

I happily went for Ameele—happy to get out of the sweltering kitchen—and when we returned, Ameele sweetly scolder the old woman, "Ma, I wish you hadn't gone to any trouble for me."

Ma Bradder said, "Now, Ameele, you can sit in the rocker, and Elizabeth and I will sit at the table. We will all have a cup of tea. Do you like sugar and milk? I don't have any lemon."

"You know I drink my tea plain, silly," said Ameele.

Ma Bradder poured the tea.

"You must have traveled a great deal," said Ameele.

"I've been around the world," Ma Bradder said. "By ship, of

course. That used to be the only way there was to travel. Alexander used to take me with him. I've been to Europe and China and Africa and South America. But I was born right here, not more than twenty miles from this house. I say the Lord gives everybody a place where he means them to be, and those that are happy don't mind staying where he put them."

Ma Bradder smiled brightly when I said, "That is a wise philosophy."

Ameele said, "Do you actually believe that's any kind of wisdom, Elizabeth? I don't. That's a philosophy of the dead. Once you're dead there will be enough time to stay where you're put. I want to see the world. I want to see the whole world through the eyes of a genius. I would do anything for him and go anywhere for him. Genius belongs anywhere and everywhere. It hates to sit where his mother happened to be on such and such a date and from that point on just wait to die."

"If that's so, my Alexander was a genius, because he was at home all over the world."

"Your husband was intelligent," Ameele said, "but that's not what I mean by genius."

"No, I'm sure you're not thinking about men like Alexander. But he was a smart man, and you won't find many as kind as he was."

"I don't mean to be disrespectful, Ma," Ameele said. She was looking directly at me. "Genius is in the world the way water is in the ocean. Genius is contained by the world and covers it. I would do anything to share the life of a genius."

Ma Bradder stopped sipping her tea. She took Ameele's hand and implored, "Anything? No, my dear. You'd be immoral. Nothing is worth giving up your virture."

"If I had to be immoral, I would be," Ameele said. She spoke with more passion than I had ever seen. "Not for the sake of immorality. I would do *anything* a genius required if I could share his vision."

Ma Bradder seemed on the verge of a heart attack. "Serve God, Ameele. Give yourself to the Lord. You mustn't give yourself to anyone but Jesus."

"Ameele, I'm surprised." I said. "Why this sudden need to commune with a genius?"

"These," she proclaimed, holding up her sketches. "I have been working long enough that I know I'm missing something. A genius of art is the most marvelous—."

"Must a genius be a man, Ameele?" I asked.

Ameele laughed. "Of course not. But you know how it usually is with a woman. All women care about is endless sentiment. I hate the sentimental. You know how little sex means to me, Elizabeth. You know because you have something of the same thing yourself. Ma talks about immorality, and she means sleeping with a man who's not my husband, but I would, even if I hated him. If he could show me what's missing in my work, I'd do anything he wanted."

I was appalled by her statement. "Even if you hated him?"

"I wouldn't care."

Ma Bradder said, "Well, my dear, I hope the day never comes when you'll be immoral, and if that day does come, that day I'll be glad you're not my daughter if I know anything about it."

"Are you angry, Ma?"

"No, not angry, but disappointed."

"Will you want me here again?"

"Of course I will, Ameele. Come to my house whenever you wish."

Ameele gathered her drawing materials and her purse. "Then I'll be here tomorrow afternoon. Elizabeth, meet me tomorrow. "

"I'll try," I said.

Ma Bradder said, "Promise me you'll come back and see me."

Chapter Eleven

My relationship with James was so a conventional that my parents would have approved. We went to school activities and to motion pictures. We walked together and went horse-back riding. We drove to the mountains in the Blue Ridge Mountains and talked the entire time. I wanted to talk about the movies but James preferred discussing art and philosophy.

Beauty and ethics occupied James almost obsessively. Once, when we were talking about a movie we saw over late-night coffee, James told me, "It's loaded with action, which was all right, but the lead man is a character, not flesh and blood. The men he kills are not actually dead. There's more worth to an ethical character's walking across the street than killing half the world if the ethical is not considered." He paused and stared out into the darkness. "Yet, this is the dilemma. The ethical nature of the artist draws him toward altruism, but he must resist. Otherwise he is not an artist; he is a nurse to humanity."

James believed the artist was threatened by two great dangers: cynicism and dishonesty. "Cynicism turns the artist into a user of circumstances and a knower of definitions. It robs him of the very spark that is creativity. Dishonesty is actually the greater danger. It turns the artist into a propagandist."

There was a time when I imagined myself married to James, but I grew to realize that would never happen. Common sense told me to break off with him. Our relationship was a purely platonic friendship. I wasn't unhappy but I feared that I would become like Ma Bradder, an old woman sitting alone. I longed to know myself as a woman with James but greater was the fear of the complex pain I saw in him. I was attracted to this pain as much as I feared it.

James was happiest when he was talking about dead poets. "I know I do compare myself with the poets," he said as we walked on the old clay road that circled the campus. His fingers brushed against mine and I thought he might take my hand. "Do you love me, Beth?" James had never asked me this question or spoken seriously of love. He laughed, "If you call anything love, it's a lie. Between us it's better without a name. Say attracted by or drawn to. Those expressions are vague enough to satisfy the mind of a priest."

I considered my answer carefully before saying, "I am drawn to you."

"You are a special woman, Beth. Most are drawn to people of simple definitions, but you are one of the very few who is drawn to the poet or the artist. I know how people, women in their way and men in theirs, gather about the famous artist or the quick-tongue player. That means nothing. They love an institution or a reputation or an image. Even if she does not love him as a woman loves a man, the woman who loves an artist is very special."

I pondered this as we walked. "I wonder the other way, too, can an artist have a man's love for a woman?"

James picked a rock off the road. He threw it ahead lightly in a high arc and the rock fell a few yards from us. "Is that a question?"

"I guess," I said, "I don't expect an answer."

"Good. Because I don't have an answer. All puzzles and puzzles. I understand myself little better than I understand the world. The world is part of me more than I am part of it, but I don't understand it. If I understood the world, I would understand myself; and if I understood myself first, I would understand the world."

"This isn't an Alice In Wonderland puzzle, is it?"

"No." James answered simply.

"Could a man or a woman be a poet if he understood the world and himself?"

"Not if he understood. If he understood, he couldn't be a poet. His understanding would be dishonest."

James ran ahead, kicking the rocks in the road like a boy. "Not so serious, Beth. Let's not be serious." He was like a child as he circled around, coming up behind me and he pulling my hair. "Red hair of Beth," he said as he ran around and around. "Pretty red fire-head of hair. The touch of her hair. So powerful and playful. I love the touch of her hair."

Breathing deeply, James suddenly stopped running and pummeled his chest like a uncaged gorilla. "I love this free air. The air goes wherever it wants, and it never decides a thing. It gives me its strength and energy and lets me take a little bit of its freedom. The air's not stingy, Beth, but the air's not generous. It has so much. No fragrance could ever be better than clean air."

Students smiled as they passed us by, a few laughed. I loved James' childlike joy. "The air's making you giddy," I laughed.

James put his arms about my waist. "More than giddy, Beth. I breathe the free air and I can forget all discipline." He touched my hair again, running his fingers down my curls. "More than freedom, the same as freedom, not more, the same, I can see how beautiful your red hair is when I touch it. Isn't that the definition of freedom? Isn't freedom the love of beauty?"

I shyly pulled my hair out of his hands. "I would say that freedom is the ability to act according to your own wishes."

"I wonder how much difference there is. Not much, I think. Your hair is beautiful and you are beautiful."

"You believe I'm beautiful. Other men think I'm rather plain."

"Believe me, Beth, not them," he said. "Those men have sold their eyes to the public and the public votes to decide how the eyes will see. But I have sold nothing. My eyes are my own. They are free, and they see beauty when I look at you, Beth."

Back in my apartment, I was so torn with what to do. To stay with James or break it off. James said he wanted me because he needed a woman yet he had never kissed me. The strange unphysical intimacy between us was the antithesis of simplicity. This fixed me to him like a servant to master, like apprentice to artist, like hound to hunter, and filled me with feelings I could not endure. Far more than being with

James, I felt myself being taken up by him, being unable to separate my own emotions and thoughts from his.

One night I dreamt I was an empress on a golden thrown who was obsessed with death. In my dream I ordered a funeral ceremony for James. As he lay in his coffin, mourners passed by, then, when we were alone, he awoke from his death and rose from the coffin. He came to my thrown and said, 'She is beautiful.' Then he disappeared and I was alone. I left my thrown and went to my family home. James was there, as were my parents and my brothers. James told me I was beautiful and said he loved me. I awoke covered in perspiration.

I longed to break off with James and to forget him as a young girl forgets her last boyfriend and wonders about her next. I begged the universe for such easy forgetfulness. I hated the impossibility. I was a captive of my own and I could not separate my nature from his. I knew I must decide. But between acceptance and decision, between the turning of the head without consideration and moving deep into the body and saying the words, the gap was very wide. I was afraid as I had never before been afraid. I had to decide, or I must no longer accept.

Chapter Twelve

Gloria was sick. Vomiting, diarrhea, and fever, which meant I was forced to do all our cooking. She sat at the kitchen table in a fluffy robe with a thermometer in her mouth. She was studying from one of her notebooks. After starting the coffee, I set the table. Gloria took the thermometer out of her mouth. "Well? How much?" I asked.

"Ninety-nine point five," she said. She put the thermometer aside and laid her head on the table. "I don't trust this cheap thing. I feel a lot hotter than that." She looked up at me. "Feel my head, Elizabeth. Tell me if I seem hot to you." I hesitated and she scolded me. "Some doctor you'd make!" I finally touched her forehead and it felt normal. "Well?" she asked. "Am I dying?"

I shushed her. "You feel like a girl who's trying to talk herself into sitting around the house another day instead of being in class where she belongs."

"How would you know? You have no heart. If you were sick, Elizabeth, you know I'd be good to you."

"Don't pout, it's ugly."

"Elizabeth, you have the feminine touch of a bulldozer."

"I know. I know," I said although 'look who's talking' was what I was thinking. "How do you want your eggs? Scrambled all right?"

"I don't care," Gloria said. She closed her eyes.

I was becoming annoyed at the drama. "Apple butter or jelly?"

"I don't care," she mumbled from her notebook.

"Take one or the other, or you'll have nothing."

She raised her head and the pattern of the notebook was embedded in her fleshy cheek. I had to cover my mouth not to laugh. "I tell you, Elizabeth, I'm too sick to think about jelly or apple butter."

"Do you really feel sick?"

She shrugged then motioned for more coffee as if she was Bess

Truman and I was one of her White House servants. "I guess I'll make it through the day."

"I thought you would," I said as I poured the coffee.

I scrambled three eggs, two for Gloria and one for me. Gloria had read somewhere that people with her health problems should limit sodium so I did not add salt. I toasted two slices of bread. I turned the flame too high and the eggs were tough. I was never a good cook. "Are you expecting a test today?" I asked.

"Vector analysis," Gloria answered as she loaded two spoonful of apple butter on her toast. Being sick didn't reduce her appetite. "I hate it. God knows I don't feel like thinking. Right now I wish I'd majored in something less exacting, maybe English lit."

I nibbled at my dry toast and picked at my one tough egg. "You know you wouldn't be satisfied. Imagine a professor talking about a poem and you mad as the devil because he can't write in one simple statement exactly what it means."

She laughed and went for my toast. "Are you going to eat that?"

"Yes!" I jerked it away as quickly as I could from her chubby fingers.

"Oh, Elizabeth, let me tell you, math is beginning to make me so despondent. I never want to think and I know why. It's because I'm too lazy. That's why, exactly."

"I thought it was an unwritten law that mathematicians be lazy."

Gloria rolled her eyes. "Foolishness. We're supposed to seem lazy, not be lazy. But I am lazy. Not just with math either. I'm sick of thinking all the time. You know what I would really like to do?"

"No, but I'm sure you are going to tell me."

"Take care of babies and change diapers and spend my life working in the kitchen and puttering around the house. I don't have any business worrying about derivatives and vectors."

"You notice something, Gloria? You didn't say a word about a husband."

"Men," she stuck out her tongue, " Worms in the apples. Babies and a house and a big kitchen. I imagine myself with those things. But not a husband. I suppose I think of a husband as just another part of the house, like an upstairs closet where I keep old shoes and raincoats."

"Gloria! Don't talk like that! You could get into trouble with that attitude."

"Is it so bad, Elizabeth, what I said about a husband?"

"You can't expect a man to enjoy knowing he was thought of as an upstairs closet."

"Sounds funny, doesn't it? Maybe a room. A living room. How would a man like being a living room?"

"Gloria, if you don't want to marry, that's no crime. You're not alone, you know. Many women I've known find it easier to love a house than a husband. And all men are not alike, of course. Some are wonderful husbands. True companions for life."

"Maybe, Elizabeth. You make it all so simple and natural, almost like plugging in to figure a dependent function."

"A what?" I asked.

"Are men really that simple, Elizabeth?"

"Very simple," I said, "especially compared to math."

Chapter Thirteen

About a mile outside of town was a cheap yet popular restaurant known for catering to students. Banners from the university's sports teams and stuffed replicas of team mascots covered the walls, with crowds of young people talking loudly and popular music even louder than the voices. The Andrew Sisters and Eddy Arnold sounded so snappy a listener might think the world was trouble free and no one had come home injured or insane from the war in Germany and Japan. I wanted to close my ears and imagine I was listening to Mozart. James ordered steaks from a bored waitress who turned a pencil end over end.

"You don't like it here, do you, Beth?" he asked.

"I wish it were quieter and less crowded."

"I enjoy the noise."

"Do you?" I said. "I'm surprised. This music is terrible. Sounds like crows fighting over scraps."

James laughed at my criticism. "There's strength here with these people, and it makes me stronger. As long as I have my own strength, I enjoy being here. Sometimes a crowd is like a beautiful flower."

I shivered as if I were cold. "Not to me."

"No?"

"I can't see a crowd as a flower."

James held my hands lightly and kissed my fingertips. His hands were still soft, just like the first time I touched them. Had he never done any manual labor? Had he never played sports? "You are so beautiful, Beth. You are the center of everything I know. You are like the crowd for me and like a beautiful flower."

I measured my next sentence. Afraid my words would be misinterpreted and equally afraid they would be interpreted correctly.

"I have never seen the room where you sleep," I said.

"I will show you tonight," James said.

"I want to see it."

The steaks arrived and were surprisingly delicious, grilled on the outside and moist inside. The blood ran freely over my plate into my mashed potatoes. I could barely eat it all. There was so much food available now, so much more than during the war. I barely remembered the Great Depression but I had heard stories from my older brothers of our mother feeding us syrup sandwiches because there was nothing else in the house to eat.

"Ignorance is not always unpleasant, Beth," James said, "And emptiness is not always the hollow madness of starvation. The emptiness which is worst, which is almost unbearable, is the emptiness of wanting. Just wanting, even when you don't know what you want. It arises from the primitive struggle to awaken painful remnants of early childhood, left over like an appendix." He pointed his fork at me, bits of flesh clinging to the tines. "You have known this wanting, Beth, not often but enough."

He saw through me easily and I felt pleasure from his knowing me.

James lived in a sprawling and poorly maintained boardinghouse. I followed him up the stairs into his darkened room. He pulled the long cord which hung from the ceiling light. The bulb was not covered and cast a harsh glare.

He had only one room, somewhat smaller than my bedroom. The walls had no pictures, no mirrors. The closet was open. The window was heavy. The half-drawn shade was faded and water-marked. The furniture consisted of one chair with an orange cover, a linoleum-topped high table, and a pipe lamp with a metal disk of a shade. Disarranged papers and books randomly filled a large and obviously homemade bookcase. A cot and a chest of drawers were opposite one another by the wall. There was a very faint odor of dry plaster.

This wasn't how I had imaged his room to look or any man's

room to look. It did not invite discourse or limelight.

James took off his coat and put it over the orange chair. He stood motionless as he watched me.

"Where was your bath?" I asked nervously.

"It's communal, down the hall."

"Oh."

"If I wanted a roommate I could afford a better place, but I prefer living alone."

I went to the communal bathroom to wash up and brush my hair. I pinched my cheeks and checked my smile in the mirror. When I returned to his room, I examined the three shelves of books. Texts and paperbacks, obviously second hand. The texts were of a wide variety of subjects: biology, chemistry, physics, history, literature. He had an old Bible, several collections of poems in English and German, a collection of modern plays, a few classic and a few contemporary novels, works of various philosophers including the history of philosophy.

I thumbed through a volume of poems. "Could I borrow this book?" I asked. "I want to learn something about the kind of poetry you like."

"Of course," James said as he went to close and lock the door. He sat on his cot and looked to me as I flipped through the book of poetry. "Beth, are you sure?"

The look in his eyes was unlike anything I had seen before. I quivered slightly as I set the book aside. "Yes," I said, the only word which was possible. All other words were vulgarities.

"Beth, undress."

I wished for darkness or at least another room where I could undress.

James said, "Are you afraid?"

"No," I said, crossing my arms over my waist. "I am ashamed."

"I want you because I need a woman," James said.

I felt myself about to fall into uncontrollable crying but I did not cry. "I need to turn out the light," I said. James didn't respond. I reached up and pulled the cord. A bit of light still came in through the window, but not much. I felt comfortable enough to take off my coat and put it over the orange chair. I took off my shoes and placed them under the chair. I quickly took off my dress and undergarments and put them on the chair.

James' voice was soothing, "You are naked, not nude, Beth." His voice calmed me and I heard for the first time the lust a man can have for a woman. James touched my face. He stroked my skin. He moved his fingers easily through my hair. I closed my eyes. He kissed my mouth lightly and slowly. His hands wandered over my body. I stood there, unmoving and rigid, feeling that I would collapse or break like a glass vase. James guided my hands to his body, and, as if I were a servant taking instructions, I began undressing him. I folded each article of his clothing as if this were a ceremony and I placed them over mine on the chair. I knelt, untied and removed his shoes, and I put them under the chair.

When I had finished, I said, "Now you are naked too."

The universe seemed a secret between James and me, and yet there were no more secrets. We moved to his cot and caressed one another. There was nothing we would not do.

"Beth, raise your hips," he said and I obeyed. James knelt beside me. Gently, he caressed my body from my knees to my throat. He kissed my mouth and my body. He kissed my eyes, my chin, and turning my head with his fingertips, he kissed my ears. He whispered to me, "Beth, lift your knees." For a moment I did not understand. "Pull your feet toward me." I drew my legs up, and James looked down at me. He whispered, "Good." His hands moved over my body. He said, "I will be as gentle as I can. I'll be careful. Don't be afraid."

"I'm not afraid."

James was gentle. He moved slowly. My thoughts seemed to pass out of my body. James clutched me tight. I held him close as his body trembled and slowly became limp. He lay relaxed on me until he kissed me quickly and got up. I turned toward the wall and heard him put on his clothes.

He kissed my shoulders and covered me with the sheet. "I'm going out now. I'll be back in five minutes."

I heard him unlock the door, close and lock the door. I drifted in sleep until I was startled by his return as James unlocked the door. I turned and lifted myself by my arms.

"Use these," he said, handing me a towel and damp, warm washcloth. I took them, not really knowing what he wanted me to do with them.

"Get up," he said. I moved away from the bed and cleaned myself. "You bled a little," he said. I felt ashamed. I balled the towel around the washcloth and put it on the floor by the yellow chair. I began to dress. James stopped me. "Not yet," he said. "I want you to stay." He lowered the window shade completely, and the faint light became almost total darkness. "Come here," he said as he sat on the bed, "Sit beside me."

I did as he said. He took my hand. Time was nothing between us. James touched my face with his fingertips, and his fingertips moved delicately over my lips and about my ears. "Lie down, Beth." I settled my head on the pillow. James said, "I am going to turn on the light."

"Please don't James."

James turned on the light and then placed his hand over my breast, which seemed to spring toward his touch. He began to play, moving his fingers in great circles, pinching and lifting as if he were playing with a child's toy balloon. He kissed my right breast, "Breast of Beth, here," and kissed my left, "and here is breast of Elizabeth. I must not neglect poor Elizabeth and her breast, but I have to disappoint her. I prefer Beth's. Her breast was much easier to reach. Someday, I think, I'm going to write a book and put one large breast and one very upstanding nipple on each page. I will undoubtedly be considered a genius and make tons of money. But the price will be high in human suffering."

He moved his hand from my breast and to my hip. "I wonder if as a woman gets older she feels less pleasure between her legs and more with her breasts."

"I don't know," I said.

"You are young."

I rose up on my elbows. "I'm twenty-two."

"Are you ashamed for me to see you naked in full light?"

"It's silly, I know. I hate it."

"Are you cold?"

"Yes."

He covered me with the sheet.

"Beth, do you think I want to destroy your shame?"

"No."

"Then what?"

"I'm not sure. Face it?"

He stroked my hips. "There must be shame or something very much like shame, or there can be no sensitivity to value and no true civilization and no true art. Danger is like shame. A person's shame is like the danger which threatens a growing, vibrant civilization. Shame is the deepest pain the immature and vibrant can know. I am ashamed, therefore I am."

I wrapped the sheet up to my chin. "I see no value in shame."

"Yes you do," he countered. "Let me tell you, Beth. Somehow, I don't remember how or where, I learned shame. Great shame. I was a child and a victim. I grew up with shame and I was totally powerless against it. Shame is many things but it is never useless."

He sat up on the bed and turned away from me. "My shame was like a terrible kind of second womb," he said. "You might call it a shell. I admired no-one. I had no heroes. I had no group. The only thing I loved was beauty. I always loved beauty but I don't think," he paused and his voice started to break. He was once again the soft-handed poet that I had come to love. I reached out to him. I stroked his back until he went on. "Tell me, Beth, do you think an artist can have that kind of beginning?"

I pulled the sheet around me and sat beside him. "You said shame was necessary."

"Yes."

"But if you were still walled in by shame you would be helpless," I said. "You wouldn't be creative. You'd be incapable of expressing creativity."

He looked at me and I saw the hurt child inside. "Do I seem that way to you? Maybe every poem I read, every play I write, is like tissue grown about a piece of glass in the flesh. Little angels must walk on a floor of broken glass that cuts into their feet."

He stood and pulled on his underwear and pants. He walked away from the cot. In the dim light, he ran his hands over the volumes of books he'd collected. "I am allowing myself to absorb as much of the world as I can."

"Turn on the light," I said. "I want you to see me."

My request clearly startled him. He pulled the cord of the light and we both had to shield our eyes from the harshness. He said nothing as I pushed the sheet away. I stretched with pleasure from my toes to my arms above my head.

James said, almost mockingly, "Beth is so free. She is a naked woman with a man who is not naked. She is free and innocent. I wish, I wish, I wish. Beth is beautiful. She is so beautiful."

James stood over me, not touching me. Of all moments I was with James, this moment was the best and the most pure. There can be few such moments, those of total nakedness without either embarrassment or casualness, when nakedness is discovery without effort and peacefulness without lethargy. I felt as if the doors, one after another, between us were opening.

James said, "I do like this hair, this red hair." He touched the hair on my head. "Here. And here." He touched the red blood stain. "You really do have bloody-red hair." He laughed and laughed. His streak of cruelty had returned. All that was good and pure had vanished. The nakedness of discovery had been crushed by vulgarity.

I turned away from him. "James, why? Why do you have to be so cruel?"

"I hate myself."

"I've got to leave."

"Don't leave me, Beth."

I remained with James all night. He took me home in the morning.

Chapter Fourteen

The day was clear and unusually warm for December. We drove to the mountains and James parked off a narrow road near an abandoned house. He wore a knapsack and cut walking sticks with his pocket knife.

The trail was obscure and we hiked past a series of waterfalls, each deeper than the one before. The journey was increasingly steep and increasingly cold. James climbed up on a crown of great rocks surrounding an icy pool. He picked up a handful of pebbles and threw one into the pool, watching the water become motionless before throwing the next pebble. I believe this was James' greatest happiness, here in the mountains. He found strength in the mountains.

As we climbed toward the next waterfall, we saw a young doe among the barren trees above us. James slipped out of his knapsack and silently placed the knapsack and walking stick on the ground. Crouching, he moved slowly toward the deer. She raised her head and twitched her ears. James dashed madly for her and she disappeared among the trees. James ran back to me laughing.

I teased him. "You know you didn't have a chance of catching that deer."

"Not much."

"What would you do if you caught her?"

He laughed playfully. "I have no idea."

We climbed higher and discovered a gorge deeper than any of the waterfalls. James dropped a stone. There was no sound. "How deep do you think that is, Beth?"

I inched close enough to peer over the edge. "I don't know. Maybe two hundred feet." I immediately backed away.

"Beth, I want you to go over to that largest tree."

I obeyed, nervously adding, "Promise me you're not thinking of doing anything dangerous."

He placed his finger to his mouth, "Shhh." He picked up a stone and moved to the edge of the gorge.

"Don't," I said, my hands close to covering my eyes. He inched until the toes of his shoes hung over the drop. "Stop! Move away from the edge," I begged. He laughed nonsensically as he teetered on the edge. He bowed low like a performer on stage, facing the hellish gorge, and dropped another stone. I started shaking with a newfound acrophobia. "Stop it!" I yelled. Finally, he moved away from the edge.

"Are you mad at me, Beth?"

I was too angry and upset to speak. He ran to me and wrapped his arms around me. "I promise I won't do anything like that again."

"It was stupid," I scolded.

"It was idiotic but it was also funny. How far can a man trust a god he doesn't believe exists?"

I pushed him away. "I don't know. I don't want to know."

"Of course you know, Beth." He pointed to the gorge. "You told me, about two hundred feet."

"That's why you risked killing yourself and giving me a horror I could never forget, so you could say something idiotic about God?"

"Don't you see the humor?"

"I'll tell you exactly what I see. I see you down there dead. And right now I don't care. I don't. Why don't you go jump off. Maybe then I'll appreciate the humor the way you want me to."

He circled around me like a madman, his arms emoting wildly. "The humor, Beth, the humor! There's humor here for everybody but you won't see it."

James grabbed his stick and knapsack, and continued up the trail, still laughing wildly. I followed, angry at my inability to resist him. He shouted at the trees and the rocks as he hiked, with every step sounding more like a king addressing his subjects. "I proclaim to the world that the idea of god is false!" He looked back at me and grinned. He knew I would follow. He waved his walking stick like a scepter. "I lean over the gorge and laugh at this false idea, and even as I laugh I trust the false god to keep me from falling. If I was a scientist I could compute my impact velocity, force, and a hundred other inconsequential matters."

He raced ahead and I had to run to catch up. He raced to the windy and cold top of a mountain. Only fir trees retained their color. All the oaks and hickory were bare. I could barely breathe by the time I caught up. I doubled over and held the stitch in my side. He took no notice of me as he stood on the rocky mountaintop and proclaimed to the valley below.

"What if I were a mystic?" He turned to me, "did you hear me, Beth? What if I were a mystic?" He turned back to the horizon. "The mystic claims there is meaning to life. Ha! That's what keeps the mystic from being an artist. Listen to me, you bootless housewives and clay-brained blokes, mysticism has nothing to do with god. I can say 'there is no god' and be a perfectly respectable mystic. That is trust."

He turned to me and grabbed my arms. He was as empathic as Roosevelt as when he declared war on Japan, as passionate as Mozart when he wrote Don Giovanni. "What if the mystic crosses that line of trust, Beth? That is the first step into the land of the artist!" He shook me as if he were trying to awaken me from a deep sleep. "And do you want to know where this land of the artist is located?"

"Stop!" I cried. He was frightening me. "Let me go, James, you're hurting me."

He held tight. "You know where it is, Beth. It's at the bottom of that gorge."

He let go and his arms fell limp at his side. His voice lost all passion. He fell to his knees and the cold wind blew his sandy hair about his face. "The artist lies down there at the bottom, and before he dies he wonders why the hell he was so idiotic."

I made a nest of soft pine straw and sat under the trees while I dried my eyes. I tried to forgive James and forgive myself for following him. The natural grandeur of the Blue Ridge Mountains brought me back to reality. The fresh, cold air cleared my head. James joined me and opened his knapsack. "Beth, I have some new poems."

"You don't expect me to read them now, do you?"

"Of course I do. Poetry is a thing that will not wait." He handed me two sheets of paper with four typewritten poems. "The college literary magazine accepted three and rejected the one I believe is best."

I read the four poems and handed back the papers. "The first is too full and irregular. But I do like the other three. Which ones did the magazine like?"

"The same ones you did." He took the two papers, folded them, and returned them to his knapsack. He fell back on the soft pine needles and I beside him. The only sounds were from the wind and the waterfalls. James said, "Isn't it so alone and wonderful here?"

"I love this now," I said.

"I wish we could sleep here tonight. Have you ever slept in the mountains out in the open?"

"No."

He rose up on one elbow. "How would you like to?"

"We can't."

"But if we could, would you want to?"

"Heavy-tailed if."

"What does that mean?"

"It's one of Gloria sayings. We couldn't possibly stay here at night. We would freeze to death."

We were quiet for a long while. I watched the thin clouds and listened to the falling water. At last James broke our long quiet. "Up here a man can be free with a woman and there's no vulgarity."

"I feel just that way."

"Do you? Beth, do you know what I want to do? I want to throw off all my clothes. I want us both to be naked and free and run in the woods and shout."

"It's too cold." I told him. "We'd die of pneumonia."

"I need to be naked. Don't you know, Beth, these mountains exist for nakedness. Here is the great womb, and here you can touch your freedom." James kissed me and opened my coat and held me to him. "We can never be free in a room, Beth. Men and women are made to love one another in the mountains, not simply to love the mountains, to say 'how lovely' and leave. Even if it's for no more than five minutes, lets' take off our clothes and be free."

"Is that really what you want to do?"

"It's what I need." James said.

I stood and took off my coat.

"No, wait." James said. "I was wrong." He took up his knapsack and the walking sticks and handed me my coat. "Beth, I want to climb to the last waterfall."

James walked on ahead of me. He was such an unpredictable man.

Chapter Fifteen

Christmas recess began and I expected my father to arrive the next afternoon to take me home. All was a rush. I packed immediately after classes and Gloria and I exchange our gifts during dinner. I bought her a small cookbook and she gave me a build-your-own crystal radio kit which, honestly, looked far too complicated for me to ever try to put it together.

After dinner, I bathed and dressed for my evening with James. As I sat on the couch and watched for him out the front window of our apartment, Gloria sat beside me and casually played with my hair. "Your James doesn't seem to care much about your feelings," she said. "I know if somebody kept me waiting almost every time I saw him, I'd wonder if he thought I wasn't worth much. When he comes, do you want me to go into my bedroom?"

"Don't be silly," I replied.

"I only thought, with Christmas and all, maybe you wouldn't want me around."

"I don't expect we'll stay here very long. I have my gift for Ameele. I'm going to ask James to take me to her apartment."

"Oh?" said Gloria.

I could almost hear her thoughts. "You don't approve?"

"Me? What's for me to approve? Do whatever suits your fancy."

It was a little after seven when James arrived, pounding on the door and shouting, "Open up for Merry Christmas!" I opened the door and James pushed an elaborately wrapped box into my hands. He kissed my cheek and then handed Gloria a smaller gift. "And for you, dear Christmas maid whom never shall I kiss. I have something less exciting than a kiss, but less infuriating."

"What?" said Gloria.

"You can't hide it from me. You're surprised by my remembrance."

Gloria blushed. "I thought you disliked me." Gloria's gift was a silk scarf and matching handkerchief. "This is lovely. Thank you, James."

"Gloria, you have the soul of a guilty woman," James said which made Gloria laugh.

I gave James a small volume of modern poems. His gift to me was a beautiful topaz necklace on a gold chain. "I read that Jane Austin wore a cross set in topaz," he said. "I forwent the cross, of course."

"This was too much, James," I said as I put the chain around my neck. "I love it." It was truly the loveliest gift I had ever received.

James read the index of the book I gave him. "No Frost and no Sandburg. Excellent! Beth, I think you can read my mind."

Ameele's hair was indifferently pinned and she wore a pair of brown pants and a plain, off-white blouse, yet, as always, she looked stunning. She was surprised by my visit and even more so by James, of whom I had told her nothing. After I introduced them, Ameele and I exchanged our gifts: simple knickknacks, minor tokens of our affection. James sat quietly while Ameele and I talked.

Ameele had plans to meet her parents in Washington and then fly with them to California to spend the holidays with her grandparents. For me such a trip would have been terribly exciting but Ameele spoke of it casually. This was merely a break in the routine of her life at the school. She was accustomed to flying cross country. Ameele asked if we would like wine. She had to ask James twice to draw his attention.

James considered her before answering, "Thank you, Miss Clark, but I don't want any wine."

"I have some very old, very good sauterne."

"No."

"Beth?"

I glanced at James before answering. "I don't think so."

"Don't you believe in drinking alcohol?" Ameele asked James

with a twist of condescension and mockery.

James ignored the question. He was looking about the room at each of her paintings. "I don't believe I've ever seen so many paintings outside a museum or art show."

"Everything you see here is my own work."

"All this, you did all this, are you an art student, Miss Clark?"

"Of course," Ameele answered.

James sat back in his chair and studied Ameele. "I wonder, Miss Clark, is there a good future in commercial art?"

A hard glow of contempt came upon Ameele's face. "Perhaps there is, but I am not concerned with commercial art. I'm an artist, not a designer."

I felt the need to explain. "Ameele can afford to ignore money. She's independently wealthy."

James seemed taken aback for a moment. "You are fortunate, Miss Clark. I bet it's nice to be immune to all the common sicknesses which afflict the working people."

"Why don't you call me Ameele. Miss Clark sound so *country*," She said, emphasizing that last word.

Instantly, James' expression changed. He looked at Ameele as if he despised her. He stood and snapped at me. "Why did you bring me here, Beth?"

"I didn't think you would mind."

James took out a cigarette and lit it. "I need an ash tray." He said as he paced around the room.

For a moment Ameele appeared to be debating what to do. Finally, she went into the kitchen and brought James an ash tray.

Taking the ash tray, James said, "I'll call you Ameele or anything else you wish."

"Ameele will be enough."

James held the ash tray in one hand and the cigarette in another as he went from painting to painting. "How many canvases do you have?"

"I have approximately forty," Ameele said. "Actually only painting interests me, but I've worked with charcoal, ink, clay, even paper and wire."

"I don't see any portraits here. Not one. Why? Don't you paint people?"

"Very seldom," Ameele said. James stopped at one canvas. Ameele said, "This was my latest work, and I believe it's the best I've done. You know how it is, I'm always trying to work toward something, and this is my best step toward that something."

"What makes you think I know how it is?"

"It's a figure of speech," Ameele answered. "I thought that was obvious."

James put down the ash tray. He held his cigarette between his lips and picked up the painting. He brought the painting into the living room. I followed him, carrying the ash tray. He placed it across the arms of a chair near a light. He took out his cigarette and held in in his hand, animatedly pointing at the painting. I quickly handed him the ashtray to keep from burning the floor. "I think I know this place," James said as he stubbed out his cigarette. "Isn't this part of Ma Bradder's house?"

"Yes, this is her parlor. I'm proud of my work."

"Really? Proud?" James queried, as if Ameele had suggested some idiocy. "I don't believe you. You're not the least ashamed to be doing something so useless? In truth, you're afraid I'll think you're a fool so you tell me beforehand you're proud to of your work."

Ameele crossed her arms over her breasts. "One must be proud to be an artist. I have no use for humility."

"Art is always foolish, Ameele. I don't see how such a fact has escaped you. No, actually, I do see. You're not a fool, Ameele. You're a nice rich girl who has found the perfect hobby."

"If you don't like my work, I don't care."

James raised his hands in mock surprise. "I haven't said one word about any of these paintings and you are defensive. But let's look at this one." He pointed to the painting he'd placed on the chair. "I can see you love bright colors. Lots of green. Green's a good feminine color. Red. Not much blue. Brown. White. But I don't remember seeing all this color at Ma Bradder's. When I was there, everything was covered by dust."

"You wouldn't understand," Ameele said. "If you think I ought to be ashamed because I paint instead of, say, studying something you would find acceptable. Perhaps nursing or teaching. You'd be dumbfounded by many of the theory of art classes I attend."

James softened, almost smiling, he said, "I might be dumbfounded, but I won't laugh. I promise. Cross my heart and hope to die."

"I don't care if you laugh or not. I'll tell you. I make sketches of a subject, and I paint from the sketches and from memory. I imagine what colors are implied by the colors I saw and remembered. I paint the hidden colors, and the hidden colors alter the form and the shape of the subject."

"Interesting," James said. "I mean that, Ameele. Your ideas are interesting. But one particular color is not quite right."

"What color is that?"

"A certain shade of red. I know an old story about a painter who wasn't able to capture quiet the red he wanted so he cut his fingers and mixed a few drops of his blood into his paint. You don't know that story?"

"I don't believe it would do any good," said Ameele.

"Yes. Yes it would. I'm sure," James said with a new excitement. With a single motion he took hold of Ameele's hand, squeezing her fingers. "Like this, with something sharp." James pushed his nail into the tip of her finger until it almost bled.

Ameele jerked her hand away. "You're crazy! You're insane!"

James laughed at her. It was laughter I recognized, a kind of calculated madness. "Do you hate me, Ameele?"

"Hate you? I think you're crazy!"

"I hate you, Ameele," James said very coolly. "I think I could take great pleasure in crushing your throat with my two hands."

Ameele took a step back. "Get out!" She yelled. "Get out and never come back!"

James laughed as reached out his hand for me. "Shall we take our   leave,   my   dear?"[i]

Chapter Sixteen

I had so much on my mind that I barely spoke to my father during the drive home to Petersburg. The land was so flat and sandy, nothing like the rolling mountains of the Blue Ridge. My father tried to make conversation. "Look at that convoy, Elizabeth," he said when we passed a long line of military trucks and tanks. "Wonder if they're heading to Camp Lejeune?" My father never served in the military. He was 4-F. Most people do not know that the term 4-F originated in the Civil War and was used to disqualify army recruits who did not have four front teeth with which to tear open gunpowder packages. Most people don't know of the Civil War battles fought around Petersburg, Virginia, that these battles ultimately lead to Lee's surrender at Appomattox. My father had four front teeth but he also had a curved spine that made him unfit for military duty but capable of work as a carpenter and running my parent's small farm.

My mother ran out to greet me as did my two brothers, Tom and Lewis, both wearing their army uniforms just for me.

This was where I belonged, yet I knew that I had changed greatly. My home had become a foreign place. My parents and siblings were distant and unreal. I had never before felt so lonely.

I had never before kept any great secrets from my parents but I could not tell them about James. I never even mentioned him yet I thought of him constantly. James was like a sickness to me. Everything I did, whether talking, laughing, singing Christmas carols, or exchanging gifts, seemed like a lie to me because I was not telling anyone about James.

How could I? My whole relationship with James involved fear. I was tempted to say something after dinner, when my father, my brothers and I were working together to clean the kitchen. Mother had spent days preparing a wonderful Christmas dinner and father always cleaned up the kitchen. He never insisted that my brothers or I help, which I thought was foolish. My brothers could be so lazy sometimes, but this time we all helped.

Tom talked about the girls he'd met in overseas and I talked in general about college. I wanted to tell them about James but there was no point. I had no future with James. College and James were quickly passing and I knew the time would come when I had to make sense of my world beyond home and beyond college.

And beyond James.

Two weeks after I had returned to school, my faculty adviser, Professor Dorothy Ellis, the only woman on the history staff, asked me to come to her office during a mutually free hour. Professor Ellis' manner was habitually authoritative and direct. "Elizabeth, sit down please," she said. I took the one chair beside the desk. The office was a small room, with bookcases overflowing with books, papers, and folders. Professor Ellis was looking through a pale yellow folder. "Elizabeth, I understand you will be going into public school teaching," she said, reading a paper in the folder.

"Yes, I suppose I will. My father wanted to teach. But his family was poor. He had to go to work early to help financially. When I began college, it was simply assumed that I would be a teacher."

"Do you want to teach?"

"No, not really. I don't think I would ever be a good teacher."

Professor Ellis was never one to mince words. "So why go into teaching? Don't misunderstand, I'm not saying anything against public school teachers. I know that an excellent teacher is truly a remarkable person. But I don't believe you would ever be content as a teacher. I have your records in my hands, Elizabeth. I see you have an 'A' in your major. At least a 'B' and perhaps a low 'A' generally. Do you have a scholarship?"

"Yes."

"Conditional?"

"No."

"Excellent. I know you to be a good student and I have spoken with a number of other professors about you. Dr. Schmied tells me you sometimes appear to ignore him in class. I can't blame you much for that. I've sat in on his lectures on several occasions. On the other hand, Dr. Schmied tells me your research work is excellent. In fact he believes you have a very unusual talent for digging facts out of the jumbles of prejudices a great many so called historians pass off as objectivity. And you can use your material intelligently. I have the greatest respect for Dr. Schmied's opinions, and in this case in particular I totally agree with him."

"Thank you." I said.

"You're welcome," she replied. "Now, I'll get to the point. I have a job offer for you and I want to know if you are interested. I have an old friend. His name was Albert Henderson, Emeritus Professor at Maryland. Albert is the author of several important studies of the American period between the Civil War and the First World War. At present he is beginning a major study of the period of the Spanish-American War. He needs a research assistant, and, if you would like the position, I am certain I could make the arrangements. The pay would be quite low, of course, but you could make this into a great opportunity, especially for a woman. But Albert is a rather progressive thinker, as many historians tend to be. Learn from the past and all that, I suppose."

I could barely restrain my excitement. "I don't understand, isn't this the kind of position normally given to a graduate student?"

"Albert is an emeritus professor which gives him tremendous autonomy."

"He knows that my area of concentration was European history?"

"That should not be of any difficulty at all. Albert likes to train his own people. What he is looking for is someone with basic research skills, a good mind and boundless enthusiasm. I'll warn you, you will be working a good deal more than now, and the work will be considerably more demanding than college work."

"I can handle it." I said, "It's almost impossible for me to believe."

"It's an opportunity, Elizabeth, and not a commonplace

opportunity."

"I want the position."

"I thought you would. I believe you will be glad in the future. Do you live in town, Elizabeth?"

"Yes."

"The address?"

"Twenty-nine Jefferson Avenue, apartment number six."

"I'll get off a letter to Albert today. I'm sure you'll have a letter from him soon, then you and he can make the specific arrangements."

I stood and shook her hand. "Thank you very, very much."

This was new life. My future had embraced hope. Simple joy had replaced the chaos and the fear I felt when I was with James.

After classes I went with James to Bonners'. I talked almost ceaselessly about my family in Petersburg and my new semester of classes, but I resisted telling him about Professor Ellis' offer. I wanted to savor the news privately for a while. James smiled and said, "Tell me what you're hiding, Beth."

"Hiding?" I said innocently.

"Don't you think I know you? You're too happy not to be keeping something from me. Now you're going to tell me what it is."

"I'm glad to be with you," I said. "That's all. Glad to be back in Charlottesville."

"I like to believe you are, but I know it's more than that."

"Maybe I ought to make you guess."

"Well, tell me, how many guesses would I need?"

"Oh, I don't know, a hundred or a thousand."

"You've done something with your hair? A new dress, perhaps? Something involving your parents?"

Every question earned an enthusiastic "No" so I decided to tell him. "I've been offered a position."

"A what?"

"A position. A job."

"A teaching position?"

"Do you think I want to teach?" I said. "No, this is something much better. I suppose you know Professor Ellis, Chair of the History Department."

"How would I know her?" he snapped.

"Don't be so impatient."

"I'm waiting very stoically," he countered.

"Professor Ellis is my faculty advisor. She asked me if I would want a research assistantship working with a friend of hers, a Professor Henderson. I have accepted, of course, and if nothing goes wrong, I'll be working in the National Archives in Washington DC. She believes this will be a great opportunity. And I agree. This is the kind of work I really want to do."

"When will you begin?"

"I don't know yet. Professor Henderson should write me soon, within a matter of a few days. My expectation is that I will begin sometime this summer."

The waitress arrived to take our order and James asked, "Are you hungry, Beth?"

"Oh, no, I'm too excited to eat."

James said, "Will you come with me to my room?"

"Yes! Let's hurry, James! Please! I want to hurry!"

When we arrived at James' room it was frigidly cold. "Mrs. Miles asked me to shut off the heat this morning." James turned the knob of the radiator. "It will take a while to warm the room."

I sat on the bed as James locked the door. He sat next to me, his face was a blank and his eyes were staring ahead. "Tell me what you are thinking," I said.

"Many things and nothing in particular. About how happy you are going to be in Washington and how funny we are sitting here. About how I have no idea what I will do after graduation. And I was thinking how pretty are a cow's utters."

I could still be astonished by the things James could say without the least affectation. "A cow's utters?"

"A cow can have pretty utters. A girl has a pretty face. A woman has a beautiful body. I wonder if your friend Ameele was right, and I am less than sane."

"I have wondered," I said very lightly, neither playing nor questioning his mind. James nodded absently. More seriously, I added, "You do have so many obsessions and visions which are certainly not very easy to understand. But I would never call them insane."

"Do you want that job in Washington?"

"Yes."

"You will have some freedom there. You need that freedom."

I kicked off my shoes and hugged my legs. "I'll probably always think of freedom as in the mountains, the way you talked about freedom. Is there any chance I can have that kind of freedom in Washington?"

"Beth, we both know the mountains are an image of *might-be* freedom. The freedom you will have in Washington will not be so pure, but it was going to be much more tangible." I nodded as James continued, "I think I know you, Beth, and I believe you will discover you belong in Washington as you have never belonged anywhere before."

James knew my fears and joys immediately, even more than I knew them. "And you, James?" I asked. "What about you?"

"I want that kind of tangible freedom," James said. "As a man in this society, I am forced to want it. But I don't belong in it or with it. Someday, maybe I will, but not yet. Now I belong in the mountains. Maybe that means I belong nowhere. Maybe someday I will sell shoes. I could do one thing then another. First, now, it's beauty and ugliness. And it's beauty and goodness. But always it's beauty. I love beauty with a pain that's like fire burning on my skin, and I seem almost to smell my skin burning. I have to clutch everything that's beautiful. But beauty dies and I know why. Because of power. The lust for power is a kind of rape. I clutch too viciously. I am too weak and too strong. Do you know? I'm too weak almost to live at all. And I'm too strong to hold beauty without destroying it. I'm like a wild animal with beauty. Beauty is a weak and innocent thing that never knows its value. I cannot be so weak and live. I know and think on and on. I think until there is nothing to me except thinking. I could almost laugh. If I were someone else seeing me, I think I would laugh. 'He has tied himself in a ridiculous joke', I would say, 'And he doesn't even see how funny he really is'."

At that moment I would gladly have died to hear James tell me he loved me. Love would be so wonderfully simple. The room had grown warmer so I threw my coat to the floor. I ripped off my clothing as if my clothing were covered with spiders.

Naked, I stood motionless beside James as he sat on the bed. James placed his hands upon my hips, and he turned me gently. He kissed my buttocks, one then the other, as if he might have been kissing the cheeks of an infant.

He said, "Nakedness is humanity against system." He seemed imprisoned in softness but I didn't want softness. I wanted passion. I wanted to strike out at him and beat him with my fists.

"Please," I begged. "James, please."

James undressed, taking time to fold his clothing and place everything neatly on the orange chair. When he came to me, there was no passion in his body. I sat on the bed and he sat beside me. I waited, and he did nothing more. I made him lie on the bed and kissed him but he did not kiss me. I caressed him but he did not touch me.

He was looking up to me, his eyes so sad, and I could almost hear him telling me: 'Beth, you are beautiful.' I hated his constant obsession with beauty. I wanted a warrior at that moment, not a poet. I wanted power, not beauty. I wanted ugliness and vulgarity, not innocence. I began to caress him with increasing intimacy. I tickled him with my fingertips. I kissed his body. And very slowly, seemingly laboriously, James' body responded to my touch and my kiss.

He put his arm about my waist. He pushed me to lie back. As he lifted my hips, I wrapped my legs about him. My body sprung upward into his movements. I pushed myself to him with all my strength. I wanted to scream every vulgarity against beauty I had ever heard but I did not scream. And this silence seemed to fester within me. I cried out, "Harder! Please. Please. Faster and harder!" I caught James' neck and bit his shoulder with my teeth.

Tears escaped. All my feelings were beneath my tears. I dropped my arms from about James' neck. I dropped my legs from around him. I lay back. I was still and my mind drained. James moved and my body began to move in obedience to his and my ecstasy increased with every touch.

The room was hot. Our bodies were wet.

"Tonight was the best ever for you, wasn't it, Beth?"

"It was wonderful."

"So soon you will be going to Washington and I'll be going other places."

"I don't want to think about Washington."

"Don't you, Beth? Doesn't a part of you want to get away from me and hope never to see me again? Doesn't a part of you hate me?"

"How could I hate you?"

"Even if we were to marry, wouldn't something in you hate me? That part of you that enjoys a victory?"

"I could never hate you," I said. "But something I fear you. I seem more and more to be becoming a part of your personality. Once I was Elizabeth and now I am Beth, and Beth seems more you than me."

"I think you are very courageous, Beth. You have the rarest kind of courage, the courage to bring together innocence and freedom. Freedom kills innocence, and innocence cannot live in freedom. You have joined them for us tonight, and we have lived a kind of miracle together."

"I don't think I understand."

"It doesn't matter."

James kissed me.

Chapter Seventeen

By the first week of February I had exchanged several letters with Professor Henderson. I began planning seriously for my new position and studying background material.

That same month, the college literary magazine published an issue more than half of which was devoted to James' work. In addition to the three poems I had already read, the issue included a fourth short poem and one longer poem and the entirety of the play James' group had put on at the Barn Playhouse. The play appeared under the title *The Death of Beauty*.

Gloria and I were doing our homework when Ameele came for an unannounced visit. I hadn't been avoiding Ameele—I'd seen her often at school—but I hadn't been at her apartment since her heated encounter with James. The tension between Ameele and Gloria was almost as contentious as between Ameele and James.

"I want to talk with Elizabeth alone," Ameele demanded as she marched to my bedroom. I made my apologies to Gloria then followed. I closed the bedroom door behind me. Ameele was sitting on my bed. She had not yet taken off her heavy winter coat. "I suppose you know about this." She held a copy of the school's literary magazine.

"Yes, of course," I said.

"Did you know of this before you brought him to my apartment?"

"James took me to see the play for our first date."

"Where?"

"It was just a group of students, Ameele," I said. "Quite innocent."

"Where!"

"Off campus," I said.

"But you didn't bother to tell me."

"The play was open to the public, Ameele," I said, confused by her anger.

"I want to see him."

"You can see him any time you want. He's easy to find on campus, but I would have thought you couldn't stand the sight of James."

"How long have you known him, Elizabeth?"

"About five months."

Ameele took off her coat and held it on her lap. "I'm asking a favor of you. I want you to bring James to my apartment for dinner. It would be purely social, Elizabeth, nothing more. I wouldn't ask you if I had anything else in mind."

I frowned at the suggestions. "No, Ameele, we both know it would be terribly awkward for all of us."

Ameele gathered herself into her most regal manner, speaking to me as if I were one of her subjects. "I don't think it would have to be awkward at all. James and I share an interest in beauty, Elizabeth, albeit he is too gruff with his opinions for my tastes." She glanced out my window and I followed her gaze. Snow was falling and that could mean classes would be canceled. Ameele continued. "What could be more natural than our simply getting together and exchanging ideas? Now that I have read his poems, I think I understand him. He demands life. That's the one great quality that goes through all his poems, and that is exactly what I need, someone whom I can respect. Someone who knows what it means to need to create."

How did I find myself in this situation? There were no two people I cared for more than James and Ameele yet there I was between them. I wished Gloria was in the room with me to help me convince Ameele. Gloria was nuts and bolts logic while Ameele was as predictable as spring water. "I'll tell you what will happen, Ameele. I know James. He insulted you the first time he ever saw you."

"The only time," Ameele said.

"He insulted you then, and if you put yourself close to him, he'll insult you again. But this time it will be worse."

"You still don't understand, Elizabeth. I don't care. I mean that.

I don't care what he says. I want to know him. I have to know him. It's for my art, you see."

"The situation would be too miserable for all of us."

Ameele pointed to a missing button on my shirt. "Did he do that?"

"I don't appreciate what you are insinuating."

"Nevermind," she said. "Will you and James ever marry?"

She was almost as bad as James at knowing my most vulnerable sites. I lowered my head. "No, I don't believe there is much chance of that."

Ameele said very coldly, "Then what are you afraid of? Do you think I'm going to rob you of your place in his bed?"

"I'll tell James what you said, and I'll let him decide."

Ameele was smiling. "Friday should give us all enough time. Ask James to come at seven-thirty."

"Am I invited, too?" I asked.

"Ameele gave a little laugh, "of course."

I met with James Tuesday afternoon at the student union. Perennial card games were everywhere and at one table a small crowd was gathered to watch two servicemen play chess. James brought me coffee and a sweet roll, and we sat at a booth.

Fatalistically, I began, "James? Do you remember Ameele Clark?"

"Of course," James said. "She's the painter."

"She read the literary magazine and asked about you. She would like to know you better. You and she share an artistic interest, she said, and she asked if you would come to her apartment for dinner on Friday. She insisted that I ask you. I promised not to try to influence you one way or the other."

James nodded as if he were solving an abstract problem. "Really?" he said with neither surprise nor emotion. "Ameele asked you to get me to go see her?"

"Yes, she asked both of us to come." I hesitated. "Actually, I doubt she cares whether I come or not, but I want to be there."

"So Ameele thinks you will be the perfect chaperon."

"More like referee," I said. "She can be very insistent."

"What time does she want us Friday?"

"At seven-thirty. Do you want to go?"

James smiled "Of course I want to go, Beth."

Chapter Eighteen

It was Friday evening and I was downstairs in the laundry room with Gloria and Alice Frost. I was sorting through laundry to find gloves for my dinner at Ameele's. I was sure I'd lost them, not that either James or Ameele would notice. Gloria had begun spending more time with Alice after her return from the hospital. She was chronically depressed and emotionally unstable. Gloria had confided in me that she often heard Alice screaming wildly and cursing. Gloria suspected that Alice beat her children and was afraid Alice would attempt suicide. Her husband had taken the night shift at the textile plant west of town and wasn't home to help.

"He wasn't much help anyway," I whispered. "All he did was get her pregnant."

"Not anymore," Gloria reminded me without mentioning the hysterectomy.

I was young and in love so all of Alice's troubles disappeared from my mind the moment James arrived to pick me up. I forgot all about my gloves and rushed upstairs when I heard him knocking on my front door. "Give me a moment," I yelled as I ran a quick brush through my hair and pinched my pale cheeks. I opened the door and there he stood, dressed casually as if we were going for a walk in the park and not to a dinner engagement.

"I'm worried about tonight, James," I said as we drove to Ameele's. "I feel like a terrible fool taking you to see Ameele again. Am I a fool?"

James laughed lightly, "I have no idea, Beth."

When we arrived Ameele greeted us with a touch of shyness. She was dressed elegantly, wearing black with pearls. She hung our coats in the closet and led us to her dining table. "Please, sit down."

The meal was unlike any I had ever had: lamb with exotic spices, fragrant rice topped with a cauliflower concoction, and her favorite sauterne wine. I enjoyed my meal but James picked at his, barely taking a bite. Ameele accommodatingly asked James questions. James' answers were brief and matter-of-fact. His major? History. What kind of writing was most difficult? Poetry. Why more difficult than prose? Poetry required deeper understanding, more honesty, did not yield to skill and eclecticism. His favorite poets? Keats and Wordsworth, but Shakespeare was more intelligent. Ameele said, "I don't know as much as I could about poetry. I used to like Masefield, the poem that begins 'I must go down to the sea again'."

James said, "Masefield is ordinary, but I have read worse poets. He's a Wordsworth without magic."

Ameele worked to maintain the conversation despite awkward gaps, until it eventually lapsed completely. I had expected the evening to be uncomfortable and it was. After dessert James complimented Ameele and thanked her for the dinner. He excused himself and went to the living room.

James was so unlike my father, who would have offered to help clear the table and wash the dishes. My father's hands were always rough and red from his carpentry work and from helping mother in the kitchen. James' hands were as soft as a girl's and his fingernails were always neat and trim. Perhaps that was why I was attracted to James. I thought my father's roughness and generosity were a signs of weakness.

Ameele had the habit of grinding her teeth whenever she was very upset or angry. As we worked through the mountain of dishes, I tried to forgive her for initiating such an exhausting evening. James came into the kitchen with an unlit cigarette in his mouth and asked for an ash tray. With wet hands, Ameele handed him the ash tray and James thanked her and left. At that, I threw the dishtowel aside. There was too much to clean and I was tired. My back ached from my long week of school and study and preparing for my new job. "I told you this was a bad idea," I said as I left the dishes and followed James to the living room.

James was spread out on the sofa as if he were a monarch. Ameele followed me in and she and I took the less comfortable chairs. We both sat straight backed as James lounged and lit a cigarette. Ameele was the first to break the silence.

"Are you going to write professionally?"

"Maybe I will," he said. "Maybe someday I'll be able to make a living by writing, but I'm not counting any future royalties."

Ameele nodded. "Money is a real problem."

"Of course," James said.

"Do you think you might teach?"

James blew smoke in my direction. "Ask Beth if she wants to teach."

I laughed sarcastically, "I hope I never have to stand up in front of a class."

"We're all agreed on that point," James said as he puffed his cigarette. "And what plans do you have for after graduation, Ameele?"

"I plan to study in Paris for a couple of years."

"Do you speak French?"

"Fluently."

"I envy you," he said.

"Do you? I'm surprised."

"Surprised by my envy, Ameele?"

"No, surprised you would admit it," she said. "I thought you abhorred weakness."

James crushed his cigarette in the ash tray. "It's Beth that abhors weakness, isn't it." He looked at me and I blushed. "Beth, tell me, do you envy Ameele?"

"A little," I said which was close to the truth. In truth, I envied Ameele quite a bit.

"So your family is wealthy?" James asked. "What is your father's profession?"

"He's an investment broker."

"Where?"

"New York."

"Your father is successful so I imagine he is very intelligent."

"He is."

Talk of fathers and success made me uncomfortable but not enough to ask James to take me home. He opened his cigarette case and lit another. "You are also very intelligent, Ameele, and attractive, especially your hair. If you let it down, would it touch your buttocks?"

Ameele laughed, obviously startled by the sudden change in the conversation "Not quite. Almost to the small of my back."

"You do have lovely hair. Tell me, do you know about a certain kind of very large garden spider? When I was in grade school, the kids called it the writer-spider. We used to tell each other that if a writer-spider wrote your name in its web, you would soon die."

"I never heard that story," Ameele said.

"I never saw any writing in the spider's web. All I saw was confused design, but I suppose nature gave the spider an instinct for order."

"Is there any point to all this?" Ameele asked.

"Conversation, just conversation," James said as he puffed his cigarette. On our previous visit, James was rather prudish about wine. Not this time. He'd had wine with dinner and now he returned to the dining table and poured himself another glass. He brought it back to the sofa and drank freely. Settling in like a king on his throne, he asked, "What do you want from me, Ameele? Why did you ask me to dinner?"

"To talk with you. I wanted to know you but you are not making that easy."

He cocked his head. "Wanted? The past tense? Have you changed your mind? What exactly did you expect? To be born again like a Baptist?" James placed his wine on the side table and smashed out his cigarette. He stood. "Beth, I think it's time to leave."

Ameele touched his arm. "Not yet, please. I have a new painting. I'd hoped to wait to until after we knew each other better but perhaps you'll take a moment now."

James looked down at her, "Show me your painting."

Ameele brought out the canvass and set it on an easel opposite James. It was a portrait of an elderly woman painted in grays and browns. None of Ameele's usual bright colors, the colors James had mocked her for earlier. The old woman's nose and lips were exaggerated and her skin was marred with age spots and deep cuts.

"This is a portrait of Ma Bradder?" James asked.

Ameele nodded. "Yes."

"I barely recognize her," James said. "Ameele, tell me, who was the better painter, Braque or Picasso?"

"Picasso, I would say."

"And tell me, as a woman and a painter, why does every woman paint like a child or a trained monkey?"

Ameele stiffened and I shook my head. I knew this would happen.

"I don't care what you say or what you think," Ameele snapped, "This is my work and this is good work. If you're not going to say anything constructive, I don't care what else you say."

James moved behind Ameele and placed his hands on her shoulders. "Ahh, Ameele, we all know that you are lying," he cooed. "You painted this specifically for my approval."

"I am not lying."

"You painted this yourself, without any help? Ameele Clark painted an old woman?"

"Are you accusing me of stealing someone else's work?"

"No, not steeling. Something far worse," James said, "You have to take a step, Ameele. One very short step."

Ameele looked like a vulnerable child. "What step do you think I have to take? Tell me."

"I'll tell you next year, after your return from Paris, if you are still alive."

"Why do you think I invited you here? For your charm? Tell me now!"

James massaged her shoulders and she let him. "Tell me, Ameele, have you ever been drunk? Not swaying a little, but really drunk?"

"Perhaps," Ameele said. "I don't know."

He left Ameele and picked up his glass of wine. He held it under the lamplight and swirled it gently. "The step you must take is something like being drunk, but much more intense. There's nothing pretty or noble about it. You, Ameele, must be killed and it must be vicious. You must be killed like a woman opening her legs for her lover and getting an icepick stuck in her breast. It's bitter cruelty, Ameele. It's an angel walking barefoot over broken glass. It's taking your soul out of your brain and knowing everything."

Ameele rubbed her shoulders, where James' hands had been, "I need some time to think."

"I'm not debating with you. What is an artist, Ameele?" James allowed her no opportunity to answer. "Ask a man in the drugstore and he can tell you. An artist paints. An artist makes beautiful objects. An artist writes poetry. But ask an artist. He could more easily count imaginary numbers on his fingers than define art."

"You are trying to smother me."

"I am giving you what you want, Ameele," James said. Ameele crossed her arms over her breasts as James drank the wine. He said, "This new painting of yours is pure art, Ameele. Pure art is trash."

"Trash?"

"Believe me, Ameele," James said. "Believe what I say. You know that you want to believe me."

"You're telling me I want to believe that my work is trash?"

"Ameele, do you love this painting?"

"Yes."

"Why?"

"Because it's mine, because I created it, because I think it's a good painting."

"You are like a god."

"Yes, exactly. I am like a god because I can create."

James laughed at her. It was cruel, bitter, ludicrous laughter. Ameele seemed stunned. She did not move. She stared at James as expressionless as a statue.

James said, "An artist is not a god. This painting is not the creation of a god. And it's not the work of an artist, Ameele. You know exactly what it is. Believe what you already know, Ameele. This was the fabrication of a young woman who has told herself, if I was an artist, I would think this way and feel this way. The young woman imagines herself knowing the heart of an artist and she pretends that it is her own heart she knows. You know too well what an artist is, Ameele. You know without any doubt that an artist is someone who paints."

Ameele kept her eyes on James as he paced in front of her.

"Your painting is trash. Do you know where trash belongs, Ameele?" James went into the kitchen. He came back with a small knife. He offered the knife to Ameele."Where does trash belong, Ameele?"

Ameele looked at the knife. "This painting is mine. It's not yours."

"You are lying, Ameele. This is my painting, not yours. You painted it for me and I don't want it. I don't want any trash, Ameele." James spoke with a great calm, as if he were a man giving instructions to his daughter.

Ameele studied the portrait of Ma Bradder, perhaps as a young woman might study the face of a sleeping lover. She took the knife from James. She had such contempt in her eyes; I feared she would strike James or turn it on herself. She did neither. She pushed the blade into the canvas. She cut the canvas many times, leaving the knife in the mutilated canvas. She turned to James, moving to him, her eyes fixed upon his face. She encircled his body with her arms. She pressed her face to his body.

Neither of them seemed to be aware of my presence. I felt more alone at that moment than I had ever felt before. I was invisible. I was nothing.

There was no kindness in James' expression as Ameele embraced him. He placed his hands upon her head and then moved them to her shoulders. He pushed her away. "Ameele, you are a whore," he said. She grew limp in front of him. With deeper cruelty, James repeated the same words, "Ameele, you are a whore."

Ameele backed away from him.

James laughed, "A whore, but never an artist. I call you a whore and laugh and you stand there like a mute. Do you want me to spit in your face, Ameele? Artist? No never, you're not even a woman."

Ameele slapped him and James smiled, mocking her. She stood a moment, transfixed, looking at his mocking smile. She picked up a small empty vase and threw it at him. It hit a chair instead. "Get out! Get out!" She ran into her bedroom. I was ready to follow but James stopped me.

"Don't go after her, Beth," James said. "It's an act. It's all an act."

I turned on him, ready to slap him too. "I wish the vase had hit you!"

"I never told her it was a bad painting." James said. "Maybe it was good. I don't care. It doesn't matter."

I grabbed my coat and stormed out the door. I walked in a fast rage back to my apartment. James followed, hurrying to catch up. "Beth, will you come to my room?"

"I can't," I said when I reached my apartment. "No, that's not the truth. The truth is that I don't want to be with you."

At the door to my apartment, James whined like a child, "I want to see you tomorrow afternoon. Please Beth, will you want to see me then?"

"I don't know," I said as I searched my purse for my keys. "Not now. I don't know how I'll feel tomorrow." James left and I went to my bedroom and cried.

Chapter Nineteen

The morning was sunny so, fortunately, we were hanging our wash outside instead of in the dank laundry room. Gloria did not ask me about the dinner with James and Ameele. She talked about Alice and her children as we stood side by side. "I think Alice is getting a bit better," Gloria said as she shook the wrinkles out of one of her huge slips and handed it to me to hang on the line. "She doesn't cry as much as she did when she first came home from the hospital." She handed me a pair of her oversized underpants and I wondered if any of my clothes had actually been washed. "She's an object lesson on the dangers of becoming involved with men, Elizabeth. Too many children and the only way to avoid more is surgery." Gloria shuddered. "No man is worth that, if you ask me."

"I didn't ask you, Gloria," I said. I wasn't about to share the horrors of my dinner with James and Ameele. She'd just gloat. Clouds rolled in and the sky turned solid dark gray. "Oh no," I complained. I was tired, and the cold wind made my hands hurt. I threw the rest of the laundry at Gloria and ran back inside. I ran all the way to my room and fell on my bed. I pulled the blankets around me and cried as the clouds came in and covered the ground with snow.

I can't say what made me give in to James. Loneliness, I guess. So many young men had died or been disfigured in the war in Europe and the Pacific, with gossip surfacing every day of madness and suicide. Most of my women friends were alone. I didn't want to be an old maid. I took a hot bath, and dressed comfortably, leaving off my stockings and girdle. I wore slacks and a loose blouse. I didn't care what I looked like for James.

James' room was warm. I said nothing as I undressed. As he

began to undress, I looked at the ceiling above the bed. There was cold emptiness in my feelings for him. James spoke my name. "Beth," and speaking my name was deeper intimacy than our sex. After, we again lay together without a sound.

"Beth?" James whispered my name, again, this time it was a question.

"Yes." I said.

He touched my face with his fingers, and I turned away from him.

James said, "You can send me away."

"What would I have then?"

"Boyfriends."

I laughed bitterly. That was the problem, wasn't it? The word became a ridiculous corruption of my girlish dreams. How could he not see the source of my anger? How could he be so brilliant and so obtuse? "I wasn't even there," I said, "You ignored me while you had your cruel fun with my best friend then you asked me to come to your bed. If you slept with another woman, that I could understand, if you wanted her for sex. But for you to play your cruel games with another woman then come to me for sex, that makes me feel like a cow, and I can't stand that."

"Would you rather I slept with her, Beth?"

"I don't know what I want." I said, longing him to care for my feelings without my having to ask.

James turned on his side to face me, "You once told me that when a man sleeps with a woman without talking with her, he makes her his whore. You don't care if I treat another woman as a whore, but you don't want me to treat you that way." James touched my shoulder. "Isn't this touch a word, Beth?"

Tears filled my eyes. My body longed for his hands and mourned for it when the touch passed.

James quickly got out of bed. "Beth, let's go out. Let's walk. "

The sky had cleared and the moon gibbous. We walked through the snow along the old sidewalks of the city, beside rows of large, well-kept houses. The streets were especially quiet and, in a comfortable way, beautiful. James tried to take my hand but I crossed my arms.

"Anyway," he said, "after last night I expect Ameele will always despise me."

"Maybe," I replied, "but Ameele is a woman, as lonely as the rest of us. If you wanted her, she would come to your room tonight."

"You think so?"

"Stop playing the fool," I said.

"As long as we are together, I promise you, Beth, I will never ask her."

"I don't want to be alone tonight."

James took me up to his room. We did not make love. I slept in his arms, comforted against the cold winter.

Chapter Twenty

Spring erupted without my notice. I was busy with my studies and had altogether stopped going to Ameele's apartment, although we continued seeing one another at school. I passed her on campus once and she stopped me. She enthused that her manner of painting was changing. "I've found a greater sense of solitude. Objects stand out as if they had no relation to backgrounds."

I was disappointed when James mentioned going to Ameele's apartment. "Don't worry," he said, "Ameele treats me as if I were nothing more than an embodiment of an artistic attitude. She believes I have enormous influence on her work." I can't say I was shocked to hear this. Both James and Ameele put art above reason.

One day, Ameele invited me to see her new paintings and I accepted. She made coffee and shared some madeleine cookies she'd bought from Silverstein's grocery. "As I paint now, I can feel myself getting better. Not just learning. I can feel myself growing, my whole self, my body and my intelligence, everything. I can feel everything about me grow." After coffee, she showed me two landscapes. Both were exceptional and I told her so. She brought out a third painting. It was an unfinished portrait. "Do you recognize that face, Elizabeth?"

I came so close, my heart raced so fast, I almost touched the still-wet portrait. "James," I whispered.

"Only one who knew James well could have recognized him."

The colors were inhuman. The piercing eyes were exaggerated, the pupils black and erratic. Ameele had captured the contradictions in James' personality. And more, I saw in the portrait James' peculiar need to coldly examine that part of himself which was nearest to madness. The painting reminded me of the time James told me of one of his recurring childhood nightmares. He was climbing the steps of a great pyramid, at the top of which he knew he would see God. He reached the top and sitting on a throne a giant albino. He ran and awoke to the feeling of falling.

I asked Ameele if James had sat for her.

"That's not my way. This is entirely from memory and imagination." Ameele was always focused on her commitment to her art when she spoke and I envied her for that. I had nothing in my life I cared about as much as she cared about art, except for James, perhaps. And he would never be mine whereas Ameele would forever have her art. "James is the perfect subject for me. He hasn't seen this, yet. I'm planning at least two or three more portraits of him. I think that the better I know him, the more telling my paintings will be." I felt the fool for bringing them together.

It was in mid-March, a Sunday afternoon, when Ameele showed up at my doorstep. She looked terrible. Her face weighted with pain. Her eyes were swollen and red. "May I come in?" Her voice was weak.

"Are you sick, Ameele?" I asked as she entered.

"I have to talk with you alone," she said. "Where's Gloria?"

"Downstairs with Alice Frost and her children. We are alone."

She said, "James made me come here. I've finished three portraits of him and I have begun another. Elizabeth, this has become an obsession with me. I want you to see all the portraits."

"You met with James? When?"

"Does that matter? James said he wouldn't see me again if I didn't tell you everything." She finally took off her coat and sat on the couch. I sat next to her, thinking I should offer her tea, but I needed to hear every word. "Thursday night I went to his apartment," she said.

"His apartment!"

"Yes," she said. "I found his address. I had to see him. You can't imagine what he did. He asked me in and locked the door. He told me to undress and not a word more."

I tightly crossed my legs and felt a flush. "I believe I can imagine that."

"I don't understand you at all, Elizabeth, how you can be so calm. Don't you care? I know you're not casual with James."

"You know that yet you went to his bedroom!"

"I know, Elizabeth," Ameele said, her voice pleading. "Pride and secrets between us are ridiculous now, aren't they?"

At that moment I hated Ameele. Yet I loved her. In Ameele, I had found another woman who understood the torment of loving James Campbell. I wanted to slap her and I wanted to kiss her.

"I should go," Ameele said.

"No, don't!" My voice had an eagerness I barely understood. I began to laugh.

Ameele's face lightened for a moment then turn dark again, "I was a virgin, Elizabeth, before James. Were you?" I nodded in response. "We are quite a pair," Ameele said and she was right. This was like a dry joke without humor. She added, "I don't have any regrets, Elizabeth. I've had others tell me they loved me, but James demands life, and that is so much more than mere love."

"Do you love James?" I asked her.

"I could hate him," She smiled. "Actually, I believe I do hate him." She laughed shallowly. "I have enough cause. When James told me to get undressed, I was petrified. I wanted to be any place but there in his room. I still can't believe I didn't run away and never look back. You know that cold expression of his? The one he had when he called me a whore? I've seen that look many times since and I have always hated it. That's the expression he had as I undressed. It was a long time, it seemed a year, before he undressed himself. He was, um, you know, Elizabeth. His voice, oh, it was so brutal. 'Make me want you, Ameele. You're a woman. Make me want you.'." Ameele stopped. She bit her lip and clinched her hands. "I can't help being ashamed."

I took her hand. "We really are the same, aren't we?"

"Yes, we're the same." Ameele's expression changed. I saw in Ameele's face love and more than love, desire, and I was embarrassed by it. "I felt trapped and frightened. I was crying, and you know I don't cry. I expected James to laugh, but he didn't. He put his hands on my shoulders and pushed me down. He told me again to make him want me. And I did, Elizabeth, with my hands first, then with my mouth."

We sat together in silence for a long while, my holding her hand. "Come to the kitchen and I'll make some coffee," I offered.

"No, I think I ought to leave. Thank you, Elizabeth."

Chapter Twenty-One

To my surprise, new warmth had entered my friendship with Ameele. We talked with greater intimacy about our respective relationships with James, especially as it involved Ameele's art. It was 1949 and my position in Washington, the future, and graduation were all quite naturally replacing Ameele, college, and James as the focus of my life.

But outwardly my relationship with James did not change. On Sunday afternoon two weeks before the beginning of the Easter recess, I packed a lunch and James and I went to the park for a picnic. In the center of the park was a pond so small a man could easily throw a stone across. The smooth water was like a clear sky and the sun glared in the water. I chose a spot near the pond. Across from us children played on swings, a slide, and a merry-go-round. As I was setting out the lunch, James was looking at the children across the lake. "I think a lot now about how much of Wordsworth I can keep," he said. "I think it's going to be a long while before Wordsworth can be read again."

"Do you want to eat?" I asked.

"What do we have to eat?"

"Beggars can't be choosers."

"And why can't we? I heard of a beggar who refused a nickel and, like an Oxford snob, said 'I never accept any gratuity inferior to the dime."

I poured tea into paper cups. "But did the beggar get his dime?"

"A story is a story. How would you like the story to end?"

"I don't think I would give him anything."

"But somebody else would, and a third person might think the beggar showed great courage and give him fifty cents. It's all just a matter of style and odds."

"I have cheese and bread, plus some carrots, celery and

cucumbers."

"Fine."

Soon a twitching squirrel came begging. James offered a crust of bread. The squirrel sniffed the bread and began pumping its tail excitedly. James laughed, "I know there's got to be a moral." The squirrel took the bread and scampered up a nearby tree. James's mood darkened. "I'm afraid, Beth. I have to be afraid. I know I shouldn't ruin the day talking about fear."

"What is it? James, tell me," I said.

"Courage, everything is courage," he said. "My courage, as much as I have, is the only thing that separates me from the world. This is why I envy Ameele, I do envy her. Ameele can be alone and never be alone. Financial independence is such an easy substitute for courage. I have only one advantage over Ameele, that I am my own courage."

"You have many advantages of Ameele," I said as I crunched on a carrot. "I know you are strong."

"Maybe, Beth. Maybe I am strong. But it's not a matter of strength. I wish it were. Strength is a more common stock than courage."

"My father was strong," I mused. "But was he brave? I don't know. The family worried endlessly when my brothers were in the war." I offered him some celery. "James, what do you intend to do?"

"Ultimately? I don't know," he said as he took the celery and tossed it into the pond. "For now, I want to write poetry as long as I have enough energy. Then what? Maybe I will write a book, a novel, maybe two or three books, but not turgid paps. That's about as ultimate as I'm thinking. Any book will have to wait until I have found something true about beauty and goodness."

"Isn't that a lot like searching for the meaning of life?"

"Not if meaning implies god. I'm willing to admit that the purpose of life is reproduction of the species. That doesn't cost me a thing. I have no interest at all in supernaturalism. Every great artist now has to have forgotten god. You might call that the beginning of a definition."

"Where will you go after graduation?"

"I haven't thought about it," he said. "Not seriously. I know I'll go to some large city. But not Washington."

"Why not Washington? Because I'll be there?"

"Yes," he answered. "And because I have to cut myself off as totally as possible from my family and friends. I know I won't have much time."

"Why so little time?"

"Energy and courage, they have their limitations. I know if I waited I would be consumed by cynicism."

I leaned against James as we watched the children play across the pond.

That week was the last time I saw Ma Bradder. I had been visiting her off-and-on since meeting her with Ameele. I watched her health and her mind deteriorate. She often forgot my name or confused me with friends long dead, and she often promised me impossible favors, even going as far as to say I was in her will. She looked back to her childhood, and as her senility progressed, she seemed to forget all the years of her adulthood. She liked to quote the lines: "Turn backward, turn backward, O time in thy flight. Make me a child again, just for tonight." The day before Palm Sunday, Ma Bradder died. She was alone.

Chapter Twenty-Two

Ameele asked me to come for a visit and showed me a new portrait of Ma Bradder. It was typical of her use of bright colors, and, honestly, I cringed when I saw the portrait.

Ameele told me, "Once she was dead, I knew I had to paint another portrait. I felt like a mortician. There's a certain idiocy about making a corpse lifelike for burial, isn't there?"

"I doubt that a mortician would agree," I replied.

Ameele dismissed my comment. "She was an old woman."

"And all men are mortal." I felt myself begin to cry even though I held little attachment to Ma Bradder. It was only a few years after the end of World War Two and despite America's victory, death still hung in the air.

Ameele, however, didn't seem affected by Ma Bradder's death, or any death, for that matter. Rather, she became quite animated. "Oh, I have another painting to show you, and I completely forgot about it." She brought out another portrait of James and set it on an easel by the refrigerator. This portrait resembled James much more than had the first. But Ameele had pictured his face older and weaker. "It's James, of course," Ameele said. She seemed to want me to say something. "This is the last, Elizabeth. I'll never paint James' portrait again, I promise. I suppose you know I don't see him much anymore."

I held my emotions close. Talking about James was never easy. "James never told me. I never had a thought."

"I'm not surprised. We're all involved with our own plans. The end here is so close. You'll be going to your job in Washington. I'll be leaving for Paris in August. Tell me, has Gloria been accepted to graduate school?"

"Yes."

"I'm glad," she said. "I suppose we're all a little afraid. And I know James is afraid, Elizabeth. Perhaps he deserves it, but I don't believe I've ever known anyone as afraid as James is right now. He's become so enwrapped by fear that just being around him makes me afraid." She pointed to the portrait. "Look. You can see it here. Compare this with the first ones I painted of him. Those were portraits of an artist. Not this. This is the face of an ordinary man. And this is exactly what James wants to be, ordinary. He doesn't want to be an artist. He'd rather be a cab driver. He simply doesn't want to push himself against inertia the way an artist must always do."

I knew that something of what Ameele believed was true. I suppose it was akin to my longing to be rid of James. Escape from obsession sounded so very peaceful. James had a longing for a life without art, for the most ordinary and routine life. Above all, he longed for life to be simple, without the quest for beauty and goodness. "You can't really believe that James is ordinary."

"To be an artist doesn't a person have to want to be an artist?"

"Are you asking me?"

Ameele picked up her painting and I followed her back to her studio. "Only rhetorically," she said as we walked. "A person who's an artist must constantly force himself to be different from others. Conformity is the death of art. Isn't every artist who's any good a unique individual? But James wants to conform."

"When did you decide James doesn't want to be an artist?"

We arrived in Ameele's studio and she set the painting on its easel. "Not in a day. There was no flash of understanding. I discovered it gradually. But looking back now, I know I should have realized it from the beginning. He condemned me for wanting to create my own reality. It's cliché, yes, but it's true. Every artist creates her own reality or she's no artist."

One of the last days before graduation, in the late afternoon, James and I walked along the dirt road through the farmland behind the college. The sun was warm and the sky unbearably blue. There were birds in flight and a great, white cloud making the blue even more vibrant. I was feeling melancholy. I had grown to love this town.

James seemed to share my mood. He said, "We have known each other less than a year, but it seems almost half my lifetime."

"I know, mine too."

"We are both young," he said. "We both have people to meet and things to do."

I could barely speak as I took his hand. "I've made arrangements at a boardinghouse in Washington. I want you to write me, James, and—," my voice cracked as I wiped away a tear, "—and tell me where you are and what you are doing."

James picked a wildflower and gave it to me.

That last night in James' room I was trembling. We had very little to say to one another. We lay together quietly and tenderly. I stayed with James until almost midnight. Leaving him that night was the most difficult thing I had ever done. I thought of Gloria's heavy-tailed if. If we could have had a life together. If we could have married and had a family. But there was no fairy tale ending. There was only a sweet good-bye.

In the morning I began packing. Gloria was back and forth between my bedroom and her own complaining, wishing, remembering. "Do you want my old algebra book?" she asked.

Hands on hips, I answered mockingly, "Why would I want anything old of yours?"

She tossed it in the garbage pail and headed back to her bedroom. "I guess I'll have to throw it away." She ran back to my bedroom and to the pail. She retrieved the book, holding it tight like an infant. "But I've kept this book for four years. This was my first college math book." She turned the pages "I hate to throw this book away. I'll never need this book again but I hate so much to throw it away."

"If you feel that way, for God's sake keep the book," I snapped.

"Tell me, Elizabeth, truthfully, do you think we will ever see each other again? Will you write to me?"

"Of course I'll write."

Gloria smiled with awkward innocence. "I do love you, Elizabeth."

Chapter Twenty-Three

The work with Professor Henderson in Washington was much more demanding than I had imagined. Perhaps my greatest difficulty was adjusting to the enormous diversity and dispersion of source material. I spent months in dusty libraries with crudely organized papers from 1840 to 1860: Letters from soldiers in the Mexican American War and the Civil War (or as we in the south called it, The War of Northern Aggression), handwritten notes, requisitions and the like, all stored loose in boxes. It was very much like those first years of studying a language, when each day you feel yourself measurably increased.

My social life was full. At first, inevitably, I compared each young man I met with James. As time passed, my memory of James grew more distant. These young men of Washington were ambitious and eager with their liberal-minded idealism so attractive in persons of ability. They were all Truman democrats, of course. I was quite aware that they attracted me for reasons quite unlike those which I had found attractive in James. They were simple where James was complex; they were sure where James was uncertain. Most seemed more intelligent than James—or perhaps not—but they seemed to have clearer vision where James' mind was deep and murky.

I wrote James twice or more every month and I received two letters from him. One marked Richmond and the other Charleston, South Carolina. Then his letters stopped. More than a year passed before I heard from him again. I received a letter from Philadelphia. From the envelope, I learned that James was living at 517 Booth Street. The letter inside was pencil written, the handwriting erratic and almost illegible. James wrote:

Beth. I am sick now, and I can't think right. I have a fever. I don't know how high. Maybe it's nothing.

*Too much sun. Probably it's nothing. But I can't eat. I
know how the play has to end. Why don't you write me? I
wish I could read your letter. I'll tell you when I can. Do
write me if you can.*

I immediately called Professor Henderson at his home to ask
for time off to visit a sick friend.

Chapter Twenty-Four

My train arrived in Philadelphia at eight on Friday evening in late August, 1952. I asked at the station about a reasonable hotel and I took a cab. I had dinner at a small restaurant close by my hotel. That evening, alone in the room, I seemed for the first time aware that I had made a decision to come here to see James. I had spent a considerable amount of my small salary and I could hardly believe that I would be with James the next day. Between the awful heat of the city and worrying about James, I lay awake a long while unable to sleep.

On Saturday morning I took a bus to where James lived. Booth Street was a narrow road made up of nothing but stones covered by broken blacktop, cars parked on both sides. The houses seemed oddly hollow and massive, like houses once owned by the rich but now had been eaten from within so only empty shells remained. The porches were high with marble steps. On one side of the street white men and women were sitting on the steps and children were playing. And on the opposite side of the street black men and women and children were doing the same.

I found house number 517, the address on James' envelope. Sitting on the steps was a small girl of five or six and a thin, old man. "Excuse me," I said.

The man took off his hat. "Yes ma'm."

"I'm looking for James Campbell. I wonder if you could help me."

"Yes'am, I know 'em, he's got a room upstairs, but I ain't seed him much lately, I suppose he's up there now, he might be, can't say I know as a fact."

I took a step back so I could see the entire front of the building. I shielded my eyes from the bright morning sun and asked "Which is his room?"

The old man pointed to a drooping balcony. "Yes'am, like I say, go upstairs, and you'll see his room at the end of the hall. Go up and go straight after the stairs."

"Thank you," I said.

The hallway smelled of spoiled milk, urine, and perspiration. I climbed the dimly lit stairs and knocked on the door at the end of the hall. I waited a moment then the door slowly, almost painfully, opened. I saw a badly scarred man. "I'm trying to find James Campbell." The man acted as if he didn't hear me. "Do you know James Campbell?"

"He ain't in here right this moment, but I'll fetch him for you." I watched as the man walked down the stairs. He'd left the door open so I looked around. The room had a cot, a table, a chair, a top coil refrigerator, a metal cabinet, and a military duffel bag stashed in the corner. It was humid and smelled of stale tobacco. I opened the metal cabinet and found a few cans of food, some cookware and tableware. On the table was a single coil hot plate. I opened the refrigerator and appreciated the cool relief from the oppressive heat. It was almost empty. The total ugliness of the room was deeper than poverty.

I went to the window and opened it. A slight breeze and the sound of traffic entered the room. Across the street a black man was pushing a two-wheeled wooden cart of scrap metal with a dog following behind. I turned when I heard steps outside the door.

I barely recognized James. He stopped, resting against the doorframe. He was thin and hollow-faced, like the photos of depression-era farmers. He was deeply tanned and his sandy hair, bleached white by the sun, was long and uneven. For a moment he did not seem to know me. Then he smiled weakly, "Beth? What are you doing here?"

"I received your letter."

James closed the door and squinted at the open window. "Close that window, will you, and pull down the shade. I'm always so cold and the light hurts my eyes." I closed the window to a couple of inches and lowered the shade.

"You don't look well at all."

"You do," he said. "You look more beautiful than ever."

My heart ached seeing him like this. "I didn't come to be complimented." I felt his face. His skin was moist and clammy. "Have you seen a doctor?"

"No. I'm too exhausted. I try to keep warm. I've been taking quinine tablets. If I take four or five of them, I don't feel much of anything."

"Quinine! Why are you taking quinine? Do you have malaria? Tell me the truth."

"I don't know. I haven't been to a doctor. I bought the tablets at the drug store, Beth. I feel like a wolf has hold of my throat. My head and spine feel filled with ice."

I led him to the cot and sat beside him. I took his hands and was shocked at how different they felt. Gone were the soft hands of the boy who'd never known work, replaced by the rough hands of a working man. His fingernails were thick and unkempt. Then I noticed a horrible scar on his palm. "How did you get this?"

"An accident. It's a burn. It doesn't bother me anymore."

I sat to face him. "What have you been doing, James? How did this all happen?"

"I've been working in the sun."

"What kind of work?"

"Hard work."

"When did you eat last?"

"Yesterday."

"What?"

"Bread and milk."

"Did you keep it down?"

"No. I think the milk was spoiled."

"Oh, James. You have to start eating." I went to the window and moved aside the shade. "Where can I find a grocery?"

"Do you have a car?"

"No, I took the train."

"You're not going to walk, Beth?"

I dropped the shade, "Of course I am, silly."

"This was a bad neighborhood."

I crossed my arms. "I grew up with two brothers; I can take care of myself. Now, tell me how to get to the store."

"Two blocks down." James tried to stand but collapsed back to his bed. He pointed in the general direction. "It's a little store. But I'd rather go with you. "

"Don't be ridiculous. Lie down. Keep still. I'll be back in a half hour. And don't take any more of those tablets until you see a doctor!"

It was a relief getting out of James' sick room and depressing apartment building. The walk was refreshing and all the people I passed on both sides of the road were pleasant, tipping their hats and smiling. I hurried to the grocery store and purchased canned beef stew and soup, cans of grapefruit juice, a box of shredded wheat, milk, sugar, bread, and bar soap. I hurried back, carrying the full shopping bags in both arms. A fat, middle-aged woman was sitting on the steps of James' apartment building when I returned. She wore a soiled dress that was at least a size too small for her and was smoking a cigarette. I asked her if she knew who owned the building.

"Some Jew," she answered as she puffed.

"Is there anyone here I could see for a room?"

She looked incredulous, "You want a room? Here? In this dump? A nice girl like you?"

"Yes."

She sneered, "You ain't one of those working girls, are you?" I stared blankly and she finally relented. "You'll have to see the man with a burn aside of his face. He takes care of the building. What little taking care as was done."

"Could you tell me his name and where I can find him?"

"Sure, hon," she said. She worked her way off the steps and pointed to the entrance. "There, first door on the left. Just knock. He's in there. His name was Lynch."

Mr. Lynch was the man with the scars on his face I had met in James' room. His voice was deep and so heavily slurred; I found it hard to understand, "You want one room?"

"One room. Yes."

He looked me over. I was still holding the grocery bags but had no luggage with me. "How long?"

"About a week." I followed him up the hallway. He didn't offer to carry either grocery bag. He unlocked a door and stood aside for me to go in. The room was much like James'. It had a bed instead of a cot but there was no refrigerator. "How much is it?"

"Fifteen dollars for the week."

"That includes sheets for the bed?"

"It does. You do your own changing and washing."

"And laundry? Do you have a laundry?"

"Machine's on the back porch. Ten cents a load. You get your own soap."

"If you will get the sheets now, I'll pay you. I have a great many things I need to do today."

The man nodded. "I'll bring the bedding."

"Oh, and one more thing," I asked, "Can you recommend a doctor for a sick friend."

"Man or woman?"

"My friend is a man."

"Methodist Hospital is on the other side of the river. That's a far piece."

"Could you take us?" I asked to which Mr. Lynch replied by raising one finger and shaking it. "Then do you know of any doctor's who'll make house calls?"

"Here?" he snorted. "Are you crackers? No doctor's coming out here."

In my new room, I placed the groceries down on the bed and opened the window. Only the side of the next building was visible. I ran my finger along the windowsill, it was thick with dust. I shook the thin mattress, hoping to scatter any hidden bedbugs. When Mr. Lynch returned with the bedding and I paid him for one week. He gave me a key and a receipt. I asked him about cleaning materials: a broom, a mop, rags. "Look out there on the back porch." I would have to clean later. Now I needed to get the groceries to James.

James looked up from the cot when I opened the door. As I put the milk and two of the three cans of grapefruit juice in the refrigerator, I told him I had rented the room downstairs.

"Why?" he asked. "You could sleep here, with me."

"You could be contagious," I said. I found a can opener and a cup in the cabinet. I opened the third can of grapefruit juice and filled the cup. "Here, you're going to drink this." He sipped with hesitation. I stood over him like a prison guard. "Not like that. All at once. Get it down fast." He swallowed, gulping loudly, and finished all the juice. "Hurts your throat?"

"Yes," He answered.

"How are you feeling?"

"Dizzy."

"Uneasy in your stomach?"

"Yes."

"I want you to eat something," I said.

"I don't want anything, Beth," James said. "I don't think I can eat." He fell back on the cot. I broke one biscuit of shredded wheat into a bowl and added fresh milk and a little sugar. I brought the bowl and a spoon to James and fed him in bed. He ate slowly. I was patient and did not urge him to eat faster. Several times he stopped, looking blankly at the bowl, almost ready to regurgitate, but he finished the cereal.

"How did it taste?"

"Not bad," he replied.

"Now, I want you to take off your shirt and your undershirt and lie down on the cot. Lie on your stomach," I said. James swayed and almost fell over as he pulled his undershirt over his head. "Lie down," I repeated. I massaged his neck and shoulders. At first, his muscles tightened under the touch of my fingers. I kept at it and he finally relaxed. "When did you last have a bath?"

"I don't know," he said. "Days and days."

I didn't say but it was as clear by the odor in the room that he hadn't bathed in days. "If you need to sleep, don't fight it. Let it come."

James said, "Thank you, Beth. Thanks for coming."

He couldn't see how very moved I was at this simple expression of appreciation. "You didn't expect me to come, did you?"

"No."

"You didn't hope, just a little?"

"You're the only person who knows my real feelings. That's why I wrote you, but I never thought you'd come here."

Gradually, as I massaged his back, James fell asleep.

I left him asleep and went back to my hotel. I checked out and returned to my new boarding room with my luggage. I checked on James but he was still asleep. I went downstairs and gathered the cleaning supplies. Cleaning my own room took two full hours and I intended to clean James' room as well. I took the broom and some damp rags to James' room but he wasn't there. I knew one bathroom was downstairs, I supposed another was on the second floor. I assumed that James was there. I swept the floor and wiped down all the surfaces with the damp rags. I took the sheets off his cot and shook them outside. When I returned to his room and he still wasn't there, I began worrying. I decided to look for him.

The outside of the bathroom door was disfigured with drawings and vulgarities. I tapped on the door. "James? Are you OK?"

"I'll be out in a minute, Beth."

I waited at the door. When James came out of the bathroom, his face was pale and his head was bowed. He leaned against the wall as he walked back to his room. I followed, ready to catch him if he fainted. He sat on the cot, took off his shoes, lay on his side and pulled the sheet tightly to his shoulders. "Were you sick to your stomach?" I asked.

"No," he said, clearly uncomfortable with this line of questioning.

"Good. Any diarrhea?"

James winced. "Good Lord, Beth. Can't a man have any privacy around here?"

"No," I said. "Not when you take quinine without seeing a doctor, you don't." I plugged in the hotplate and asked, "Which would you prefer, soup or more cereal?"

"I don't care. Really, Beth, I just want to lie still. I don't want anything to eat."

I opened a can of beef stew and put it on the hotplate to warm. "James, you have to eat. Tomorrow I'm taking you to the nearest doctor. Understand?" I set the table with a bowl and a spoon for each of us then I went to help him up. "Come to the table," I insisted. "No more eating in bed." James did not move. I took hold of his arms and pulled. He pushed me weakly.

"I hurt so, Beth." His face was raw with pain.

"Get up!"

"My spells. They come and go."

"Yes, yes, I know," I said, clucking like a mother hen. James swung heavily off the cot and I helped him to the table. I poured a cup of juice for each of us and served the stew. James sat shivering, his arms folded at his waist. I ignored him. I began to eat. He sat a few minutes, and then he ate his dinner. I asked, "Do you have any more quinine tablets?"

"In the bag, there by the bed."

I searched his duffle bag and found the tablet box. I put it in my pocketbook. "I don't want you taking any more of these tablets again without a doctor's approval. If you have malaria that's one thing, but if you don't, well, these pills could be causing your problems." James nodded passively. I said, "I haven't seen many people here, and I didn't have any trouble at all getting a room. We shouldn't have much competition for the bathroom or the hot water. What do you have in the way of clean towels and underclothing?"

"Probably nothing. I don't know."

"I want you to get a hot bath right away, before somebody else gets to the bathroom."

"Beth, no, I can't," he said.

"I'm going to help you and I'm not listening to excuses. Either you let me help you and get up this instant, or I'm leaving. I didn't come all this way to twiddle my thumbs."

"I'm too dizzy. I'll be sick to my stomach."

I left him there to finish his dinner. I found some laundry detergent on the back porch and used it to wash out the tub. I partially filled the tub with hot water, and then I returned to the room for James. I picked up a robe and gave it a sniff. Not horrible. "You'll have to wear this for now. I'll wash your clothes in the morning." I took his arm.

James stood up from the bed, swaying like a toddler just learning to walk. "Would you really leave me, Beth?"

"Yes, now where is your door key?"

James fumbled through his pockets until he found the key and gave it to me. I locked up his room behind us and locked the bathroom door behind us as well. James sat on the closed toilet as I topped off the half full tub with hot water. Steam filled the room.

"Beth, I can do this by myself," he said as he tried to stand but I did not release him. I told James to take off his clothes and held him so he wouldn't fall as he undressed. I helped him into the tub. It was a long tub and he was able to stretch his legs. I gave him the soap and washcloth. He was confused and uncoordinated.

"Scrub harder or I'll wash you," I told him. He dropped his soap several times so I scrubbed him and washed his hair. "You need a shave," I said gently.

"Not now, Beth. I can't keep my balance."

"When do you want me to shave you?"

"Tomorrow, Beth. Let me wait one more day."

I helped James stand but as he stepped out of the tub, he collapsed. I could not hold his weight and he fell forward onto me, pushing me to the floor. I groaned and pushed him off of me. I had to catch my breath before I was able to help him up.

"I'm not hurt," James said.

I wiped the sweat from my face. "Well, bully for you," I said. It was so hot in the room I could barely think. "I'm not hurt either, thanks for asking."

In the morning, I began my search for a doctor. I went to the telephone booth near the grocery and opened the phone book. All I knew was that Methodist Hospital was the closest, according to Mr. Lynch. I started there until I was able to make an appointment. The first spot available was at the end of the week. Nothing else.

I returned to James' room and prepared a solution of warm salt water for his sore throat. I helped him as he shaved and then washed his clothes and linens. James pointed to his duffel bag. "Get my wallet." I opened the bag and found his wallet. "How much do I have?"

"Twenty-two dollars and change."

"Take the money," he said.

"No, you'll need this to pay the doctor."

I also found his bankbook in the duffel bag. He had less than two hundred dollars. I sat on the edge of his bed and showed him the numbers. "Just how long do you think you can live on two hundred dollars?"

"Not for the abstract future. Very soon I'll be able to work again. I am feeling better, Beth, since your arrival. Every day I feel better."

I stroked his face, brushing his hair out of his eyes. "Good," I said. Good, indeed. It felt good to be appreciated. He had changed so much.

James ate cereal again for breakfast and very little for dinner. "Tomorrow you'll be having scrambled eggs for your breakfast." I told him. The next time I went with him to his bath, he did not need my help. "Soon you'll be well enough to take your own bath." I massaged his neck and shoulders.

When I thought that James was asleep, he asked me, "Have you written to your employer? What was his name? I don't remember."

"Professor Henderson," I said. "I wrote him last night."

"When did you tell him you would be back in Washington?"

"I didn't."

"He must be very tolerant."

"I hope he is, I enjoy working for him."

"I'm glad." James said simply, and he smiled.

"What happened to your car?" I asked.

"I sold it. I needed the money to get to Philly."

"From where?"

"I was working in South Carolina."

"Your letter was postmarked Charleston."

"I was there for a while," he closed his eyes. "Please, no more questions. I'm too tired."

The next morning, James was able to walk outside. We walked to the highway and back, and we sat on the front steps. "How are you now?" I asked.

"A little tired, but I'm getting stronger all the time. You can cancel that doctor appointment. I need the money more than I need the doctor."

I canceled the appointment and hoped this wasn't a mistake.

During the next several days, we maintained this routine of walking. We walked longer distances and at night we talked. James asked me about my life in Washington. I told him everything. I enjoyed sharing my life with James. He said, "I'm happy for you. You will always have a good life, Beth."

"I wish I were so confident."

"You are confident. I know you are."

"I've found myself as a part of a vast system and I love it. There's nothing for me to do but to grow."

During our second and final week together, James showed me the city, or as much of it as was possible with our limited amount of time and money. We visited the iconic sites: The Liberty Bell, Independence Hall. James told me everything which had happened to him since the graduation. Some parts he told superficially, others in great detail. I understood the changes I saw in him.

As I have since then lived my own life, I have understood much more. James Campbell was a poet and it is commonplace that poets write for the next generation. As I write these words, probably no more than a few thousand persons have read the poems of James Campbell. Even more than his being the first man of my adulthood, James Campbell was a true poet. And you never forget a true poet.

Never.

Part Two

The one thing about James I most failed to understand when we were at school together was his fear. I never appreciated the depth of James' fear and I never knew its origin.

—Elizabeth Brewer

Chapter Twenty-Five

Everything, I imagine, must begin at home.

James spent only one week after graduation at home with his parents. This one week was one of the few periods James could not talk about with ease. He left home as soon as respectfully possible. He could not endure spending a long time with his parents. He was physically repelled by the house of his childhood.

It was my own opinion that far from hating his parents, James loved them more than would be considered the natural obligation of a son. James' father was a kind, gentle man whose eyes were bright and expressive. He loved to laugh. He did not smoke, drink, or use profanity, and his happiest moments were spent singing gaily off key in church. He often suffered great physical pain, which he traced to a childhood injury.

With pain came depression. James' father would sit for hours moaning, never hiding his pain. Fits of rage followed pain and depression. Apologies followed rage. Then cheerfulness returned. Twice he had attempted suicide, or so James thought the both times he found his father in the closed garage with the motor running. As James grew into young adulthood, he lost respect for his father. He never lost love but he did lose respect. In his father, James saw the same weaknesses he saw in himself: Indecision, oversentimentality, and gullibility. This had left James' father struggling with creditors and left James longing to belong to a wealthy family.

James' mother was unlike his father. Her life seemed devoid of joy. Her only pleasures were vicarious, of seeing the smiles of another, in particular of her children. She was morose, uncomplaining, and rigid. The only touch she took pleasure in was that of a crying child she could comfort, and she withdrew from every other physical contact, especially that of her husband. She worked slavishly and was forever asking James if she could do something for him, as if she were trying to mend some great guilt. She was obsessively asking him about his health. I wondered if this was the origin of James' obsessive tendencies as well as his inability to hold his tongue. Rude and critical comments had landed James in the principal's office when he was a schoolboy, and had given him more than one bloody nose.

James never spoke of siblings that I could recall. Just the cryptic statement he's said years before: *the mountains have strangeness, like a brother who hates you.* This was a mystery I would never unravel.

When James left his parents' home, he drove east. He had no destination. He decided on Richmond. There was no reason, only a decision. James had no interest in that city.

Near the river, near warehouses and rail tracks, James took an apartment of two clean rooms and a private bath. He seldom saw the owner-manager, a middle-aged widow named Mrs. Pratt.

He also met the couple who lived downstairs, Mr. and Mrs. Davidson. They were in their sixties and Mrs. Davidson took a motherly interest in James. She asked him many times to dinner. He accepted a few times. His attitude toward Mrs. Davidson and her husband was one of self-interest. A circumstance might arise when he would need their friendship.

James found a job as an attendant at a near-by service station, about a mile away. He walked to save money. He quickly established a routine. His employer was an honest, quietly religious, mechanically gifted man of fifty-five named Plymale. Mr. Plymale's single permanent employee was named Al.

Al was the kind of man nobody ever calls mister. Just Al. He was taciturn with what little he did say punctuated by quick vulgarities. But he was a good mechanic. Al always did exactly what Mr. Plymale told him, never more, never less. He never asked James questions or volunteered anything.

James seldom went out. He seldom talked with others at the apartment house or at the station. With ever deepening singularity he immersed himself in those questions he had long puzzled over: Which was more important, goodness or beauty? What was the relationship between the two?

The newspapers were full of articles about post-war Europe: The poverty, the destruction, and the horrors. James had a deep respect for nineteenth century German music and philosophy, but Nazism had taken this respect and mangled it. War illustrated the antagonism between beauty and goodness. Yet James knew of no artist who had analyzed this antagonism in a serious fashion. James was convinced that if this antagonism could be understood, the spirit of the artist—and perhaps only the spirit of the artist—could define and ultimately resolve the very core reason for the conflict.

James considered Keats' famous lines *Beauty is truth, truth beauty, that is all ye know on earth, and all ye need to know* to be more a logical puzzle or a play on definitions than a true sentiment. The statement, read literally, has no meaning and it gains meaning only if beauty is defined into meaninglessness. Such was the nature of James' thoughts. He wrote poems for practice. His skill was increasing. He kept each poem for a few days then destroyed it.

Then came depression. He was spiritless and doubtful. His poems were flat and hollow. He was learning nothing. He asked himself how much he was sacrificing. Law school? Many people had suggested he attend law school, but he was working in a gas station. James read the poem he had written. Worthless. He tore the paper into shreds, packed it into a tight ball, and threw it into the wastebasket. *Who doesn't laugh at a poet?* he thought.

Nobody laughs at a lawyer.

James ate his lunch outside, just a sandwich and a coke. A drunken man across the street was waving a whiskey bottle at passing cars. The man fell over and wiggled languidly onto the grass. He curled prenatally. Moments later three teen-aged boys walked up to him and stopped. They stood over the drunk. One of the boys pushed the drunk with his foot and turned him onto his back. Another boy picked up the whiskey bottle and poured what remained on the drunk's head. He threw the empty bottle down the street, shattering the glass in the road. The drunk got up and staggered away.

James watched with indifference.

Later in the afternoon, James had a car over the pit. As he worked, the image of the drunk returned. James tried to grasp the meaning, like a craftsman with a new, very unusual tool. The craftsman must first discover the function of the tool before he is able to learn how to use it skillfully.

After work, James walked back to his rooms. He prepared an easy supper and tried to write. He paced the floor. He took a bath. He lay across the bed, face down, staring at the scars and scuffmarks on the wooden floor. He saw the image of the drunk there on the old wooden floor. He got up, and, duplicating the actions of the drunken man, he walked about the room with a stagger. He sat on the bed and dropped his head between his legs. He fell over onto the floor. He repeated this pantomime several times. Many hours passed, and James, physically and mentally exhausted, sat at his table. The image of the drunken man fell soundlessly through his mind, and he became aware of a single word.

Corruption.

He repeated the word aloud several times. He wrote the word on a piece of paper. The relationship between beauty and goodness wasn't antagonism. It was corruption. The drunk was a corruption of something. Nazism was a corruption of something. But what? Beauty? He flipped through the newspaper and returned to an article he had seen earlier about Nazism and art. Hitler was a painter and wanted to fill his Reich with stolen art from across Europe. This was the worst corruption of the best? Could beauty be a corruption of goodness? Did every good have a corruption?

What about the drunk? Drunkenness could be a corruption of many things. But beauty and goodness? That was James' problem.

Could beauty be a corruption of goodness? Something was missing. What? James didn't know. All James knew for certain was that he did not have enough experience to discern the truth. Without more experience no amount of thought would be enough.

James crumbled the newspaper and threw it in the trash. "Everything I've done has been to know beauty and goodness directly. But what more could I learn if I allowed myself to be overcome by corruption?"

James knew had to submit to corruption, to make himself as weak as the drunkard on the street. He knew what he had to do.

For several nights James walked to downtown Richmond, by the closed banks and government offices, where men who had the greatest power over others became themselves institutions. He walked along the riverfront, near the bars and shady motels. The streetlights failed as James crossed over to an even darker street that reeked of garbage, sweat, and gasoline. Over the door of a dingy tavern, the neon script read *air conditioned*. Everything was dirty and he knew he would hate this place.

The bar was short, only a few stools. At the few booths and tables, half-dozen men and women sat as ragged music crushed all conversation except the loudest shouts and squeals.

The man behind the bar was soft and fat. James did not like beer, but he motioned for a beer anyway and gave the fat man a dollar. He motioned to keep the change.

James waited at the bar alone. The music quieted and people behind him at the booths and tables chattered but he didn't listen. He lit a cigarette and sipped the beer. A woman took the seat beside him. She was at least thirty, maybe forty. She had unnaturally red hair and conspicuous make up. Her skirt was tight. The fat man behind the bar said to James, "You wanta buy her a drink?"

James took another bill out of his wallet. The fat man gave him no change. The woman shifted toward James. "Thank you," she said. Her voice was melodious, with a form and shape James could almost visualize.

"You're welcome." James was aware of the childishness in his voice.

"What's your name?" The woman asked.

As James watched her, he imagined a sweet smoked ham in a cloth sack hanging in the back of a store, still turning after a customer had looked at the price and decided not to buy. "James Campbell."

"James Campbell," she said, repeating his name like a roadside vegetable seller repeating the price of beans.

James asked, "Do you want to tell me your name?"

"Susan."

James offered her a cigarette. She took it. James put a cigarette to his own mouth and his hands trembled as he lit both. She thanked him. James said, "I'm not from around here."

"I see."

"I just graduated from the University of Virginia last May," he said. The woman smiled like an impatient mannequin. "How much is your time worth?"

The woman shrugged. "The price of a beer."

"Do you have a place near here?"

She shrugged again and stood. She headed to the door. "Coming?"

James followed her outside and walked beside her down the dark street. "How much do you want?"

"Twenty."

"I think ten's enough."

She stopped. "Twenty dollars."

"I can give you ten, no more."

"Fine," she snapped. She had an air of cold majesty. Of the various city sounds—trains, cars, music in the distance—James heard only the quick repetition of her heels on the concrete sidewalk. He followed her up a narrow stairway. She took a key from her purse. James had no desire for her, but he put his hand on her rump. "Can't you wait another minute?" she said sharply. She switched on the light. She hooked a night-chain but left the door ajar. "This room hot as hell!" She threw open the window and shade.

"I hate open shades at night," James said. He pulled it closed.

"I want it open."

"Then maybe I ought to leave now."

"Prick," the woman said but she left the shade down. She put out her hand. "Give me the money." James gave her ten dollars. She put the money in her purse, and it seemed as with one single motion that she undressed. Her pubic hair was black and thick. James sat on the bed. She stood, her hands on her hips, appraising James professionally. Behind her the bathroom door was open. The light was on and James could see the toilet. She went into the bathroom and came back with a roll of toilet paper which she put on the floor beside the bed. She stretched out on the bed. "You gonna just stand there?"

James undressed and lay on the bed beside her.

"You ready?" she asked.

"What a dammed dumb question." He pointed at his flaccid cock. "What do you think I can do like this?"

"Don't blame me, friend."

"You'll have to help me."

"I don't do sucks, friend."

James touched her. Her body was rigid. Her breasts were like hardened muscle. Her swollen abdomen was firm. James put his mouth over her breast and aridly held her nipple with his teeth. He moved his hand through her pubic hair. She pulled his hand away. "I don't like you doing that."

"Then you do something. You have the money."

James took the woman's hand and moved it between his legs. Her fingers moved like wooden sticks guided by a blind man. James got out of the bed. He took one of two condoms from his pants pocket and tossed it on the bed beside her. He said, "Now I know why men beat their whores."

"You think I'd do this if I had a choice?"

James had never before been with a prostitute, and he had never before wanted to beat a woman. But, looking at her, he knew it would be pleasure to beat her. Instantly, James took hold of her ankles, jerked them up and pushed her knees to her shoulders. He fell on her, pinning her, keeping her legs up with his arms. "Use your hands," he growled.

The woman's composure melted under his harsh stare. She fumbled like a novice but quickly brought him to arousal. James moved his hands to her breasts and pressed his weight on her. He hurried with the condom. She did not move with him. She made no sound. For James this was nothing but the lifeless release of fluid. After, the woman sat on the edge of the bed and cleaned up using the toilet paper. James went to the bathroom and flushed the condom down the toilet, washed, urinated and flushed the toilet again. He dressed as quickly as he could and left.

He walked to an amusement park filled with boys in buzz cuts and girls in hoop skirts. He walked along the fence, watching the fun from the outside. Roller coaster, Ferris wheel, Tunnel of Fun. He felt more isolated watching the crowds than when he was alone in his apartment. Autumn was approaching but the heat of summer lingered. He stopped at an ice cream parlor and asked for a cone. He watched the girl as she dipped the ice cream, her hands and her face. Her every movement seemed unbearably significant, as if when he accepted the cone and left the shop he would walk into the eternity they talk about in churches.

"Thank you," the girl said with a smile. James sat at the counter and ate the ice cream. He wanted to say something to the girl, and he imagined that she wanted him to speak, but he finished the ice cream and quietly left.

James returned to his apartment. He took a warm bath and went to bed, but he did not sleep. "Beth," he said. "Beth."

What had he learned? That sex without the aesthetic was vulgarity? That sex without closeness was emptiness? No, he already knew these. What new information had he learned? James tried to fit the woman and the institution of prostitution into his theory of corruption. What did this mean? That prostitution was a corruption of what? Of business? Of womanhood? Of sex? Maybe, yes, probably, that was the meaning. But it was an obvious and shallow meaning. He knew he was looking for something much deeper. James knew one thing beyond doubt, that he was growing closer to the true relationship between beauty and goodness. With the prostitute he had found the opposite of both beauty and goodness.

James had wanted to beat the prostitute, and that fact was the center of everything for him. He would have preferred any reaction— hatred, screaming, anything—to her wooden indifference. The hard emptiness he felt had not grown from his wanting to beat the woman. That he could explain away. But he had no pity for her even though she deserved pity. Was she the embodiment of institutional corruption or the result of it? He could think about wanting to beat the woman; he could think about his intercourse with her; he could think about beauty and goodness; he could theorize; he could use the woman, but he could not pity her. To pity her was to pity corruption.

James returned again and again to that same part of the city where he had met the prostitute. One night he met a girl his own age, around twenty-two. She was unlike the prostitute, more like a runaway in search of dangerous adventure. She was dark and beautiful, probably a mulatto. She took James to her room and undressed wantonly for him to watch. She smoothed her long, ink-black hair. She caressed her breasts. James had never seen areolas so dark. "You think I'm something worth looking at, don't you?" she said. James merely nodded. The girl sang, "*I'm thru with Love,*" as she swayed from side to side. She said, "Honey, the things I can do for you, you wouldn't believe they could be done."

James asked, "Do you have to sell yourself?"

"Don't be that way, honey. I hate boys who ask me dumb questions. I like you." She undressed him as she danced, her hands moving knowingly over his body. She kissed his chest and bit his nipples. James reached for his condom. "Give me that dammed thing," she said, tearing open the packet with her teeth. Her fingers moved with skill. Pulling James onto her, she groaned in quick repetition. Her name was Darlynne. She wouldn't tell her last name. James offered to give her money but she refused. Although she fascinated him, she was not what he needed to learn and he never saw her again.

On Sunday, Mrs. Davidson asked James to accompany her to church and he accepted. He had not been inside a church since his freshman year of college and was curious to know what he would feel. He had rejected Christian doctrine as untrue while in college, likening orthodoxy to a tightness of the spine and stomach.

Mrs. Davidson belonged to a small Methodist church. James didn't listen to the sermon but he did enjoy the hymns. He thought of his father's love for singing in church. He watched the sun illuminate the dust as it came through the stain glass windows. As music filled the sanctuary, he felt lifted away, as if by a great metaphysical bird, to a place where he could clearly see the solar system. He could see the sun and moon and stars. He could see earth with all its oceans and continents. He could see himself sitting on the fifth pew, three seats in, and it had no meaning to him at all.

For several days after James was deeply depressed. He returned to the same part of the city but he had no idea what he was looking for. He ignored the women on the street. He went from one cheap bar to another. At one bar he sat beside a loud and dirty man. Almost shouting, the man introduced himself as Gus and asked James, "Look here. You ever used a rubber on a girl?"

James looked forward, watching the man's reflection in the mirror behind the bar. Gus wore coveralls like a stevedore and had hands as thick as a bear's. "I have," James answered.

"Sure gets to be a god dammed nuisance, don't it. What I mean was you got to work at it, pulling it on. And then you don't feel nothing. Listen! Don't use one! Don't use a rubber. Sure, sometime you got to use one if you want a bit. But if you don't got to, don't use one."

"Sometime? You mean disease?"

"Sure."

"And what if she gets pregnant?"

Gus laughed into his glass of beer. "Hell. Fuck the kid. That's the cunt's worry. But you want to know how you can figure when you don't need a rubber, I'll tell you. Trick I picked up down in South America. Works every time. You got a lemon, see?"

"A lemon?" James asked.

"Sure. A lemon. You bite off the end. You make her spread good, see? So you squeeze the lemon, all the juice, all of it, on the cunt. So if she don't yell none and don't flinch none, then you know she's clean and you don't need no rubber."

As James watched their reflections, he seemed to be watching large spiders in a glass case. He was sickened by the man, who continued an incessant flux of gutter humor, toilet-stall jokes, and beer-and-urine stories. Then, in the mirror James saw the reflection of a young black man come in and sit at the bar beside them.

The bartender said, "Sorry, buddy, we don't serve colored in here."

Gus looked indignant. "Him? You throwing him out? I fucked lots of whores blacker'n him, and they never said a word about how white I was. What's it you care about? The color of his skin or the color of his money?"

The bartender said, "I don't own the place. No colored, that's the rule."

Gus slammed his hand against the bar. "I'll be god dammed. Hell, he's good as I am. He goes, I go. Simple as that."

"No colored."

Gus slid off his bar stool. "Let's go," he said to James.

"I'll stay," James said.

The man left, cursing. The black man remained seated a minute or two, then he got up and left. He had not said a word. James waited a few minutes, glad to be alone, and then he left. He walked slowly, wondering. The man's words—'What's it you care about? The color of his skin or the color of his money?'— arose like a great, undefined shadow in his mind. James knew instinctively, as he had known when he saw the drunk stagger across the street by the gas station, that he was changing, that tonight he had seen something profoundly evil. He could not identify the evil. It was not the easily recognized, easily condemned evil. This evil was deeper, more subtle, more deeply buried, more deeply covered. James knew by his instinct that this evil—the seeing of this evil—was to be the place at which he would begin to find definition; he would begin to be an artist.

The hull of James' mind was numb, as if this inner part of his existence was deadened, paralyzed. But day by day James' body became increasingly sensitive to everything about him, hideously sensitive. Seeing or touching anything, knowing anyone, talking with anyone was great pain. A man, an artist, any person can lie to himself or he can lie to his father or he can lie to his friend or to his enemy, but he cannot lie to his body. James loved everything living. He loved universally, not with sweet, melodious love, but with hideously painful love absorbing all pain, love which knows that to see a man was to cry, that if you do not cry when you see him, you do not see him.

Weeks passed the same. Then there was the accident which left the scar on the palm of his hand. James was unsure who was at fault. Al was soldering and James was helping. They both moved at once. Initially, James felt no pain—his body seemed to empty as if he were bleeding through an artery—and he fainted. Someone carried him to the chair in Mr. Plymale's office. He felt a damp, cool cloth on his forehead. He heard Mr. Plymale saying, "If I think he needs a doctor, I'll take him to one, don't you say anything otherwise. Understand?"

"Yessir," Al said. "Don't say a word."

James opened his eyes and his hand began to throb. Mr. Plymale asked, "You got much pain now?"

James gritted his teeth. "Enough."

Mr. Plymale wrapped James' hand loosely with gauze. "This don't look bad as some burns I've seen. I don't think you'll be needing a doctor. I'm getting Al to drive you home. You know somebody who'll see to you if you need help?"

James should have gone to a doctor but he was in too much pain to think. All he could do was answer the question. "Mrs. Davidson."

"Fine. Now, if you do think you need a doctor, go on. I'll pay the bill. But if you don't go, I'll let you have a few days off. Maybe a week. With pay, of course. Then you can come back here and work for me again."

James felt dizzy, close to fainting again. "Thank you," James said. Al drove James to his apartment and James went immediately to Mrs. Davidson's. She removed the gauze and was horrified at the sight. His hand was massively swollen. It no longer looked like the hand of a human, rather like the flipper of a beached whale.

"Oh my Lord. I've never seen anything like this outside a hospital. Who wrapped this for you?"

James could hardly breathe. Would his hand ever be normal again? Was this permanent? He thought of the crippled war veterans with their scarred bodies and blank eyes. He thought of the pity he'd felt for them, and the superiority. How foolish they were to place themselves in danger, and yet he had done the same, without even a commission to show for it.

Mrs. Davidson repeated the question, "James, dear, who wrapped this? Did you see a doctor?"

James blinked and shook his head. "The man I work for," he whispered.

"Awful, just awful. You poor dear." She carefully rinsed his hand with soap and cool water, gave him two aspirin and applied ointment from a tube. "Did your employer make you walk home?"

"Another employee drove me."

"At least that shows some good sense. You'll stay here for supper. You and Henry can talk. He'll want to know how this happened. He'll know what to do." Mrs. Davidson wrapped James' hand and James felt close to vomiting from the pain. He couldn't imagine wanting any dinner or conversation.

When Mr. Davidson arrived, he asked how James had been injured.

"Soldering, eh? Dangerous business. Not as bad as welding, though. You can get a welding burn in your eye. Known lots of men had a blind spot that way. Singes a spot on the nerve I'm told and afterward you've got a blind spot there. Get enough you'll start to see everything full of black holes. You ever been on a ship?"

"No." James wanted to return to his apartment and rest. He didn't want to talk about burns or boats.

"Ship's got steam lines, wrapped in asbestos and canvas. Used to be they'd only use canvas. Some still do. The older ships. You got to take care of the pipes. God, that steam comes out boiling when she comes. New ships run at a thousand pounds pressure. Too hot for canvas. That's why they now use asbestos. Steam'd cut a man in half. I never saw that. But I saw a young fellow lose a couple of fingers. Steam cut his fingers off."

James felt increasingly queasy.

"Course, that's not near the worst thing I've seen. I'd say the worst thing I ever saw was in Charleston. I was on the deck watching the loading. Tracks come up to the pier, all crossing this way and that. Anyhow, I saw this man on the track behind a freight car. Then come another car. He never saw what was happening. I was yelling like a madman, but he never moved. Cars coupled right through him. He was sort of bouncing. I could see him just as clear. I'd say he lived a good minute or more. When they finally got the cars apart, he was dead."

Mrs. Davidson called from the kitchen. "Supper'll be on the table in five shakes. And Henry, no more talk about accidents. You've got the sense of a polecat. Can't you see the boy's hurting? And here you are telling him tales that'd scare the bite out of a bulldog."

Mrs. Davidson served meatloaf. James had eaten her meatloaf before and had enjoyed it, but now it looked too akin to burned flesh. Mrs. Davidson appeared injured.

"I'm sorry," James told her, "I can't eat. I need to rest."

Mr. Davidson spoke up, "I know, son. Don't apologize. I know when you're hurting you can't enjoy your eating." She took the plates to the kitchen and Mr. Davidson called to his wife. "Dear, don't you have dessert? I think James could eat something sweet. Couldn't you eat something sweet?"

"I have some pudding, James."

"Eat some of her pudding, son," Mr. Davidson said, smiling, he patted James' shoulder.

"No, I can't." James thanked the Davidsons, excused himself and went up to his room.

James did not take a bath. He washed with warm water without soap. He tried to read, but reading was impossible. He listened to music on the radio, but any sound, even the sound of soothing music, grew unbearable. His body grew stiff with pain, from his arm to his shoulders and spine, into his legs, into his eyes; the pain would relinquish its hold for a second just to take hold again. James expected the pain to lessen but throughout the night the pain grew.

Images moved through James' mind: Soldiers at war, prostitutes, veterans without arms and legs. He fell asleep and dreamed he was waiting in a white tiled hospital room for an attendant with the huge enema bag because his bowels have no nerves. James woke with a start and the pain coursed through him.

In the morning, James was afraid to stand. He longed to be able to faint, longed for oblivion. He sat a long while, images moving through his mind without control. Before the accident, when he had been unable to control his mind, when images, even good images, drove him almost insane, he would read obscure philosophy or study mathematics.

Not now.

Now he could not read or study or think. He had no strength at all against these images. The pain was everywhere. The images were everywhere. His pain and the images were the same, as if his body absorbed all the pain from all the people he had ever known or seen. If you see them, and you do not cry when you see them, you do not see them. James loved, and love was pain and universal love was total, constant pain.

Mrs. Davidson brought James a tray with lunch. He thanked her and she left without objections. James left the tray on the table. He ate nothing. As evening approached, the room grew dark. James did not switch on a light. He could not endure artificial light. He felt himself growing insane. He felt no hope, no power of will. Pain was too constant and too unchanging. He was without power to control himself.

In the morning Mrs. Davidson came up and saw the untouched tray. She changed his dressing. James said nothing. She questioned, and James answered by turning his head. The meaning of her words was emptiness behind the unbearable sound.

Did he want any food? James shook his head.

No breakfast? James shook his head.

Did he want her to call a doctor? James shook his head.

Each question Mrs. Davidson asked was more a threat than an enquiry. She was less than a woman, less than a person. If a superior will had ordered James to kill her, he would have killed her and gone back to bed. James ate nothing that day. He remained in bed. The third night passed without his sleeping. James had become utterly confused. Objects seemed to move chaotically in the dark room, and his body seemed to wander aimlessly among the moving objects. Images occupied space, and each image was pain and without meaning. Silently, James cried: Why? God help me. God, please help me. Why? Many times he silently repeated the word *why*?

By the next afternoon, James felt somewhat better. The pain was rather localized in his hand so he went down to the Davidson's apartment and she prepared breakfast.

James was able to think. He realized that never before had he truly known anything about helplessness and that never before had he experienced total pain. It changed him greatly. He could no longer be a young man believing that maturity was for most men only the acceptance of mediocrity, but not for him. He had seen a new enemy: the why? Not why do I exist? But why do I have to suffer such pain? He knew the power of this new enemy, which was much stronger than shame or culture or pity or hate. He took this to be the greatest of all enemies. Civilization may be based upon the knowledge of the inevitability of pain and progress may be based upon the illusion of continued good health, but why? *Why* must be an enemy, and it must be fought as any enemy was fought.

Mrs. Davidson dressed James' hand. His skin looked like raw chicken. Mrs. Davidson's eyes were kind and sympathetic. She said, "You poor dear. I know how you've suffered so much." James felt suddenly naked with her, and he began to cry.

Chapter Twenty-Six

James returned to work and for a number of days he did little more than pump gas. Even as the pain diminished, his emotions and his thoughts were still chaotic. He had become another person, as if he had lost a kind of virginity. He needed time and energy to see through these new experiences to uncover beauty and goodness or, at least, to regain a sense of their presence. He looked at experiences like a hungry boy looking across a room to a table full of Christmas treats. They were a luxury he could not now enjoy. Later. He could taste them later. James had to wait.

James identified this time of waiting with the time required for his burns to heal. This pain which was simple and physical became, in a way, something of a friend. Reason was useless. It was like arguing with time to go backward. As days grew shorter and colder, James very slowly yielded to the inevitable, to dissipate like smoke from a dying fire, to move with the breeze, to settle awhile among the leaves of a thick brush. When he finally saw clearly the image of what he had to do, it seemed so obvious.

James went to poorest, ugliest part of town, places where, when a man drives through with his wife he reaches over her shoulder to lock the door beside her then locks the door on his side of the car. Streets were crowded. Buildings were decaying. There was no canopy of genius or superior will or old authority to guide him. Shame and fear were rats eating his intestines. Physical pain—now that it was gone—seemed so simple in comparison. He wished for courage, not a pose or strength or casualness or degeneration or intoxication. But rats ate his courage. He was naked, yet he hated his nakedness, which needed his courage and consumed it. He could not know beauty or goodness without nakedness. "Why are you laughing?" he yelled.. He pressed his hands against his ears, "*Stop! Stop!*" He had to retain courage enough to endure their laughter, but each person drew off some blood of his courage. He could not do other than absorb and tend to understand, and they held hundreds of blades cutting him.

On the corner, where two back alley streets met, was a place called *Jake's*. The name, in large block letters, was painted on the glass, which was discolored with street grime and dirt. Inside, a squat oil stove stood against the rear wall. Crude and heavy wooden tables and chairs were painted dark green, and the counter was a sickly lighter green. The bartender was a fat albino. A younger black man worked the grill. James asked for a coke and a pack of cigarettes. The bartender filled a glass with a squirt of dark cola syrup, ice, and seltzer water. He stirred the concoction and handed it to James. "That's all?"

"For now," James said. He moved to one of the green tables back beside the stove. He opened the pack of cigarettes. An elderly woman, wearing a long plaid dress and a black coat, her legs bound with red cloth, came in. She bought a six-pack of beer and a carton of cigarettes, then left. A heavy, wheezing man sat at the table nearest James with a bottle of beer.

Those first few times James visited Jakes he was very much afraid. He was not at all physically afraid—James had always been able to control his physical fear, facing it with a kind of dullness or stupidity. Dullness and stupidity, James believed, was the core of strength. James wanted to discover courage which was neither dull nor stupid. He needed to build his courage slowly, and to do this he needed a particularly vulnerable subject, a woman, of course, an outcast to explore the relationship between goodness and beauty, and the *why* behind endless pain.

James asked the albino behind the bar how late Jakes remained open. "Somedays ten, somedays twelve, somedays eleven. Twelve all the time in Summer. Now, not so long, unless business is real good."

"Many people come in at night?"

"Sure. Lots of business. Most business starts about eight," the albino said as he scraped the grill clean with a long handled brush, "You's the only white man I ever seen in here. What's it you want here?"

"I'm looking for someone," James answered.

"Who?"

"I'll know when I see her."

James began going to Jake's every night. He ordered his drink and sat alone. He watched the people coldly, and in turn, they were unsettled by the presence of this lone white man with piercing eyes. In time, they ignored him. They danced and sang. James could not understand them. They clapped their hands to a rhythm they all seemed to hear effortlessly, their bodies transformed into one single living organism. James was aware of the rhythm, but he could not distinguish it.

A group of men were playing cards, but James had no interest in them. From them he could learn no more than was known by a soldier who has been with only men for many months, who has become simply male and less than human.

Among the women, however, was one that did interest James. She was repulsively ugly. Her dark face was blotched and knotty. Long tufts of hair grew from a deep scar on her cheek. The men tormented her, one making ape sounds and gestures. "Didn't know the circus was back in town." Another pulled the tuft of hair and she kicked him in the groin. A second kick and he fell to the floor.

"You ain't got nothing worth nothing," she growled.

The man slowly pushed himself up, sputtering vulgarities. He pulled out a knife. "Bitch!"

The other men jumped back, "Hey now, put away the knife, Reggie, she ain't worth going to prison for."

The woman with the tuft of hair on her cheek left Jake's before he could sheath his knife.

James followed the hideous woman along the dark alley beside

Jake's and down a covered stairwell to a basement. A cat hissed at him. A dog turned over a metal trash can. James couldn't allow himself to think. If he did, he knew he would convince himself to return to his apartment.

There wasn't a hint of moonlight. He lit a match. The door was blotched with thick white paint as if someone had painted over offensive words. He knocked and waited. He knocked again. The door opened. The hideous woman answered. She held a corked bottle of wine by the neck like a club.

"I want to come in to talk to you," James said. She squinted at him, keeping the wine bottle high, ready to strike. "I saw at Jake's. I saw you kick the man who insulted you. I'm not with the police. May I come in?"

She grunted and lowered the wine bottle. James entered the room. He closed the door behind him. The single room was small, the furniture was old but well-tended. The walls were concrete. A wooden crate full of empty bottles was on a table. The room smelled like fried pork rind. James asked, "Do you have any children?"

The woman crossed her arms over her heavy breasts, "Why you want to know?"

"I am curious."

"Did Reggie send you? Where's my money?"

James hesitated, not sure how to answer. If she was a prostitute, she was the homeliest one he'd ever seen. "I have it."

"Sure, I know, you got it, but I ain't got it yet," she snapped. "I heard that one before."

"I want to give you the money. But I have to talk with you before I can."

She looked at him like he was spoiled meat. "What you want to talk about?"

"I asked if you had any children."

"No, I ain't got none. I had a girl once. She's dead."

"How old are you."

"What kind of fool question is that?" James didn't answer her. She said, "Forty or thereabouts. I'm just this side of forty years old."

"What's your name?"

"What kind of—," she balked but James persisted.

"I simply asked your name."

"Martha Lee."

"Is Lee you last name?"

"Riddick. That's my name. Martha Lee Riddick. But my name don't tell me a thing about that money."

James said, "May I visit with you."

She frowned. "May I visit? What kind of fool white-boy talk is that? Who sent you? Why you here? I bet you ain't even got my money. You said your name was what? How old are you?"

"James. I'm twenty-two."

"Shit. That man I kicked, everybody done call him Spaghetti Man. He owed me five dollars for cleaning I done for him." She looked James up and down. "You don't even know what I'm talking about, do you boy?" She lowered her arms. "You know what it means when a white man visits a colored woman? It means he ain't good enough to please the white women. But you don't look like that kind to me. And I sure know. I see lots that kind of white trash. It don't make sense, not a bit, not to me. Men my own color don't want me 'til they get skunk drunk, and here's a white boy wants to visit with me."

James took five dollars out of his wallet and gave it to Martha Lee, holding her hand for a few seconds. "I will come back tomorrow at nine-thirty."

She stuffed the five dollars into her bra. "Let me get this sure and straight. You just let it all settle in my head. You mean to be here again tomorrow night?"

"Yes."

"You ain't got some meanness in your head you're planning?"

"No meanness," James said. He opened the door. "See you at nine-thirty tomorrow."

James felt a strange calmness as if years of tension had slipped away in a moment of utter relaxation. Martha Lee was not part of a crowd. She was a single individual. He could be himself with her.

Restful and without pain. If she were beautiful, he could never know her without pain. But Martha Lee was ugly. She was the opposite of beauty. It was a new sensation, this restful calm he felt. He started to whistle as he walked the dark streets back to his apartment.

Chapter Twenty-Seven

The alleyway could have been a well-lit path in the mountains, with the warm sun and a waterfall at the end of the hike. The stench of poverty could have been the pleasant aromas of trees and clean air. The brutalizing filth could have been leaves moving delicately with mountain winds. Pain could have been immortal youth. Cruelty could have been kindness. Song could have been real.

James touched the outside wall of the building, running his fingertips on the brick and mortar. The bricks were cool, the days were getting shorter. This time James did not wait at the steps. He knocked and the door opened. Martha Lee greeted him wearing the same tent-like dress she had worn the previous night.

"What you want?" she asked.

"I told you last night. I gave you five dollars, and you took it. I'm not going to push my way inside."

"You bet you ain't," she snorted.

"Please let me come in." He waited. She stared at him, not moving to close the door or to open it fully.

She finally swung open the door, "Come on in, then." She locked the door behind him. The smell was unchanged but the room was more orderly, the crate was gone from the table.

James said, "Right now you're thinking, 'when's he going to give me another five dollars?'"

"Boy, you're mean," she said. "You see I got barely enough money to keep rags on my back and something in my belly. You think I live like some mange dog so you got to treat me like something that gots no pride. You're just a dammed mean white boy, that's what I see."

"Do you intend to let me sit down?" James asked.

"Do what you please."

James sat at the opposite end of the sofa. He patted the empty space beside him. "Please sit down."

Martha Lee didn't oblige. She sat in one of the two straight chairs. "Just how long you expect to be here?"

"Longer," James answered. He studied Martha Lee's face as she looked at him. He was indifferent to her suspicion. He knew she didn't trust him, and he accepted her mistrust. It did not touch him at all. Whatever she might feel toward him meant nothing. This was an experience and all that mattered was what he learned. He asked, "How long have you lived here?"

"Six years."

"Do you work?"

"I scrub floors at the Lindbergh Hotel. You know the hotel?"

James shook his head. "Are you from Richmond?"

"No," she said. She held off silently, her eyes filled with contempt. She said, "I crossed here from North Carolina, from out of Greenville."

"Why did you come here?"

"I don't have to tell you."

"That's true. You don't have to tell me anything. Were you born in Greenville?"

Martha Lee became increasingly agitated. "Why should I tell you that? Anyway, why'd you want to know? And what are you doing here? What's it you want anyhow, you coming here?"

"I told you, just to visit."

"Stupid. Know what you sound like? Like some stupid white boy. I'm ignorant, I know. I don't know much, but I ain't stupid." She snorted and looked him up and down. "You don't look stupid."

"If I don't look stupid, maybe I'm not." James was very aware how foolish he sounded. He looked around the room, avoiding her eyes.

Martha Lee asked, "What's it you hunting for? Nothing here's worth taking."

James crossed his arms, feeling defensive. "I was wondering

how many rooms you have," he lied.

"Here and a bathroom and what passes for a kitchen. Most colored folks everywhere don't have a bath inside. I guess I'm blessed a few pennies worth. Know what? I forget what you called yourself."

"James. Should I call you Martha or Martha Lee or Miss Riddick?"

"You don't need to call me a thing, boy. I don't hear nobody calling me Miss Riddick unless they're trying to sell me something, then it's like they had something dirty in their mouth they want to be rid of fast as they can."

"I'll call you Martha."

The sat in silence for a few moments until Martha Lee broke the quiet. "I don't like you staring at me."

James looked away. He asked if he could light a cigarette. She got up, went into the kitchen and came back with an empty mustard jar she'd filled with half inch of water. James took the jar and lit his cigarette.

The cigarette helped James regain his confidence. He began to feel the calm he had felt the night before. He crossed his legs. "Tell me why you left Greenville."

"Not worth the telling."

"Six years is a long time."

"Sure, maybe so. People don't ask me things, and I don't say. Always been that way. Know what I mean?"

James nodded.

"Toad's blood, you know!"

"I've eaten swell-toad."

"Never heard of it."

"Swellfish, some call it, a fish that blows itself up when you rub its underside, like a balloon. Most people won't eat them. Some people say the fish is poison, and other people say only the organs are poison."

Martha Lee scowled. "What's that got to do with you knowing how I feel? You is a rich white boy."

He puffed his cigarette. "I'm not rich, Martha, I won't be able to give you money every time I come."

"Sounds like you got some plans. But you listen, boy. I never said a thing about letting you in that door whenever you be there knocking."

"You don't have to let me in. I know this is your home, and I can come in only if you allow."

"Boy, you know you're right. I can kick your fanny out that door whenever I got a thought to do it."

James felt warmth, and at the same time, analytical toward Martha Lee. To him, her words were like echoes which measure the depth of a pit when the bottom cannot be seen. James drew meaning from the sounds. He and Martha Lee were very similar. They shared a common fate beyond the obvious. Both Martha Lee and James were victims of an evil which was too distant to be seen, too powerful to be overcome. They both knew of this evil by their isolation from society and from their pain.

James rubbed his arms. "Is it always so cold in here?"

Martha Lee laughed, "You cold? Ha! It's barely November! Let January come round, then you know some cold."

"Was it cold in Greenville, Martha? Were the winters as bad there?"

"No. We barely ever had snow. We had us a fireplace and all the pine logs we needed. I was born right in that house, that's where I'd go now, if I could. That house is where I want to die. Sometimes I say that day can't be too soon." Her legs were together and her hands were folded below her knees.

James closed his eyes. She was terribly ugly. James had never known anyone so ugly. Her skin was like gravel on a freshly asphalted road, black and gray with splotches of white like some unseen assailant had splattered her with thick paint. She surpassed even the hideousness of the veterans with faces half destroyed by gunshot wounds and bombs. He felt shame for his inability to see beyond her repulsiveness.

"Tell me, Martha, what did you do in Greenville?"

"Growed tobacco mostly. Not on our own land, you understand.

We never owned any land. We had our garden and some pigs and chickens. I was the oldest after mama died. I stayed 'til poppa died, too. Then I had to leave, so I come up here."

"Why here? What made you choose Richmond?"

"When I come then, I had my sister here. But a couple years ago, she went out to California with her man and her kids. Now, I don't have no other place, so I just stay here."

"Do you hate this city, Martha?"

"Here or another place, it don't matter no more. I got nothing here but this room. Someplace else, I'd still have nothing." Martha Lee brooded. "Where'd you come from, boy?"

"Not far."

"You a farm boy?"

"No."

"I knew you weren't. And you're no rich boy, either."

"I'm a gas station attendant."

"That all? I thought you was more than that. That's no good paying job, that I know."

"It doesn't pay much, Martha. I won't be able to give you money every time I see you. I'll give you money when I can. "

"Boy—."

"Use my name, Martha."

"Sure. James, look here, I don't know what gives you thoughts you need to give me money."

"Martha, I want to be able to visit you."

"And that sure don't make a bit of sense. Maybe if I was smarter. You know, I don't have much education."

"You don't need any more education, Martha, and you're smart enough." Martha Lee looked at James quizzically, with softness in her face. James saw it clearly. It was not softness of innocence, but softness of finally not being alone. James said, "Martha, don't you see that you and I are much alike?"

"How's that? How's that you're like me?"

"I can't tell you, Martha, because I don't have the words. You'll have to see for yourself."

She rubbed her broad nose with her sleeve and shook her head. "No, boy, we're nothing alike. You're a young white man and I'm an old black woman. You can go anywhere you want, do anything you want. You can go into the Lindbergh Hotel and get yourself a room if you have the money. Don't matter how much money I got, they won't let me do nothing there but clean the floors. If you see us alike, you're fooling yourself."

James knew she was wrong. He couldn't go anywhere or do anything. He was trapped by his fearfulness as much as she was trapped by prejudice. They were both victims of some distant evil which he could not see. James felt comforted sharing his prison with another prisoner. As comforted as a boy who was dying might be comforted by his mother making plans for some pleasant event in the far future, and he begins to make his own plans, which for a while are wonderfully tangible.

"What you smiling at?" Martha Lee snapped.

"Nothing. I didn't know I was smiling."

"You had a face like a sleeping pussycat. That sounds good to you, the idea we ain't much alike?"

"But we were alike."

"Sure sure, you keep believing that. How long you mean to stay here?" The softness had left Martha Lee's face. She looked tired.

James said, "If you think I'm calling you ugly names in the back of my mind, you're wrong. I'm not. I don't wish to mock you. If you want me to go now, I will."

"I gotta get up early to go to work, you know."

"I know. May I come back tomorrow night?"

"Do what you want."

James took a five dollar bill out of his pocket and put it in her hand. "Take this. I want you to keep this money. But you have to know I won't be able to give you money every time I come here." Martha Lee said nothing. Her hand closed about the bill.

For the first time in months James had a good night's sleep. In the morning he was filled with energy of body and mind, giving equal life to many diverse thoughts and feelings and ideas: the poetry of Milton and Wordsworth; Martha Lee's face and voice; his life at the college; memorized facts of history and dates, the mechanics of meiosis; the laws of physics. James did not try to organize his thoughts.

He knew strength to be the illusion of courage and his courage took life from his love of beauty. He knew great emptiness, which meant his hold upon beauty was weakening, not growing stronger. He feared the emptiness. He feared life without beauty. This fear settled upon him like unalterable darkening, and he grew physically afraid, as of an enemy. Within him, a pair of gnarled hands seemed to reach out for escaping beauty. He was like a dying priest trying to keep a crucifix from falling from his fingers.

At work James was almost effervescent with energy. He felt infantile, open and easy. He moved unconsciously yet expertly. He was proud of his work. Each accomplishment, no matter the significant, was important. James knew, of course, that this high mood could not last. But he tried to keep it as his work day ended. It was not possible and he accepted the inevitable with little resistance.

As he walked back to his apartment, he lit a cigarette. He read the inside of the matchbook cover, an ad for an art school. He heard his father's voice, which surprised him. He looked around but saw only strangers. His father was talking to him, but James was not able to understand the words.

His sweet mood fell away. He spoke to a stranger who passed him. "I do hate art and poetry. I'm doomed to love them. I guess that's why I hate them." The stranger veered across the street to get away. James shouted after him. "I do envy people who can be so indifferent to art. A man who has had a strong father is a lucky man. He could never be an artist." The stranger disappeared around the corner.

This thought comforted James. Perhaps it made him feel superior or perhaps it gave him masochistic pleasure. James looked at his cigarette. There was something undefinably ludicrous about the cigarette. He thought about Ameele and wondered what she was doing. Was she in Paris? Probably. What time was it in Paris? Midnight? Not that late, maybe eleven. Had she found a French lover?

She could be married, of course. She will marry, but not so soon. She can do whatever she likes.

If a man could live like that, and not ask too many questions, that would be the best life. Nothing would ever be surprising, not really. Nothing would be unethical. What does unethical mean, if not unpleasantly surprising? "Maybe I should feel remorse for how I treated Ameele," he said to his cigarette. "No, she's too simple. What could Ameele ever really care about my little meanness?"

But Beth. James did regret his treatment of Beth. He wished he could have Beth with him. He shook his head and threw down his cigarette. He crushed it on the sidewalk as if it were vile. "Then she would decide for me and what would I be? A follower of a woman?" he shouted. A shopkeeper came to his front door and told James to move along. James looked at him. "I loved her and I never loved her," he announced and the shopkeeper threatened to call the police. James stared at the shopkeeper for a moment then continued to his apartment. He felt certain that Beth knew he could never love her the way a man ought to love a woman. But maybe no man can ever love any woman all his life. "I do miss her," he said, tears in his eyes. "I do love her." A dark and hollow feeling grew over his eyes, burning away the tears. "Everything is a lie. Everything. When I think about Beth, that's a lie, and if I don't think about her, that's a lie, too."

He ran back to his apartment and pulled out a sheet of paper and a pencil. He wrote:

One old sea-lover, grown old
Forty years for Oklahoma
Dry dirt and oil rigs
Came back to the barge,
Where as a boy
He had caught crabs with
Fish-heads.
The old sea-lover came back
To wait quiet days to die.
The barge lay dry; the first buoy
Squatted in green mud. He moaned:

"There is no sea.
A man walks on dry land
And he gathers shells of dead
Oysters and city trash where
I rowed my skiff when I was a boy.

James did not want to go the Martha Lee's that night. He was tired and emotionally exhausted. He put his head on the table and rested a few minutes. Then he read what he had written. He began to destroy the paper, hesitated, and read it again. He recognized an imperfect value. Its imagery was commonplace. He had never before written anything of more despair. James did not destroy the poem. He sat at the window and looked out at the lights. He read the poem again and put it among his books and papers.

Chapter Twenty-Eight

Martha Lee was wearing an oversized dark violet dress with a tan jacket. She smiled briefly, or her mouth twitched, James wasn't sure. Was she glad to see him? Maybe he saw only what he wanted to see. But he assumed the role of the familiar guest. "How are you tonight?"

"How good can I be?"

James did not say anything more. Perhaps he had been too light. He took his usual place at the end of the sofa. Martha Lee, he decided, would have to be the initiator. She sat in one of her high-back chairs and rubbed her hands. Finally, Martha Lee said, "I got a hot pot of coffee made. You want a cup?"

"Thank you," James said.

"I got sugar and evaporated milk. You want them?"

"Fine," James said. He'd never noticed that she walked with a slight limp as she went to fetch two brown mugs.

"Watch it now, this here's hot coffee."

The coffee was strong and bitter. James sipped but Martha Lee drank it fast, making loud noises. She finished quickly and put the cup on the floor. James said, "You do know how to make a strong cup of coffee."

Martha Lee said, "I don't care a thing if you drink all that coffee or not. Do what you want. Hear."

"I wouldn't drink the coffee if I didn't want it."

"Well, like I say, you do what you want with it."

"I want it, Martha. Tonight I need something strong."

"That so? You just bring a bottle here if you want. I don't care none of it. Right now with a good bottle I'd be glad enough to drink it empty."

"What kind of stuff do you like?"

"Anything at all. No matter. Anything at all when I get to need a drink."

"Was today bad for you?"

"Boy, every day I got to live's another bad day. I ain't seen no good day so long I don't know the time. Preacher man tells us poor folks we'll be happy when we die. I'm good and set for that day 'cause nothing's like to be one bit harder than I got right now."

"Martha, tell me. If you could have anything, any one thing, what would you ask for?"

"I know it don't mean a thing, but I'll tell you. I'd ask for a place to live that's clean and that's warm in the winter time."

"And what about a husband and children?"

"No. A warm, clean place, that's what I want."

"You told me you wanted a man who was worth something. I thought you wanted children, too."

"I never said such a thing."

"I thought I remembered you telling me you once had a child, and now he's dead."

"No, I never said such a thing." She turned away. James finished his coffee and put the empty mug on the floor. He was sure that Martha Lee was lying. He knew also that her telling him about the child would be the first part of the greater honesty he wanted with her. James watched as Martha Lee twisted her long tuft of facial hair with her fingertips. She was still looking away when she said, "I think I know you ain't that kind with the meanness you can see. Maybe your meanness ain't meant to be mean. Maybe you just can't help it. But fact is still I don't know the why of you being here."

"I told you I wanted to visit you."

She turned on him like a bulldog itching for a bone. "Don't you go on saying them words that don't mean a thing! You know I got a full right to know what it was you want." She folded her hands on her lap. "Maybe some white boy at one of them big schools put you up to all this business. Maybe you really are rich. Maybe you don't work at no gas station. I've been wondering about all that. You sure don't seem like somebody I'd see round a gas station. Could be you got some money bet against some other white boys someplace."

James shook his head. "Nothing like that. I don't want to hurt you, Martha. I have no wish to make fun of you or talk about you. I need to know things."

"You need to know what kind of things?"

"Whether you will like me."

She wrinkled up her face. "Boy, you still ain't saying nothing. Whether I like you? What the hell does that mean?" Despite her words, a softness entered her voice; an easy, poetic lightness that lifted James as if he had seen a pretty, young child playing and laughing.

"Do you like my coming here, Martha?" She shrugged and he pressed. "Tell me, Martha."

"I suppose I do," she said and James quietly enjoyed a small victory. They shared another cup of coffee and Martha Lee asked, "Are you married? I guessed you weren't."

"No, I'm not married."

"You got a girl?"

"I can't afford a wife. I can endure poverty but if I made my wife live that way, neither of us would by happy. Martha, if I ask you something, would you tell me the truth?"

"Maybe I'd say the truth, I'm not promising you nothing."

"I want you to tell me about your child."

"I don't want to say."

"Was it a baby? Did the baby die?"

"I tell you I don't want to say." But the answer was in her face. She rubbed the glistening sweat out of her eyes before finally answering. "A girl. My baby was a girl. Not two years old. Rat bit her, so she died of bleeding. Rat bit her neck. She was dead when I found her. That man. That man, he don't know. He was drunk and he don't know. I was working to keep us living. My baby was asleep right in our bed. I know I wanted to kill that man. He just don't know. I tell you I pushed that man right out the door and he never come cross that door again." Martha Lee's face tightened.

James got up. He felt very weak, as if his muscles would crumble beneath him. He kneeled beside her and lifted her hands together. He held them gently and looked into her eyes. "How long ago did she die?"

Martha Lee sniffed hard. "She's dead for two years."

"Two years? I am sorry, Martha. I am sorry."

James kissed her hands. He was filled with warmth and peacefulness.

Then he looked up to her face—her hideous face. He hurriedly stood and stumbled to the door. He ran outside and leaned against her front door, his legs almost buckling under him. He wanted to drop to the ground in a faint. He wanted to vomit. That would give him a reason to leave. But he was not able to faint. He was not able to vomit. He knew that if he did not go back inside now, his opportunity would be lost.

Martha Lee was still sitting in the chair when James returned to the sofa. For a long while he watched her, as if she were oblivious to the fact that he had run away.

Then she finally said, "Why did you come back?"

James struggled to find an answer. "I'm sorry. Maybe your coffee was too strong for me." It was a stupid lie. Martha Lee was looking at him and he felt like a child under her gaze. He seemed about to die of emptiness. He lowered his head like a whipped school boy. "I got sick to my stomach."

Martha Lee said, "Don't want you spitting out your supper all over my floor."

James looked up at her and joked, self-consciously, "Then we would have had a real mess. My supper was hot dogs, beans and spinach."

She laughed. "Your supper goes on that floor, I tell you, I won't be cleaning nothing up. Sure. Believe me, I get plenty that kind of work every day enough to satisfy me."

"I know you do," James said. The depth of her understanding astounded him.

"You don't know nothing," she said. "When my baby was dead and I had to go back to scrubbing floors before she was cold in the ground, ain't nobody ever hurt so much. That's the kind of hurting you don't know nothing about if you ain't seen that day with your own eye. I remember that floor. Oh, did I hate that floor. I was scrubbing and my eyes was crying. My heart was bleeding and my back was hurting me awful. Lord, I hated that hard floor. But you know I got to put some food in my mouth." Martha Lee rubbed her eyes. She said something James could not understand. She lowered her hands and folded her dress. "Never any more. Not that way. No more. You know I'd soon die."

He thought of the wine bottle she held when he first came to her door. Of course she must have something to deaden her pain just as he needed his poetry to deaden his.

The next time James visited Martha Lee talked more freely. "There was seven of us kids. Near'bout every woman my momma knowed lost one child, at least. Lots she knowed about losing two or three in the winter. Sometime we didn't see a family all winter, then we'd see them, and the woman'd tell momma she'd lost a child dead getting born and not later on. My momma always said for Lord's truth that okra seeds had a magic against all the evil you'd ever have to think about, so momma had all us wearing a sack of okra seeds 'round our neck all winter, and spring we'd have to plant half our seed. We always got fifty seeds. It was always the same. Don't you ask me why, 'cause I sure don't know. Anyhow, in the spring we'd always plant twenty-five seeds. When they come up, they was our plants that we'd have to keep alive. Any rabbit will go for a young okra like they was starving, so we'd put out chicken blood 'gainst the rabbits. Maybe she knowed something real. Momma used to say to us she knowed them okra was magic 'cause it's got a skin like a snake. You know? You go to pull up a whole plant of okra when you're about to take the seed, and the skin's all slick and skins off in your hand. Momma used to say to us she knowed them okra flowers was just too pretty for a plant had a skin like a snake, so she used to say to us God made this plant special and magic.

"And I come to think maybe us lived past them years 'cause

momma had them sacks of seed 'round our necks. Maybe if— no, ain't no use now. No use. I was next to youngest. My baby brother was four when I was five. That's the earliest time I can remember. It was funny. All us had the smallpox the same time. But I can't remember me being sick. It's afterward I remember. All us wanted to get out, and momma kept us in the house."

"Smallpox," James repeated. A sudden rush of fear coursed through him, as if she were still contagious after all these years.

She started laughing. A hard, jarring laugh, like something hot made of glass that the glassblower dips into cold water and it cracks, but the glass does not break through or shatter. It just cracks.

"Maybe I won't five. Maybe I was a little older. All us had the scabs falling off the same time. I remember all us picking off the scabs and all us putting our scabs in piles so to see who had the most scabs. I was so full of pride 'cause I got scabs all over. On my arms, my stomach, my face. I got a higher pile of them scabs than any of the rest. You'd never think how proud I was. I wanted to save them scabs to keep them forever. That's the very first thing I can remember. Them days, you know, things was special. Things meant something. It was like the whole world was talking to me all the time, and it won't just words. The world had things it wanted to give me."

She talked about happier times. She smiled more. "My poppa, he was like that, wanting to give me things. My poppa was a strong man, a big man, and he knowed things, so many things I used to think every day he'd know something I didn't think about before. I remember one time in special. I remember 'cause it was funny and it made me kind of sick, too. Poppa had a tobacco mule. Poppa was good with any animal. He could keep them alive when they'd be dead with somebody else. I was about nine, I guess. A boy that worked for a white widow up the road a couple of miles come and said the widow wanted poppa to come over, said she had a mare that looked about to burst open. Poppa went and he took me with him. Poppa felt the mare's underside, and then he took off his shirt.

"First he asked the widow if the mare'd been eating any weed or vine. She didn't know. Then poppa took hold that horse's tail, and he poked his hand and arm up her back end to his shoulder. That horse sounded more like a mule than any horse I ever heard. Poppa pulled out a fistful of vine. He told me to walk the horse out. She walked like she was carrying a ton, and every step she took, out come a hush of wind. When I come back, I found that widow fainted dead on the ground." Martha Lee laughed so hard tears ran down her cheeks. James laughed, too. She wiped the tears away. "My stomach and me didn't know what I wanted to do, laugh or throw up my breakfast."

"Which did you do?"

"Neither one. Poppa went out to scrub his arm. He told me to help the widow to her feet, and I did. After that I told everybody I could find to tell, especially how the widow fainted. But poppa never talked about it. He just won't like these men I see now, with their mouths going all 'a time and saying words that don't mean nothing at all." She gave James a sly grin. "Like some white boys I know," she added with another laugh. "I don't see no use for these men with their flapping tongues. Poppa was a better sort."

Before his next visit, James purchased a pint bottle of whiskey and brought it with him to Martha Lee's. At first, they drank from glasses. James drank little—he did not want to risk being drunk. Martha Lee drank much more. After a while Martha Lee grabbed the bottle from James. "This way!" She put the bottle to her lips and tipped her head back, drinking long and hard. "Whew!!" She smacked her lips. "That's the way I like my drinking. Here, try it." James took one small swallow from the bottle and winced. Martha Lee laughed and took the bottle again. She drank as if she were drinking cola. "My way's better," she said.

"Do you like the taste?" James asked.

"You know I do! I love you baby!" She kissed the bottle and caressed the label with her fingertip. Again she offered the bottle to James.

He waved her away, "I don't want any more."

"Good," she said. She belched and slid off her chair to the floor. "More for me." She patted the floor beside her. "Come sit by me. Get one them cushions and put it here on the floor beside me." James picked up two cushions, one for himself and one for Martha Lee. Martha Lee waved him to put the second cushion back. "Just one, hear." She swatted her backside. "I got fat enough where it counts."

James placed the one cushion on the floor beside Martha Lee.

Martha Lee took another drink of whiskey and licked her broad lips. "I sure don't need nothing to sit on, 'cause I ain't one your dainty-tailed white women. Know? I got enough bacon fat where it belongs, where it does the most good."

James lit one cigarette after another while Martha Lee emptied the bottle. She pushed the empty bottle across the floor. The bottle rolled on the concrete and hit the opposite wall, not breaking. Martha Lee lay back on the sofa. She said, "Know what I want now?"

"What do you want, Martha?"

"A thousand dollars and a sack of okra seeds." She laughed and covered her mouth before adding, "And I want another bottle, a full bottle again."

"Those are three things I can't give you."

"Not three things you can't give me. A thousand and three things. Least a thousand and two ways."

"More if you count the fifty seeds. That would make it a thousand and fifty-two things."

Martha Lee pointed to his lit cigarette. "Give me that."

"I'll let you have another one." James reached into his shirt pocket.

"No, not another one. I want that one you got in your mouth!"

James placed his cigarette to her lips. She sucked and coughed violently. "Mule. You're a skinny, white-hide mule. And I hate you!"

"Martha, you don't hate me. How can you hate me?"

"Easy, easy enough, I tell you. You're a no-good man and you got that worthless thing up your legs, so I hate you. And you're white, too, so I hate you. Them's two fine causes I got for hating you."

"Maybe. But I don't think you hate me, Martha."

"Suit yourself." She swayed from side to side. "Mostly 'cause you're a man. Men, they turn me to sickness. A time I seen a man on a man, front on back, drunk and up, grunting like two hogs there for anybody wanted to see. One of 'em was yelling 'I got to be on top, 'cause I'm a man' while the other one just grunted. I say let 'em be like that. Better they bothering each other than bothering me, for sure."

Martha Lee went on talking, more slowly. Her head dropped to James' shoulder. Her hands were folded on her legs.

James felt her body twitch against him like an animal dreaming in front of a warm fireplace many hours after it has fought another animal and its body repeats the fight over and over in miniature.

A long time passed. It was after midnight. Martha Lee was asleep and snoring loudly. James shook her. She moaned. James said, "It's time for you to go to bed and for me to leave."

"Uhh."

James stood and lifted Martha Lee's under her arms. "Get up! Stand up!"

She moaned. "No more. No more."

James released her. He went to the far side of the large room which served as her bedroom. He put the piles of clothing she had stacked on the bed on the floor and straightened the bedsheets. The sheets were stained, the blankets were army surplus. James helped Martha Lee to the bed. He removed her shoes. On the bed she turned to her side. James pulled the sheet and blanket to her shoulders. He turned off the lights and left.

Chapter Twenty-Nine

Martha Lee did not answer her door Monday night. Tuesday night was the same. On Wednesday James had dinner with the Davidsons and did not go out. Several nights thereafter he remained in his room. Depression overwhelmed him as he sat hollow-centered; staring at the nakedness of his table like an artist who stares at a bare canvas when he fears he has lost the strength for his art. Lonely dread tortured James after the peacefulness of familiarity he had had with Martha Lee. It was a dread of not knowing where she had been the two nights and of not knowing why he had stopped going to her room and of not knowing if he had strength enough to see her again. He wanted to rekindle the peacefulness he felt with her and the drive to understand her.

At the gas station James worked with greater skill and economy of movement than usual. But lucidity did not alter his sense of dread and emptiness, like the helplessness a very young man feels with an experienced woman the moment of orgasm before ejaculation, when his mind is very clear. James knew without doubt that if he were going to see Martha Lee again, he would have to see her very soon, before dread darkened to weakness too great to overcome.

James left the gas station early and walked in the afternoon. He passed old warehouses and locked gates. From within the warehouses and from behind the locked gates came sounds of machinery. He walked slowly, not wanting to be alone in his room, wanting the life of the city to strengthen him.

Ahead, four black boys, about ten or twelve years old, played kick-the-can. James walked by them. They stopped playing and watched him as he passed. Then he heard them playing again. One of the boys ran behind him, calling, "Mister, you give me a nickel!"

James smiled and asked, "Why do you think I should give you a nickel?"

"Ice cream, mister. I want ice cream. Hurry, mister, you give me the money before they go off and leave me here."

James smiled. He took a few coins out of his pocket. He gave the boy one of the coins. The boy said nothing, took the coin and ran.

What could be more joyful than watching a child run for ice cream, yet frigidity and an absurd panic flushed throughout James' body. He seemed threatened by something without form. He tried to visualize the threat. He knew of nothing. All courage drained from his body.

He was like something fragile when he climbed the stairs to his apartment. He pushed his weight against the wall. His legs felt weak. He unlocked the door and slammed it shut behind him. His legs gave way. He fell to the floor. He pushed himself to his knees, his head low. His consciousness seemed to drown within something he could not touch at all. Emptiness was sucking all of his energy. He thought the words: Beauty rules tomorrow. Power rules today and kills tomorrow.

The words were mere simple sounds without meaning. James remained motionless. He repeated the words in his mind. He got to his feet and found a sheet of paper. He wrote the words, putting them together in the form of verse.

> Beauty rules tomorrow.
> Power rules today and kills
> Tomorrow

James studied the words. They were not happy words but he felt stronger as he read them. He put the paper with his other papers. He shaved and took a bath. He ate dinner. Fate governed James now as he went to Martha Lee's. His actions and her actions. He must be passive, something of a *vaso de eleccion*, an empty glass, if fate so chose or go some unknown way if fate did not. He felt relieved of all decisions, almost like a schoolboy free to accept his own interpretation of some obscure reading after obtaining assurance from the teacher that his interpretation was acceptable. Peace overcame James and he almost did not care at all if he saw Martha Lee tonight or if he saw her again at all.

James hardly noticed the crowds about the storefronts or the people who were on the walk. They too obeyed fate. They were destined to obscurity and insignificance. This was a new pleasure. Power was strange and gave him a new, narrowed yet very clear vision. It was the power and the vision of a man who, pretending he was blind almost believes himself blind, and of the people who move away for his blindness even though it wasn't real.

James hurried to the alley, hurried in the darkness between the two buildings, smelling the rotting garbage, seeing a stray mongrel, hearing a cat hiss. James was certain, totally, as if he had been told by a woman he trusted, that he would find Martha Lee. When James knocked, Martha Lee immediately opened the door for him.

The room was warmer than before. James removed his coat and put it over the back of the sofa. Martha Lee was wearing an ankle-length quilt housecoat. Clean but faded. Martha Lee stood back and surveyed James. "I was thinking maybe I'd seen the last of you."

"You don't mean wishing?" James said with a smile.

"I'd of said wishing if I meant that."

"I wanted to see you," James said.

Martha Lee smiled freely. "I know." Her voice seemed to lift by degrees, like the sound of a small bird hurrying upward on wooden perch. "Most times you keep your coat on. I know you feel something different in here."

"What was it, Martha, another stove?"

"Almost. Only this was better. I got a 'lectric heater. And this ain't just something with a cord taped up. I got a new one. I bought it out of all that money you give me." It was a small bathroom heater with a disk reflector and a screw-in element. The heater was on the floor in front of the heavy soft-cushioned chair and a foot rest, which was in reality just a soft drink case with a cushion of newspapers.

"It does look warm, Martha. I think I could sit in front of that heater and never want to move."

"I guess now you can sit wherever you want."

For an instant James felt discomfort, as if he knew her words should bother him or frighten him. Martha Lee seemed very free and content. James was certain she had not been drinking.

"I haven't given you much, Martha."

"Now don't say that. You done more for me than anyone since my momma and daddy and I'm grateful. I thought I'd never see you again. I'm glad I was wrong. I do think you and me are truly friends."

James nodded and asked her, "Where have you been?"

"Somewheres," she answered coyly. "You want a cup of coffee?"

James said yes and added, "Is there anything I can do to help, Martha?"

"You just do whatever you want. I got to start the coffee now, so you know it's going to take a while."

James imagined himself sitting in the soft chair before the heater, his legs stretched, bare feet on the soft drink case. It would be much better than sitting at the window in his room, watching the outside traffic and hearing the coal trains in the distance. James took his usual place on the sofa. He watched the changing patterns of light on the walls and ceiling about the electric heater. When Martha Lee returned with two mugs of coffee and gave him one of the mugs, she asked, "Why ain't you sitting by the heater?"

"I didn't feel right."

"Too hot there for you?"

"Not too hot. I did want to sit there, but I just didn't feel right about it."

"Sure. You got a right," She smiled with affection. "Listen to what I'm saying. Now you and me, let's go over there, take our coffee over there by the heater and drink it there."

"If that's what you want. Take the chair. I'll sit by you on the floor." He took a cushion from the sofa. He followed Martha Lee and sat beside her, his back resting against her heavy chair.

"I bet you're wanting a cigarette now. Men and coffee and cigarettes, you won't see two of them for long without the other one. I forgot. I did. I'll get you something to drop your cigarette in."

"Don't get up, Martha. I'll leave some coffee in the mug and put the butt in there."

She brushed away his concerns. "You can drop your ashes on the floor, if you have mind to. My floor can't get much dirtier than it is now."

"I would never do that, Martha. I would never leave a mess for you to clean up." James sipped his coffee. "I can wait for a cigarette until I've finished my drink."

"I like the smell of your cigarette smoke. Most times I hate that smell, but you know I do like it when I got you here smoking your cigarette."

James put his mug aside and lit a cigarette "Do you really like the smoke?"

"Good smell," Martha Lee said attempting a sensuousness that only emphasized her ugliness. "It's good, your cigarette and this coffee and this warm feeling on my legs. It's all good."

James looked away, struggling to hide his repulsion. He thought of the piles of smallpox scabs, many of which surely came from her pitted and scarred face. He inhaled deeply and let out a ring of smoke. "Where were you, Martha?"

"Sometime I go to work 'cross the river. Over there they got a place for me to sleep. You know what? I was thinking 'bout you them nights, thinking you'd come here and you'd missed me and I'd never see you again. Worried me lots. It's funny. Sure is." She sniffed and pulled a handkerchief out of the pocket of her housecoat. "It's good. It's good seeing you. You know? I'm getting ready to cry."

"Martha, don't cry for me," James said.

She wiped her eyes. "I'm happy now. I am. You don't know, boy, it's been so long since I cried 'cause I had a friend who cared if I lived or died. Any old woman, even some woman like me that works on her knees every day she's alive, needs to cry sometime just 'cause she's happy. If she don't, it sure makes her sick and mean. I know 'cause I been sick and mean much as I ever want to remember."

Martha Lee did cry, and her crying was pleasant to James. He put out his cigarette in the vestiges of his coffee. For some time he sat quietly beside Martha Lee. Her legs were outstretched and covered by her long quilted housecoat. Her feet rested on the wooden case. The varying current from the heater's element produced changing light through which the moving dust created a mesmerizing complexity of patterns and illusions. Illusions equivalent to those imagined by Don Quixote when he dreamed of the Great Necromancer setting fire to all the fabulous books, illusions which almost separated James from things which were spiritless or ugly.

James said, "I have known times when I couldn't endure the sound of any music. But now we should have music. Then I think everything would be almost perfect."

Martha Lee looked at him, surprised. "What kind of music you like, boy?"

"How about Schumann?"

"Huh?"

"The kind of music you like when you feel sad, but you don't mind feeling sad."

"Oh, you're talking about The Blues. I gotcha. Sure. That's like the feeling I got right now in my bones." She began humming a tune that James had never heard before. Low and vibrating, like cattle calling at sunset.

James stretched out on the sofa and laid his head beside her on the seat. He closed his eyes. The warmth of the heater and her rhythmic humming were deeply relaxing. His muscles stopped twitching. The tension eased. His chest slowly grew light and his heart stopped it's hectic racing. Martha Lee gently stroked his head. He was startled, as if he had been shaken out of a daydream in which nothing in the world seems more important than a drop of water hanging from a faucet across a small room, and time waits patiently for the drop to fall.

Martha Lee lifted her hand. "Sorry I done that."

"Don't stop," James murmured.

Again, Martha Lee stroked his hair. She returned to humming the slow melody James did not recognize. "You like this music?"

"Yes," he answered. "See there, Martha, we are alike."

"Maybe so," Martha Lee said. "Maybe you're mostly right. Maybe you are like me, maybe I am like you. I don't know. Lots of things I don't know. I sure don't have to tell you. There's lots I don't know. I like you sitting here and having you here with me, and if you like sitting here too, maybe we are something alike. You know I got my legs warm. So they don't hurt me as much. I ain't pushing that scrub brush around in my head at night before I can get a little rest, and I don't have to end up down at Jake's with them I don't want to be with just cause I don't want to be here alone by myself. Maybe we are alike some ways."

James moved his head to Martha Lee's lap, or, rather the strength of fate moved his head. He did not know. Martha Lee continued stroking his hair and humming. She said, "Tonight you're not so nervous like I seen you before. Sometime I watch you, and them times I can't stand seeing you twitch about so much. But tonight you're not like that." She finally rested her hand on the side of James' neck, and he could feel one of her fingers tickle his ear. He heard Martha Lee breathing, and he heard the sounds which her body made.

He smiled, "I can hear your stomach, Martha. Sometimes I hear a thumping sound. Now it's a squirting sound."

"That so, boy," she said gently. She was twisting his hair around her fingers. James was looking away, as one who is young in the spring when the air is cool and the sun is bright. One who stands by a motionless pond and sees the colors move and merge on the still water. He almost hears lyrical poetry, and his sensations are shaped by something within him he does not try to understand, sensations which must be obeyed if he was to have any pleasure. But only pleasure and torment are possible, so James heard the sounds made by Martha Lee's body and felt her heat and saw the bizarre patterns created by the radiating white and red electric element.

"Martha? Would you like me to rub your legs?" he said. Martha Lee did not answer. James told himself that she may not have heard him or understood him. But the question was irrelevant. James opened the bottom of her quilt housecoat. Martha Lee's calves were as scarred from the smallpox as her face. As he massaged, Martha Lee rested her head on the back of the chair and moaned. Her body sounds quieted, her breathing and her stomach. So it was a long while, until James asked, "Did your man rub your legs?"

"Now and again," she said. "Sometimes he'd do it." James stopped massaging and she looked up "What'd you stop for, boy?" James pushed the heater a little away. He lifted Martha Lee's legs, first one then the other, and he took off her shoes. He lowered her legs on his legs. James opened the quilt housecoat to her knees and rubbed her legs. "I ain't comfortable this way," she protested. "I got to strain to keep my knees up."

"You'll let yourself relax when you want to, Martha."

"Not so hard like that!"

James massaged her legs from her ankles to her knees. In the warm light from the electric heater her legs appeared dark red. At her knees her legs thickened with heavy waves of loose flesh. Peacefully, Martha Lee said, "You got good hands, boy."

"Do I?" James asked. He moved his hands firmly and slowly from her ankle to her knee, one hand above the other, his hands working to a soft rhythm he could almost hear. "Do I have good hands, Martha?" he asked again. She laughed in response. "Martha? Do I? Tell me!"

Her voice was low and quiet. "Your hands is good hands. I know a man can't be worth much, not to a woman anyway, if he don't have good hands. That's a thing any woman ought to look at in a man, seeing what kind of hands he's got."

James lightly touched her skin with the tips of his fingers. He moved his fingers down inside her knees, and Martha Lee allowed her legs to drop apart. James hardly noticed. He massaged the soft, loose flesh behind her knees. Martha Lee said, "Your hands feel like they do care something about me."

James did not say anything. He moved his hands over her knees, then above her knees. Then he stopped. Then he pulled his hands away, not touching her at all. His body quivered, as if a great worm had coiled about his heart and now was moving, after it had lain motionless for a long while.

"What?" Martha Lee asked. Alarm was in her voice, but she did not move. "What's wrong with you, James?"

"Nothing." James heard the lie he told.

"Boy, I know that's not so."

"No, not true. I want to know what you're thinking. I ask myself if you still dislike me. You told me you hated me."

"Not any more. I'm glad you're here tonight."

James was still and quiet. He looked into her eyes. James leaned forward and touched her face with his fingertips. Her lips moved almost imperceptibly, as if she was going to smile, but she did not smile. James looked down at her legs, which were uncovered to her knees. He unbuttoned the quilt housecoat, starting at the bottom up to her waist. He drew the garment open to her waist and tucked it under her hips. Her undergarment may have been white, James knew, but in the radiant light it appeared red and orange. James rubbed her legs above her knees. "Martha, tell me that I have good hands."

With gentle affection, Martha Lee said, "You sure got good hands."

The loose flesh between his hands turned like a soft, circular, resilient springs wound casually about a hard core. James could feel her hard muscles. He moved the cushion up against the chair. With his arms he encircled Martha Lee's waist. His touched the flat of her back. He allowed his head to fall slowly, and his head rested on her abdomen.

James waited for Martha Lee to say something, to object or to accept. But she did neither, and her body rose and fell as she breathed. So it was for a long while, until James unbuttoned the quilt housecoat all the way up to her throat. He opened the housecoat fully, exposing her great breasts. They were smooth and full, the only part of her body that wasn't scarred and pitted from the smallpox. Martha Lee's feet fell from James' legs as he lifted himself and took her great breasts into his hands. Martha Lee placed her hands on his head. James rested his head between her breasts, hearing the beating of her heart. And he heard another sound.

"Martha? Are you crying?"

"No." Martha Lee said. But James heard her crying. He squeezed one of her breasts gently. He kissed her breast. The time was, for James, short and long, as if there were no time at all.

James said, "Martha, I'm not a baby."

"I know, boy. I know you're not."

"I could almost lie here all night and never move."

"I want you to do like that."

"I can't, Martha."

"Sure. I know you can't."

James moved, and Martha Lee pressed his head against her body. She said, "Not yet. Just a little longer, boy. Just a bit longer." She released him, and James lifted his head, looking into her eyes. "Do what I need, boy. I'll be whatever you want me." She cupped her hand below her breast and lifted it. James smiled with tenderness. He kissed her cheek, and he kissed her lifted breast. He took her nipple into his mouth. Martha Lee very slowly hummed the same melody. After some time Martha Lee said, "No more." She lifted herself.

"I will," James told her. He put his fingers under the band of her undergarment.

"Too fast and you'll hurt me."

James removed the garment, and he dropped it on the floor. She was naked. She moved back in the chair and sat erect. Martha Lee's ugliness almost forced him to turn away, but he didn't turn away. Naked, she possessed dignity he had not noticed before. He had a new, great respect for her. She had endured so much in her life: poverty, disease, death, yet here she was, with him almost as a woman is with a man. His respect surprised him, and greater was his surprise because he thought it strange. Her silent, naked dignity and the repulsion he felt together seemed altogether necessary at that moment, as if obedient to a natural law, as if the one were not possible without the other.

Martha Lee asked, "What do you want to do with me, James?"

More to himself than to her he said, "I don't love you."

"I know you don't," she said. "I know you ain't staying. But just stay a few more minutes, will you, and then when you go it won't hurt me so bad."

James stood and took a bill out of his wallet. He left it on the table without looking at the denomination.

On the street, walking in the light of stores and streetlights, James' eyes were wet and wandering aimlessly with his pain. His eyes burned from the cold wind and the bright lights. Only one knowledge was in his mind, and he repeated the words compulsively: "This is all the end of goodness! This is all the end of goodness!"

James did not wait for morning. He did not think of money owed him. The one knowledge pushed all else from his mind. With the panic of a fleeing slave who will not be beaten again or work anymore in tobacco fields under the killing sun, he packed his belongings and took his suitcase and his canvas bag to his car. He drove out of the city. He had no thought of where he was going. A sign on the road marked with an arrow pointing south. He turned that way and kept going.

Chapter Thirty

Two narrow lanes, driving in the dark. For long distances James was alone. Seldom did another car pass in either direction. James drove slowly. Distance was unimportant. Twenty miles or a hundred miles, that was not important. Movement and time and the gravel under his wheels, these were important. He had a growing affection for the back roads he traveled. It was not the mere passive element of road and automobile, the road was almost living, almost caring for him, as if it knew him by name and took a humane interest in him.

Time lay stretched out, shaped by the turns of the road, lengthened for him, so each minute he drove was longer, fuller, more significant than the arbitrary sweep of the second hand of his watch. This was finally, truly leaving Virginia. James drove through many small towns, all seemed to be decorated for Christmas. James hated these towns. Here time tightened and drew up like segments of an exposed, drying earthworm. Here James was like a man running with a strong, cold wind, when he must stop to rest, and the wind which had helped him now beats upon his sweating skin, and he feels sick.

James drove all night through the darkness, and then he drove through the broad orange of the morning and through the long shadows across the road. He drove past farms and over unsteady bridges. He stopped to purchased several cans of heating compound, a small saucepan, cheap utensils, sundry small necessities and food which he could heat and eat alongside the road.

And this was the pattern of living which James established: keeping out of towns, eating beside the road, sleeping in the car, allowing his beard to grow, going unwashed, no cigarettes, remaining alone most of the time, talking when he came upon someone who wanted to talk.

James took to this new way of life easily. The city slowly fell away from him. Only the image of Martha Lee was strong, but that image was also falling away.

All past remnants of injury, death, and disease grew weaker, but in its place grew a crust of dull and mechanical sadness. The mechanical sadness was like a banal phrase he had once heard, and, now remembered, could not be forgotten. James struggled to throw off this mechanical sadness. He turned to poetry, to Wordsworth, the one poet who had always given him beauty and strength. But against this growing sadness James could feel his sense of the importance of Wordsworth's poetry breaking apart. Words which for years had seemed as tangible as food now seemed little more than pretty phrases, and more, because they had such little substance, near vulgarities.

> Thanks to the human heart by which we live,
> Thanks to its tenderness, its joys, and fears,
> To me the meanest flower that blows can give
> Thoughts that do often lie too deep for tears.

James loved the words. But now the meaning was no more life-giving than a flat inscription on a tombstone.

> Ye blessed Creatures, I have heard the call
> Ye to each other make---

This was empty, insubstantial, and more vulgar than T.S. Eliot's cruel parody:

> I have heard the mermaids singing, each to each.
> I do not think that they will sing to me.

James put away his book of poems. For two days he had been

in one place, by a stream. Dead leaves moved slowly in the water. An uprooted tree lay fallen, its top submerged. James sat on the trunk of the tree. Across the stream tall grass clogged the bank, and in the water quivered the image of the steeple of a white church across the stream.

James stood and called out to the steeple, "Why did the Jews reject Christianity?" James had never before asked this question. He knew almost nothing about Judaism. But he recognized inevitability in his wondering, and at once he knew that he had to understand the answer to this question. In the glove compartment of his car, James kept the Bible his mother had given him when he was eight years old. He began reading Genesis. These were all familiar stories: Adam and Eve, the Flood, Abraham, Lot's wife, Jacob, Joseph and his coat of many colors. One incident seemed to James most tangible and important:

> And the children struggled together within her; and she said. If it be so, why am I thus? And she went to enquire of the Lord. And the Lord said unto her, two nations are in thy womb, and two manner of people shall be separated from thy bowels; the one people shall be stronger than the other people; and the elder shall serve the younger. And when her days to be delivered were fulfilled, behold, there were twins in her womb. And the first came out red all over like a hairy garment; and they called his name Esau. And after that came his brother out, and his hand took hold on Esau's heel; and his name was called Jacob: and Issac was three-score years old when she bore them.

The significance was obvious. God accepted responsibility for Jacob's actions. Could this be the reason the Jews refused to accept Christ? Christ added to responsibility, he didn't accept it. James read the books of the Law—Genesis, Exodus, Leviticus, Numbers, and Deuteronomy—but he knew that he did not understand what he was reading. The rules seemed endless trivialities. What to eat. What to wear. Something dark seemed to hang between his mind and what he was reading. He knew there had to be more significance than he saw. James put away his Bible. He continued driving south.

The New Year, 1950, the new decade, had arrived by the time James crossed into the South Carolina Low Country, yet something seemed vastly wrong. He seemed to be going nowhere, toward nothing, learning nothing. He had to know what he was going to do. Among his papers James found the sheet of paper on which he had written:

> Beauty rules tomorrow
> Power rules today and kills
> Tomorrow

James allowed his thoughts to be led by his intuition and instinct. He made a decision: to look at his intuition from a position of total powerlessness.

He stopped in Nabal, a small town northwest of Charleston, on the Cooper River. He parked in front of a grocery. He had little money. Seven men were standing and sitting near the entrance. They quieted and looked at James with curiosity as he got out of his car. They were of various ages, from old men to teens. James saw a single, familiar facial expression, that of a man who knows with no doubt what he will be doing tomorrow and next Saturday night, and each day after that, and the man waits passively for the common order of things to direct him.

The storekeeper, holding the hem of his full-length apron, hurried from the back as James walked in. He was a tall, thin man, long-faced and hollow-cheeked. James approached the storekeeper, "I'm looking for work. Would you be able to help me?"

The storekeeper's mouth tightened. "I thought you were a customer."

Several of the men from out front wandered in. One man wearing blue coverall mocked James. "When was the last time somebody give him a good scrubbing?" They laughed, but James did not look at them. "Don't he smell just like a yard full of niggers?" They laughed and stamped the wooden floor. "Listen here, I got a better one. Don't he smell like a house full of niggers plucking chickens?"

To James the men could have been dogs fighting in the street; they had nothing to do with his purpose. The storekeeper grinned at the joke. It was a restrained, sheepish grin. His grin disappeared when he spoke to James. "I don't need any help," he said.

The other men laughed and James saw an opportunity. "Could any of you help me? My name was James Campbell."

The blue coverall man slapped his knee and pointed at James. "Listen to him. He knows his name. I'd never of believed it by looking at him."

James said, "I never expected to work here in the store, but I thought maybe you might have some information about somebody who might give me a job. I'm not looking for anything special. Any kind of work will do."

Another man said, "Tell him to go see Buck Tanner. I understand Buck's looking again." The men laughed.

"What kind of work does Mr. Tanner do?"

"Oh, Mr. Tanner is it?" the blue coverall man said. "Don't let him hear you call him that. He'll get to thinking you're a fancy boy." The men laughed.

"Painter and roofer," said the storekeeper. "You ever do that kind of work?"

"No, but I've worked with my hands. I'm sure I could learn. Do you think there's any chance I could find a job with Mr., um, Buck Tanner?"

"Sure," said the storekeeper, and he gave the other men a smirk, as if he were trying to restrain himself while telling a funny story. "Buck knows his business, no doubt about that. Well, I can't say for sure, you know. But chances are Buck's looking for a good worker."

A short, stout man of at least fifty, put his hat on the counter. "Listen here, James? That your name?"

"That's right."

"Don't you pay any mind to this bunch of pinheads. You don't want to go to work for Buck Tanner. He's nothing but a dammed butcher. That's a fact. That's the way he is, and if he didn't have a lot more luck than justice on his head he'd be swinging where he belongs—and that's at the end of a rope. Listen, I'll tell you what kind of man works for Buck Tanner, and that's the kind of man that's had his nose up some whiskey bottle all his life and his belly up against some dog sleeping off a drunk. Tanner'd work you like a mule, and when you go, you'd be lucky you got the money you had before you saw him the first time. Right there, you look at that mule-headed son-of-a-bitch!" He nodded toward a tobacco-spitting man with teeth as brown as pine bark, "That son-of-a-bitch might not have sense enough to know his dick from a salamander in broad daylight, but he's got brain enough not to work for Buck Tanner."

The tobacco-spitting man took offense. He spit a wad as big as a mouse into the spittoon and his face started quivering from corner of his mouth to his eye. "Mapp! Keep your talking up. I might just throw a blade up your gut."

The blue coverall man chimed in, "Elroy's got a cause to be feeling against you, Mapp. You don't watch your tongue, one day a couple of the boys goin' to stamp your face quick and proper."

Mapp laughed. "Elroy? Nope. Not Elroy. No, Elroy's not about to stick nobody, leastways me. That right, Elroy? Sure. Elroy remembers. Last year who was it had his pickers out at your place, Elroy? Who else was there? What if it won't for me, Elroy's place'd be up for debts, and Elroy's wife be standing on a street corner someplace with niggers looking at her."

The tobacco-chewing man's eyes fell and he twisted his fist in his hand. "Things weren't that bad for me, Mapp."

Mapp slapped Elroy on the back like an old friend. "Anyhow, Elroy, how'd you like working for Buck Tanner?"

"Thereabouts you're right, Mapp. No man'd work for Buck Tanner if he had a little hope in his stomach. I'd never want to work for Tanner."

James said, "Tell me about Tanner. Does he live alone?"

Mapp said, "What for? You're not thinking about working for him are you?"

The blue coverall man said, "Buck lives with the ugliest pair of witches I ever seen. They's his wife and his wife's mother. Tanner brought them over from Germany back in '45 after the war. He was in the army, see, stationed in Frankfurt, that's in the American section. He left for Europe in '43 a single man and came back in '45 a married man with a Nazi wife and a baby on the way. The old mother-in-law doesn't speak English."

Mapp chimed in, "He didn't leave Germany in '45. He was dishonorably discharged in '44. Brought that Nazi wife home when he come." The men laughed.

The blue coverall man countered. "You don't know that for a fact, Mapp." He turned to James. "Buck came back from the war addled, you know, not quite right in the head."

The shopkeeper chimed in. "All I know I wouldn't touch either one of 'em if I was paid by the sheet." And the men laughed.

"Don't matter about them two," said Mapp. "Pity the boy. Tanner's son, he is. I'd have to call him an idiot. Maybe he's nothing but deaf and dumb." Mapp picked up his hat and smoothed it in his hands, picking off pieces of dirt and straw. "There's a story told about Buck and that boy, and could be it's not true, could be it is. I say it might be true, and I believe it. Says after the boy was born he used to cry all night, reason was he was sick right out from the start. And seems one night Buck just went all crazy with the boy's crying. Winter it was and Buck took that boy when he weren't more'n a couple of months old out and put him in a garbage can. Way I hear the story, the boy was out there all night. I don't know why the boy's mother didn't do something. Story was she found him next morning. Been my wife, she'd had me in jail or dead. But Buck Tanner's wife, could be she didn't care more'n he did, I don't know."

The storekeeper cleaned the counter with a rag, wiping up the dirt and straw from Mapp's hat. "My wife too. I'd been in jail. Hard to believe any woman could care so little about her own baby."

"Them people, them Germans, they don't care 'bout their kids like we do," said a man chewing on a pipe. He lit a match on his trousers and put the match to the bowl of the pipe.

Mapp said to James, "Now you know the kind of man Buck Tanner is. And like I say, if justice had its right way with him, he'd been dead years ago, or at least in prison."

"How do you know?" James asked. "I mean, how did this story about Tanner and the baby become known to everybody?"

"I don't know for sure. Could be Buck told Happy Smith, and Happy told any number of people."

"Yeah, could be," said Mapp. "It'll be like Buck to brag off to Happy. Buck'd think it was something to sing about if'en he had a good drunk on. I can easy think about Happy and Buck full of jar-whiskey and Buck bragging about something like that."

Finally, James interrupted. "Would one of you tell me how to find Tanner's place?"

Mapp said, "Go to hell!" He stormed out and the whole store was quiet, as if a vital part had been lost.

Then, apologetically, the shopkeeper said, "Don't mind him, he's always had a short way when anybody crosses him. But you ought to know what he says is true. Buck Tanner's not somebody you'd want to be working for."

The blue coverall man broke in, "Son, you go on about a mile, and there's a rail crossing. Take the next left down a half mile. That's Tanner's place on the left."

Chapter Thirty-One

Two majestic poplar trees were absurdly out of place beside the simple house, as if once, among others, they had stood beside a path to a rich home, and now everything else was gone. Amongst orange clay and spindly, moss-covered pines, deeply cut by thick, woody vines, Tanner's house was narrow, one story, and white, the paint blistered and peeling. The yard was large and overgrown with high grass enveloping several rotting stumps. The porch, half the breadth of the house, was uncovered, with grass grown up between the wooden steps. Beside the house were an open-front shed and half-dozen hens that followed a very large rooster to a field of dead cornstalks behind the shed. Away from the house a rusted car was propped up with cinder blocks.

James parked beside the poplars. He got out of the car and stepped over a chained dog, thin and mangy haired, like an underfed Doberman. The dog didn't move, not even a twitch. "That dog must be dead." James said aloud. James hesitated at the steps. Before his eyes he had the image of the baby in the garbage can, and, half consciously, he looked about for the can. There was none. James was not able to make himself go up the stairs. There was about all this something ludicrous, almost humorous, about his dilemma. He imagined a puppet show, and the puppet waited as he now waited, but waited for what? A hag to come out with a frying pan and hit him on the head?

Humor allowed James to move in freedom. He went up the stairs and knocked on the door. Two or three minutes passed and the door moved very slowly, opening little more than an inch and then closing again. The heavily accented voice of a woman was loud but single-toned and unexcited: "Es ist nicht Buck, Mama."

The woman opened the door again. Looking rigidly at James, the very symbol of hungry suspicion. She came out and closed the door, holding the knob behind her back.

The woman was almost frightening, a kind of naked, bony anger without strength. She was thin almost to starvation; her face was mere skin stretched tight over angular bones, without any expression other than deep, fragmented anger. Her yellow hair was long and dreary. The dress she wore hung about her body like something dead.

James said, "Mrs. Tanner?"

She nodded.

"I'd like to see your husband."

"Buck ist not here."

"When do you expect him?"

"I do not know?"

"Some men in town told me I might find work here. May I wait here for him?"

She pointed to the steps. "Ja," she said and went back into the house.

James longed for a cigarette. He hadn't had a cigarette since he left Martha Lee. He sat on the steps as the chickens returned from the dead cornfield and pecked at the dirt in front of him. His mind wandered over many things: people, faces, voices, the humor of his current situation. The future was unimaginable. He thought about his Bible, its cover and pages, not its words. Then, suddenly, without intention, he saw very clearly the darkness which obscured his understanding. He had been reading the Bible as a holy book, as if written by God. This was the darkness. God. Christ as god. He smiled at the revelation. He realized he needed to make two assumptions going forward: that the Old and New Testaments were unrelated and that each was to be read as if it had been written by a single author who had a specific purpose. James picked up a small stone and tossed it toward the chickens. They pecked at it wildly.

An old, light-weight truck pulled up behind James' car. The roof of the truck had been repaired with a sheet of unpainted steel, bolted in place, and the sides replaced with boards. A hard-bodied, middle-aged man stepped out wearing dungarees and a flannel shirt. His hair was buzz-cut and his eyes were steel gray.

"Trade you this truck for your car, and I'll throw in twenty."

James stood up from the steps. "Can't use a truck."

"How's your rings? Got good rings, I'll make it thirty. "

"I wouldn't use high-grade oil."

"That so? Burn oil?"

"I don't want to sell or trade my car, Mr. Tanner."

"Mr. Tanner? Hell, boy, my name's Buck. Gospel-spreaders call me Mr. Tanner. First thing them dammed spreaders call me is Mr. Tanner. Last thing they call me is sinner. Got me dead, planted, tried, condemned and roasted. But sinner, that ain't nothing against what I call them. You here to save my soul?"

"I don't care about your soul."

"Fine. It's like what I say about jokes, if it's a clean one I don't want to hear it and if it's dirty, I heard it already." He had an easy, infectious laugh that James found disarming.

"I was told I might be able to find work here."

"Where'd you hear about me?"

"At the grocery."

"Know any names? Lay it you saw some crowd."

"The only name I remember was Mapp."

"Mapp told you to keep the hell away from me, right?"

James kicked at the dirt. "Well, um—."

"Damn him. Know what, I'm in one sweet, front-up mood today. One time it was Mapp was right. Used to be I was the wildest, happiest son-of-a-bitch you'd ever want to see. No more. Army changed me." He turned deadly serious. "War ain't no trifling thing." He glanced at the house. "Ain't not one good thing ever come from it." For an instant this powerful man looked small, defeated. Tanner pulled his box of tools from the truck. "You see my woman?" James nodded. "The old woman?"

"No."

"I'd guess you ain't had a good meal awhile. Look! Watch this!"

Tanner put a finger of each hand to his mouth and whistled. The black, underfed dog resembling a Doberman barked wildly, leaping repeatedly on its short chain. Tanner laughed and whistled again. "Stupid dog." He grabbed the dog by the chain and held him high so the dog had to dance on his hind legs so he didn't choke.

"He was asleep," James said.

"That so." Tanner released the dog. Head down, nose to the ground, the animal disappeared under the house. Tanner asked James' name and James told him. "That's it?" Tanner said. "No nickname."

"No," James answered.

"I always say every boy ought to have a nickname. That's him, that nickname, not some gutless Sunday school name, a name that's his. Me, my name's Buck. Nothing else I care about. Nobody ever calls me nothing else. You know, I'd bet some men I've knowed all my life couldn't tell you my real name."

"Like Happy?" James said.

"Sure. You know about Happy, do you? That's him, all right. Happy. Damn him."

"Can I get work here, Buck?"

"Maybe. Listen, don't rush me. Things I got to know and think about. You come in with me."

"Should I move my car?" James asked.

"Leave it," Tanner replied.

James followed Tanner into the house. Tanner removed his coat, hung it on a hook, and James did the same. Inside, two women were standing together like an impossible pair of Siamese twins, each motionlessly holding the waist of the other. They were both thin to starvation, their faces sunken and without any expression. And yet there were differences. No skin of the older woman's face was not wrinkled. Her hair was gray, cut square and short.

Tanner said, "He's here to eat. Could be he'll be working for me. Get him a spot at the table."

"Good afternoon," James said and smiled. Neither of the women said anything or moved at all.

"His name's James. This here's my wife, Greta, and her mother, Mrs. Hammerhand."

James nodded, "Good to meet you Mrs. Tanner, Mrs. Hammerhand."

"Call her Greta. Mrs. Tanner is my mother's name." Tanner snapped his fingers at his wife and barked at her like a drill sergeant. "Set him a place."

Greta released her mother and went into the kitchen. Tanner made no attempt to hide his contempt as he stared at his mother-in-law. He said to James, "The old woman, she don't speak English but she understands a little of it. Don't you old woman!"

James asked to where to wash before supper and Tanner pointed to the back room. The soap was hard and brown. The water was very cold and frothy, and it smelled of sulfur.

Supper was brown bread and a thick stew unlike anything James had tasted. He told Greta he enjoyed it, which was true.

Tanner asked, "Why ain't Frank eating?" The two women ignored him. Tanner banged his fist against the table. "Greta, I'm talking to you. Why ain't Frank eating?"

"He ist to bed."

"*In* bed," Tanner said. "Not *to* bed. I want Frank here and eating his supper like a normal boy."

"Nicht, he ist sleep."

"Greta, right now, you bring Frank in here to eat like everybody else, you hear."

For a moment Greta seemed quite suspended. Then, loudly, she said, "Ja, Ja." She left the room.

After Greta was gone, Tanner turned to James. "She weren't like this when I married her," he said. "She was a scared little kitten that I rescued." He shot a look at Mrs. Hammerhand. "Might still be that way if it were just her and me and the boy."

Mrs. Hammerhand silently twitched her fingers.

When Greta returned, she held a shaggy-haired blond boy, his legs wrapped about her waist. The boy hid his face in the hollow of his mother's shoulder. He was about five or six. He wore underpants, nothing else. Bending with strain Greta lowered the boy to his chair, between her place at the table and Mrs. Hammerhand. The boy clung to his mother. With baby talk and physical urging she made him release her, and she pushed his chair to the table.

James watched closely. The boy appeared normal, although he seemed a child who had known constant fear. He breathed fitfully, like an asthmatic. The boy looked from one parent to another, neither of whom paid him any attention. Then he became aware of James and his expression changed from fear to curiosity. But his heaving did not vary. His mother spooned the stew into his bowl and cut a thin slice of bread. The boy's eyes were fixed on James.

"Frank!" Tanner shouted. The boy did not respond. "Frank! Listen!" Tanner pointed to his ear, then to his mouth. "Eat your supper." Again, the boy did not respond. Mrs. Hammerhand caressed the boy's bare stomach and he grinned up at her like an infant tickled by his mother's hair. Tanner pushed Mrs. Hammerhand's hand from the boy's stomach, and the grin fell away from the boy's face. "Eat your supper!" Tanner ordered.

Frank's mouth dropped open, and he fell to a motionless incline over the table, as if he were about to regurgitate.

"Get me more coffee, Greta," Tanner snapped.

Greta took his cup to the kitchen. When she returned, she asked if James wanted more coffee. He declined.

Frank's small fingers were stiff as he clutched his spoon. As he began to eat, Mrs. Hammerhand again began to caress the boy's stomach.

Tanner told James, "You've got stuff in your car needs washing, bring it all in when you're finished eating and put it all in the back. The women'll take care of it."

After dinner, when Greta was cleaning the kitchen and Frank had gone to bed, James asked Tanner about Frank, if the boy could understand conversation. "Frank hears what he wants to hear. You seen how he ate when I told him. But he don't talk. Never has. Never said his first word. He'll let out a good scream when he don't get his way. But he never puts his madness into words. Once had a preacher come in here, telling me Frank's my cross, saying I got to carry my cross so I'll start to believing what he tells me."

"But what have the doctors said about Frank?"

Tanner shifted awkwardly and held his hands together tight, as if one might escape away if he let go. "Hell, anybody can see the boy's got no mind. I know you ain't seen him much, but you ought to know that much. Times there's a county nurse comes around. She says there's nothing to be done for Frank, says he got something he was born with. Preacher tells me it's the will of God."

Odd contradictions about Tanner drew James' interest. Tanner seemed ordinary, almost gentle on occasion. At other times he was bizarre and cruel.

Tanner stood up and stretched. "Cold beer in the kitchen. You want a bottle?"

"No thanks."

Tanner went into the kitchen and came back with a bottle and a tall glass. He took his usual seat at the head of the table and poured the beer down the center of the glass. He sucked off the foamy head and emptied the bottle. He said, "Listen, I got something to tell you about the kind of men we've got ourselves around here. You want to listen? Say if you don't. No sweat off me. Sometimes I'll have a man here won't listen to me when I want to talk. You like that, you just tell me now." Tanner drank the beer, and he looked at James with solemnity.

James said, "I want to listen."

"That so. Well, you take Mapp. I knowed him all my life. He's a lot older than me, you know. You come in down there out of nowhere, and Mapp don't know you from Adam, but he starts in right off talking against me. Fact is Mapp's the hardest case I know. He wouldn't care a speck driving by you in his car, and he's got hisself a nice car, not if you was laying out on that highway with your head running blood. Mapp'd drive around you, just as pretty. And he's not the only one like that around here. Listen. Couple years past, for a long time I couldn't find work. All them I'd known years knowed I needed work. Willard Swift and Clyde Wakeman, men I'd knowed years, they knowed a man in need of good painter and wouldn't tell me. You seen Elroy Lane?"

"There was somebody called Elroy in the store."

"You'd know him if Mapp was there. Nobody ever called him anything but Elroy, and Mapp treats him like a baby with his pants messed."

"I saw him."

"Fact is, Elroy told me Swift and Wakeman was talking how they knowed this man looking for a good painter and how they wouldn't put in a good word for me 'cause they think I'm not decent. Hell, them two knowed I was needing work and they knowed I'm a good painter. Tell you one thing, I
wanted to lay an ax up aside their heads. Right now, I wouldn't take a job from either of them if they begged me. 'Course, I know that's not about to happen."

When Tanner finished his beer, he told James, "we'll be more comfortable in the parlor," and led the way to the main room. The room was sparsely furnished with a store-bought sofa long enough for a man to sleep on and hand-made end tables. The one bookcase, devoid of books, was a makeshift shrine displaying US Army medals, insignia from an army uniform, and a Nazi helmet. Mrs. Hammerhand was sitting in a wooden rocking chair but she wasn't rocking. Her few movements were stiff, as if she could not move without considerable pain. She watched James as if he were the enemy. The windows of the front room had neither shades nor curtains, and the room had none of the small things of glass or porcelain or any photographs or pretty things a woman would want.

James and Tanner sat on the sofa.

"So, you was just driving through town and heard about me, right?"

"I was looking for work."

"A man just going through and looking for work to pass awhile wouldn't mind having a handy place to stay. Then most of them don't have their own car like you do. So, what'd you say to staying here? Sleeping here and eating with all of us? Won't be free. But, hell, nothing's free."

"How much would you pay me?"

"Fifteen cent on the dollar."

"That's if I live here?"

"Right."

"How much if I stay in town?"

"Same. You see, I want any man working for me to live right here. That way I can get most for my money." Tanner laughed. "Look, say it's free, the roof and the meals. Do that, take it as being free."

James nodded and asked, "Are you working now?"

"Got a painting job starting in the morning. Say, you're not fearful getting off the ground, are you?"

"I'm not afraid of height."

"Good. See, that's always Happy's trouble. I'd put Hap on a thirty foot ladder and you'd see him kill hisself trying to get down. What good's that kind of man?"

As Tanner talked, James saw that he was different from the image he had formed listening to the men in town. Tanner's roughness was no worse than many men James had known. He seemed practical, and as hard-working and honest as any other man.

But the two women were strange. He had never known such women. They seemed hardly alive and were constantly watching for something which they could never see.

"My house and my land," Tanner said, "Been here twenty years. More, of a fact, twenty-two years, if you count my time in the service. I got me ten acres. Cost me five hundred dollars in nineteen and twenty-eight. And all cash it was I paid, not a borrowed cent. Not that I knew a soul who'd lend me a cent. I weren't even your age then, just a kid. Come a few years after I wished I had that money, but I had my land free when many another was living hard."

Mrs. Hammerhand was all the while in the rocking chair across from the couch, staring at James. Tanner called out, "What's you looking at, old woman? Got a spider in your mouth?"

Mrs. Hammerhand wrinkled her nose at Tanner. She called out, her voice high-pitched and unpleasant, "Greta! Meine füße sind kalt!"

From the kitchen Greta yelled, "Bewegen um dem ofen, momma."

With great effort, Mrs. Hammerhand scooted her rocking chair by the wood stove. Neither Tanner nor James helped the old woman.

Tanner laughed. "Old woman wants Greta in here so they can pet on each other. Same as two alley cats licking on each other, that's Greta and the old woman."

"I've never known anyone named Greta," James said.

"It's German. I picked her up in Frankfurt after the war. She wouldn't come with me 'less I brought her mother to America too." He leaned close. "Wouldn't have messed with either of 'em if she weren't pregnant. Now I wish she'd just gotten rid of the baby. Wouldn't be living with no two Nazis and a moron if I had a choice, that's a fact you can take to the bank."

Mrs. Hammerhand was still watching James with unmoving eyes. James smiled to her. She turned her head slightly, her eyes not moving from him. She made no other response.

It was ten o'clock before James was able to shave and take a bath. The water was painfully cold. Greta had shut had off the oil. The tub was concrete, set in the floor. James put on pajamas and a robe. The others had gone to bed. Greta brought James a wool blanket and a sheet and pillow so he could sleep on the long couch. She said nothing.

Mr. Lawrence was gray, small and nervous. In contrast, his house was large, colorful, and expensive. He'd hired Tanner to paint it bright yellow with white trim, like a giant daisy. James grew to enjoy the work. Winter in the Low Country was nothing like winter in Virginia. It was more like spring with pleasant temperatures and fresh air. Mr. Lawrence inspected Tanner and James' work frequently, demanding, complaining. James was able to shrug off the nitpicking but not Tanner. He brought the anger home and yelled at Greta over every little thing. His morning coffee was too hot, his eggs were too cold, she was too ugly to screw, but his worst was reserved for the boy.

Tanner called Frank lazy and stupid, and cursed at him until the boy cowered so deep between his mother and grandmother that he seemed to disappear. James knew Tanner wasn't sleeping at night and more than once he'd heard Tanner shout in his sleep about an unseen battle.

Several days after they had begun, James, high on a ladder, was painting about an upper window when he dropped the brush. He climbed down and found Tanner at the foot of the ladder holding the brush. Tanner screamed wild vulgarities, calling James every abhorrent name possible. Apologetically, James took the brush from Tanner and cleaned it. Later, in the truck, they did not talk. For some time after that, James was hesitant about climbing the tall ladders and didn't spend his evenings sharing a beer on the front porch with Tanner. But as he grew accustomed to the work, he lost all fear of heights and his body hardened. James worked laboriously without complaint or objection.

In the evenings, when the house was quiet, James returned to his Bible. He returned to the books of the law, to Genesis, Exodus, Leviticus, Numbers, and Deuteronomy. He read without the cloud of the Christian god, and he felt as if he was reading the books for the first time. He felt himself changing, growing tighter and stronger, not just physically but mentally and emotionally as well. The tangible grew more tangible. His delusions deteriorated. Images faded. He was able to focus. His mind would no longer flow over a thing and see it in many ways at once.

The law pressed the mind to tangible reality. The law replaced subjectivity and married reality with dream. Imagination was limited by the tangible. Everything was half of something greater, two halves mechanically connected, two halves moving opposite one another as in a balance, as in the obligation which implied the reward.

James read until he could no longer endure the mechanical limitation.

Chapter Thirty-Two

After James had been with the Tanner about a month, he met Happy Smith. James knew immediately the accuracy of the name. Happy was an incessant talker. A small, dusty-skinned man, Happy said whatever entered his mind and smiled at anything. Happy brought a giant dog, a half-grown mongrel that looked a mix of Rin-Tin-Tin and a St. Bernard, which he praised extravagantly for its intelligence. And he praised Tanner in the same way, recalling good times and bad times, how the bad seemed invariably to turn toward the good.

Happy said to James, "This here's a bear dog. Never was a dog smarter. This dog, you'd teach him something, and he'd snatch it up like you'd snap your fingers." James petted the dog and decided calling him a 'bear dog' was an accurate description. The dog was still just a puppy but its paws were the size of James' palm. Happy said to Tanner, "I commenced to thinking right off when I seen this bear dog, I commenced to thinking I wanted to give it to my good friend Buck."

"I'll take the dog, Happy," said Tanner.

"Yeah, Buck, I knowed you'd want this good bear dog right when I seen him. You recall that time last year when I was locked up in, um, what was the name that town anyhow."

"Daviston."

"Sure was. Daviston. You sent me the bail money. I don't forget, Buck. But you know I hadn't done a thing but put on a good drunk. You know, Buck, truthfully, I can't remember half the jails I've been in. But that one, that's one I remember good. God-O! What a stink! I been in some jails had some stinks, but that jail was one to remember. And no sleeping it off and trotting in the morning, not out of that place. Soon's I get a chance, I says, I'm going to do something good for old Buck.

That's what I was thinking when I seen this bear dog, how as this't be a good chance to do something really good for old Buck."

Tanner sat on the porch, his legs apart. He dropped his head between his legs.

"Buck, what you need's a drink."

Tanner looked up and called out, "Greta!!" She did not answer. Tanner cursed and again shouted, "Greta!" She did not come out or answer. Tanner told James, "Get in there and bring me out a couple of beers."

"Buck," said Happy, "I could use a real drink."

"You want a beer or nothing, that's all you got to say."

"Sure, Buck, I want a beer."

Tanner turned to James. "Go get'em!"

James went into the house, and Greta was alone in the kitchen making corn bread. She mixed milk and two eggs together, shells and all, and folded them into the corn flour. "Did you hear Buck?"

"Ja, I heared him," she said.

"Buck wants two beers."

She raised two fingers. "Zwei? You drinking beer now?"

"No," James said. "Happy Smith is out there with him."

"Oh mein Gott! If they start, um, what the word?" She pantomimed a boxing match. "Krieg? You know word?"

"Fighting?"

"Ja, if they start fighting, you come in here. Be safe."

James laughed. This was the first normal conversation he'd had with Greta. A small part of him wanted to stay in the kitchen and talk with her instead of returning to the porch. He opened the bottles and took them out.

Tanner had nailed boards to a tree and had drawn a target. He and Happy were taking turns throwing Happy's long folding-knife when James came out with the beers. Happy, handling the knife with skillful familiarity, easily hit the target from ten feet. Tanner's throws were awkward, unskillful; and the knife spun, the handle striking the board or the blade striking at an angle and not sticking. Tanner and Happy took the beers and offered the knife to James. He shook his head, "I'll just make a fool of myself."

Tanner threw again with disappointing results.

"Buck, you're too fast," Happy said. "You got to toss it smooth and easy. Watch me again." Happy threw and hit the target. "Say that's a Chinaman's nose. You just look him in his eyes. You got to be cool. Easy. Throw it at his nose."

"Happy, one day maybe you'll have a real chance to use your knife on a Chinaman."

"Hope I do get a chance. I wouldn't mind a bit sticking a Chinaman. Way I hear there's so many I'd throw blind and never miss." Happy laughed to the sky. "What I say time again, while we're fighting the Japs, we should go on through and cleared out all them Chinamen. And the same with the Germans and the Russians, gone through with all the guns hot."

"Give me that knife!" said Tanner as Happy pulled the knife out of the target. Tanner threw and missed the board. He threw twice again and missed. "Hap, you know a dammed lot about killing for somebody who's never done none. You think you'd throw right if you had to live or die according to how you used your knife?"

"Buck, I'd bet any kind of money."

"Sure, Hap. But you ain't got any kind of money. How's my ten dollars against your nothing?"

"Can't beat that."

Tanner stood by the tree and put his hand over his head. "One inch top of my head, Hap. My ten says you can't do it. If you can't, well, then you're out nothing."

Happy folded the knife, and he put the knife into his pocket. "That's a bed I don't dare take, Buck. Don't dare."

Happy remained at Tanner's for almost two weeks, sleeping on the floor near the oil stove, wrapped tightly with a woolen blanket, loudly snoring, and keeping James awake. James left the couch and slept in the shed, swearing he'd return only after Happy left for good.

Happy was there when Tanner and James went to Mr. Lawrence's house to paint and he was there when they returned. After the paint job was done, Tanner spent every moment with Happy, most of the day outside, and Tanner said nothing more about work.

No work gave James time to study his Bible. He began to see clearly that the law produced a god-like quality of thinking for power without exercising any will. The constriction of heart and mind were almost unbearable, yet the Law held a fascination for James.

He tried to read the poetry of Wordsworth. Each word was before his eyes as objects occupying spaces and waiting to be reached, held, and manipulated by fingers which might be skillful or unskillful, examined, then placed in a new position.

James understood: The perfect merchant, the perfect user of the balance, this was the ideal. First on one side of the balance; then on the other. And to use this, the most effective means of gaining power, was the will of god. The ethical serves power. The merchant, the perfect merchant, was the chosen enforcer of the will of god. The long term interest of the Hebrew people was the measure of the good. The root of such power was a kind of self-deification obtained through pushing the simple binary problem-solving system into the mind with enough force to destroy subjectivity and the aesthetic. The chains which bind the heart to the earth, of all things which can be seen, those must be the most unbearable to one who hates them or the most pleasant to one who loves them.

By the self-deception of the anthropomorphic god whom the Hebrew merchant had ordered him to do what he wanted to do, the Hebrew put the absolute stamp of institution upon mankind, defining man as a creature created by the universe, whose proper function was to serve the universe. The universe was a machine, and to have non-dangerous power a man must also be a machine. Individualism was inefficient. Imagination was the by-product of inefficiency.

The individual was the aesthetic. Those who hated beauty did not hate it for itself, but because it was the bearer of individualism. James finally understood why the love of beauty was the first sin in the

Bible.

As James became more and more a fixture in the Tanner household, he took to telling Frank a children's story after supper. James did not know how much Frank could understand, but the boy laughed and smiled more with James than with anyone else. Perhaps he was only responding to the tone of James' voice or to James' exaggerated enthusiasm. James, Frank, Greta, and her mother would gather in the main room, Frank and James on the sofa. Tanner spent his evenings outside drinking with Happy. Frank would hug James goodnight when his mother or grandmother took him to bed. Greta and her mother also enjoyed James' stories.

James grew fond of Frank. He saw that the boy's life as empty and repetitious, and being with James seemed to give the boy's life meaning. Frank grew increasingly attached to James. He wanted to be with James and to imitate him. Whenever James worked in the shed, Frank would wander in to join him.

James began to use a piece of sandpaper on a section of lumber. Frank watched with great interest. James smiled and winked his eye, and Frank laughed excitedly. James gave the boy a piece of the sandpaper and a section of lumber, and Frank sanded the wood eagerly. James inspected Frank's progress frequently, testing the wood with his fingertips, having Frank do the same, directing the boy's attention to areas not yet smooth. James gave extravagant praise for what Frank had accomplished and put great importance upon what had been left undone.

Greta often came in to watch them, as if James' interest in Frank renewed her own interest in her son. As if James seeing value in the boy gave Greta reason to see value as well. "Danka," she said to James as she took Frank's hand. "You are good man."

James was of two minds. To one, Greta and her son were indolent creatures, imperfect, unworking parts of a mechanical device, and from them James was far removed. Yet his other mind knew Greta and Frank as symbols of something larger, as he knew them, lived with them, moved with them. And it was like beauty and goodness together when beauty and goodness were impossible together.

James was cleaning the shed, hardly aware of the time. But he looked at his watch when he heard Tanner's truck. It was almost three o'clock. James stepped outside and saw that Happy was with Tanner. Each man was carrying two canning jars. Tanner took his two jars into the shed and hid them behind a board on the floor. He ignored James as he passed. Back outside, he took a jar from Happy, unscrewed the cap and drank. He offered James a drink. James took one swallow and felt a wave of revulsion greater than any. It made him feel feverish and achy, like he had been poisoned. He couldn't stand any more.

Tanner appraised the jar as if he were a skilled workman appraising work well done, "We got to get at some hard drinking, Hap."

Happy sat in the dirt among the chicken scratchings and rested his back against the shed. "Sun's so warm. So sweet."

"Happy," said Tanner. "Far's it go with you, things was always warm and sweet. You hearing a bird in your head?"

"Always do, Buck; always when I got a warm belly, all them other sounds drift off so all I hear was my little bird."

Tanner turned to James. "Cleaning out the shed? That's what you been doing?"

"Yes."

"Got to keep going, right? Where's Frank at? That kid'd rather be about you than me any time." Tanner laughed. It was the laughter of a childish man disguising his unhappiness.

"Frank wants to help me, and I enjoy letting him do it."

"Sure you do. Frank's a good enough kid, but he can't talk." Tanner laughed, almost hysterically, but with a definite string of anger in his laughter. "I ought to throw you out of here. Days now we don't work. Still you're here, still you're eating whatever you want and sleeping warm. And you don't care to take a drink I offer you, and I bought the liquor. Hell to you."

James did not answer. He began to sweep the board floor of the shed.

Happy called out, "Buck, you know where's the dog I brought

you? The bear dog I brought special for you?"

Tanner watched James work. He screwed the cap on the jar and put the jar on the floor. "You're doing it all wrong! I'll sweep!" He took the broom from James, and he swept with fast, long strokes. Dust, dirt and debris filled the air. Coughing, James ran out. "Coward! Lazy coward!" cried Tanner. "You'd of been shot for desertion if'en you'd been in the Sixth."

James shook the dirt from his clothing and out of his hair. Happy, still sitting on the ground by the shed, said, "Don't feel hard about old Buck. When Buck's drinking and feeling a little good, he thinks he's got money. I know lots like Buck; drink a little, and they got the whole world."

"But not you, Happy?"

"Not me. That's come they always called me Happy. I drink, and I don't care. I know what I am, and I don't care."

Tanner came out, and he had the jar in one hand and the broom in the other. He raised the broom like a spear and threw it into the shed. He unscrewed the cap of the jar and took a long drink.

Happy asked, "Buck, whar's that bear dog? Whistle him up, Buck."

"I don't want that dog."

"James, you'll whistle him up for me, won't you?"

James whistled, and Buck's dog got up and moved slowly to the end of his chain and looked at them without excitement. Out of the field of dead corn the bear dog ran to James and to the others. Happy held the dog close, and the dog licked Happy's face, and Happy hugged the dog and rubbed his cheek to the dog's neck.

Tanner, laughing, told Happy, "Kiss the dog. He wants you to kiss him, Hap."

Happy patted the dog's head affectionately. "This bear dog loves me. This dog's got more feeling than them I got to run with."

"Hap? Mor'n that broke-jaw woman you was shacked with, I'd bet. Hap, what was that woman's name, anyhow?"

"Mary was her name. Buck, she's dead, you know. Don't you start against her again. She was a good woman. Far's a thing goes with me, she was sweet and kind as any woman I'd ever want to know."

Greta had come out to the porch. She had two small rugs. She shook one then the other. The three men watched Greta. She looked their way then went back into the house.

Tanner said, "You ever taste a woman?" Tanner and Happy looked to James. Tanner's face was ugly with a broad grin, and Happy smiled weakly. James did not answer. "I'd lay it you ain't," said Tanner. "And you say
you'd one it, I'd figure you was lying. What say, Hap?"

"Maybe."

"You're right, Buck," James said. "I'd lie."

"Hell on lies! Hell on lies!" Tanner cried out, almost in pain. "I was all lapping for good front-up tales, and you got to lie, what's not half bad, but you got to tell me you'd be lying, even when you don't tell me a thing. You're there making me miss what's best about drinking in a bunch, telling good front-up lies, good honest lies that nobody'd more than half believe, and the best part, slipping in a truth here and again and knowing the rest won't but half believe that too. So why can't you be a sport?"

"Buck's saying the truth," said Happy.

For James, Happy's words were like a knife of pliable rubber. James sat down on the wooden floor of the shed, beside the dog, whose head and forelegs hung over the edge of the floor.

"Sit there," said Tanner. "You're hang face as a tomcat with the stones. Know what the matter with you? I'll tell you. I seen it lots since you come. You think too much. Can't make out what it is you think about so much, but all the time I see you at it. So you tell me, what's it you think about so much?"

"Buck, everybody's got problems," James said.

"I know that. I got problems I ain't seen in twenty years. Hap, what say? Same with you? You got problems you don't think about?"

"I got my troubles, Buck. And mostly I don't think about 'em."

"You don't want to think about your problems, that so?"

"That's a fact."

"And I don't love thinking about mine. Tell you what, Hap, you think about my problems and I'll think about yours."

"Sounds good, Buck."

"Don't it. Don't it though. One problem worth thinking about, Happy."

"Buck, I got the answer to your problems."

"What's that?"

"Easy. Stop drinking."

"Happy, goddamn you!"

"No need you to get flashy, Buck. First thing you'll be sliding out of your sweet place, and a sudden you'll be switching tracks not knowing what's going on. Too many time I seen you drop men, never looking at the turn."

Tanner laughed as Happy rubbed his chin. "And you got the scars to prove it." James looked at Happy with new eyes, suddenly noticing the multitude of scars and obviously broken nose. He glanced at the kitchen window and wondered about the story of little Frank left in the garbage. Did Tanner threaten Greta when she tried to save him? Or maybe the old Mrs. Hammerhand?

Plaintively, Happy said, "You put them there, Buck."

"Hap, try to shame me will you and you're playing for a mean game!" Tanner raised the jar to his mouth, took one deep swallow, and stretched his arm and lifted his chest, breathing deeply.

Happy drew his spread legs to his body, his heels to his thighs. Between his legs he held the jar with both hands. Half moaning, half singing, Happy said, "Mary oh my Mary, Mary oh my Mary, Mary oh my Mary." He said, "James, listen! Will you? Mary won't no pretty woman. Mary was in a wreck took her jaw. Hurt all nights so bad. Mary was a woman sweet she was. Nights she'd set quiet, so still times I couldn't say she was alive or dead. Sometime we'd talk. Mostly I'd do the talking, and she'd listen to whatever fool stuff I wanted to say. Sometime she'd say, 'Hap, you're a good man.' And then to me I'd say, 'Hap, you got to do something special for this woman 'cause she's sweet.' I didn't, never. Couldn't. What'd I have to do something special? Nothing. I'd want to do something special so bad it'd seem like my heart'd drop out like in the toilet. Not to the day she died did I do a thing special for her."

With a singsong whine Tanner parodied Happy. "Oh Mary, oh my Mary." Tanner burst into an ugly, mocking laugh. Pointing with his hand which held the jar, now almost empty, he said, half laughing, half groaning, "Know what the damned fool did? Most fool thing." Again he fell into uncontrolled laughter.

Weakly, Happy said, "Damn you, Buck."

"Happy, tell him about the wrist watch you gave her!"

"Mary had a right, Buck."

"Dumb talk, Hap. Always go the dumb way. She was dead."

"Buck."

"I don't care about saying. This fool takes every cent he's got, and he buys that dead woman a wrist watch. She was in her box, and Hap sets the watch right, and he puts it on her arm. Was the most fool thing I ever seen."

"Won't my every penny, Buck. Watch was twenty-five dollar. I had mor'n that. Before Mary died I figured I needed that money. But afterward, when she was gone, I come to know I didn't need that money so much."

Tanner grinned, ready to attack. "Hap, know what I believe? I think one of them gravediggers at the hole opened that box and took that watch off her wrist. Bet that's what happened. Bet if you dug up the box, you'd find out that watch was gone."

Happy sat quietly. He looked out at nothing, not to Tanner, not to James. As with great pain, he raised the jar to his mouth, and he took another drink. Then he put the jar on the ground beside him. He drew his legs together and joined his hands under his knees. He bent his body and placed his forehead on his knees.

Tanner dropped his empty jar and with the side of his foot kicked it across the yard. He squatted, raised himself, squatted again, several times, as to prove his sobriety. "If'n I had a woman now, I'd let her pooss there. Pooss, pooss." Tanner slapped his mouth. "Honey, oh that's warm, sweet honey. Yeah, even Happy's no-jaw whore. But she's dead." He laughed "Pooss, pooss." He laughed. "Sometime I say old Hap's so sweet I love him." He laughed. "So sweet sometime I love him.

Another time goddamn if I don't look at him so I can't stand him, and I want to smash his teeth."

Happy shifted in the dirt like a beat puppy. "It was my money, Buck."

"What money was that?"

"The twenty-five dollars. That money bought Mary that watch."

"Hap, you can bet, in ten years you never had twenty-five dollars didn't most of it one way or other come outta me."

"Never a penny I didn't work for, Buck."

"On my back. I carry you, Hap. What good's a painter won't climb a ladder. Maybe you'd get up on a ten foot ladder. But I work at thirty foot. You won't climb. You'd sit and you'd cry like a baby and maybe you'd starve, yeah, you'd starve in front of a thirty foot ladder before you'd climb up."

"Fact is, Buck, I done lots on your account. Always, I'm saying, what can I do for old Buck? I brung you that bear dog. I wanted to do something for you, Buck."

"Think I care about the dog? I don't want that dog."

"You don't mean that, Buck."

Tanner did not answer. They all fell into a silence of minutes. Then Tanner asked Happy for his folding-knife and Happy handed it over. Tanner opened the knife and clapped his hands. "Come here, dog, come here to me." Wagging its tail, the big pup ran to Tanner. Tanner lifted the dog by the scruff of the neck. The dog only whimpered, and Tanner drove the knife hard into the animal's chest. He dropped the bleeding, howling dog and mumbled, "Got to sleep. Got to get some sleep." He went into the house.

Happy got to his feet and staggered toward the road.

"Get in my car," James told him. "I'll drive you home."

"Do that for me, will you?"

"Yeah," James said. The dog wasn't dead. Not yet. Its eyes looked up at James and its tongue fell out of its salivating mouth. James thought someone ought to put the dog down but he did nothing. Just left it there to bleed to death in the dirt.

Happy lived about two miles from the opposite side of the town. His home was little more than a shack. James waited and watched as Happy urinated beside the front door then staggered inside. James drove back to Tanner's. The dog was dead by the time he returned and he buried it between the shed and the cornfield.

Chapter Thirty-Three

Fate. James saw the fullness of fate, the ugliness of fate, that fate could be an enemy or a friend, and if it was sometimes a friend it can also sometimes be an enemy. James saw the fullness of that final fate, the mechanical solver of problems with the seer of images: either may be a lover of justice, either may be a hater of tyranny, either may be a hater of cruelty, yet, together, the one, upon the earth, his feet rooted into the earth, must attack the other, who was the liver of the fullness of life. And those seers of images must grow weaker and still weaker until they must attack or fall into degeneration, and they will attack, they, too, obedient to fate with the inexorability of the fall of a stone or the working of a soulless machine.

Fate. And the heart of man was a thing of death; self-knowledge was the stuff of slow death; individualism was weakness; all power was based upon self-negation, self-deception; the seer of images must search out fresh, new self-deception in which to find strength. Individualism was inefficiency.

Fate was as tangible for James as his own body, and fate was like dry feathers in his mouth. James needed to touch beauty, but he could not. James dreamed of melody, and melody was mechanical, ugly. Only death had melody. The word, above the words he loved, had a melodic superiority, as beauty which was merely the absence of ugliness; he was like one who was blind and who sees a kind of beauty when all else remembered was ugliness. The love of beauty was too weak against power, yet power was too weak against fate.

James knew he could not save himself through beauty. He no longer struggled to gain his strength through beauty. As a man who was dying has moments toward the end, as when a nurse, expecting no reply, asks a question, and he was not apart from her or apart from the world, when he was a simple unit in the world, not needing to hope, so James knew and admitted that beauty was too weak.

But unlike such a dying man, James did not admit any needlessness of hope. Rather, he saw something distant, yet reachable. Something which, as the balance lifts above simple superstition could lift above fate. James saw something which must have the strength of law, law greater than fate. That distant structure, which he had to reach, would be the place at which he would be able to create new art.

Mrs. Hammerhand died as the warm South Carolina winter turned into a hot, humid spring. The undertaker came, a small funeral, with only Greta, Tanner, Frank and James in attendance. Mosquitoes haunted her funeral and buzzed louder than any of the mourners, certainly louder than Tanner.

The next day, Tanner took the truck and left. James found Greta on the couch, crying. Greta was holding Frank, The boy was whining and gasping. "Buck beat Frank again," Greta said. "Bad. Bad. Poor baby. Poor baby." She caressed the boy's shoulders. She kissed Frank then she wiped her eyes and looked at James apologetically. It was a look which James hated to see. "He was not drunk," she said. "And he still beat Frank."

James turned Frank around. His back was reddened, but not bleeding. Apparently Tanner had not used his belt. Frank pulled away from James and buried his face in his mother's dress.

James asked, "Why did Buck beat him?"

"Like before," Greta said. "Frank mess pants. He cannot help. Mostly, he goes to toilet. Sometime, he forget. But Buck, do not understand Frank. He do not love even a little."

Again Greta looked to James, and her face and eyes were apologetic. "Before Frank born, Buck say he never clean up a baby mess. Buck say, when he was boy, his momma screamed mad. Cursing. You understand?" Greta shook her fingers, as if she were Buck's mother scolding her son, "You ugly. You stupid. You scheußlich. Call him awful names. Throw slop on him, and long time he have it on face and clothes. Now, he bad to Frank." She kissed the top of her son's blond head. "I wish I go away somewhere safe. Take Frank somewhere safe and good."

"Back to Germany?"

"No! Never! Bad men everywhere. Everywhere bombed. No place safe for woman and child."

James thought about his classes in nineteenth century German history. He thought about his study of the Bible and the laws of the Hebrews. "Do you hate the Jews?" he asked.

Greta folded her arms. "None of that my fault."

"My question isn't one of blame but rather of upbringing. From your statement, I assume the answer is yes."

"They killed Christ."

"They invented Christ."

Greta looked startled and James was sure she had never considered the lunacy of genocide as revenge for the death of a mythic being.

"Holding modern Jews responsible for the death of Christ is akin to holding modern Greeks responsible for Poseidon's rape of Medusa in Athena's temple. One must begin with the realization that both Christ and Poseidon are myths and that everyone involved in the creation of these myths is long dead. And, more to the point, the purpose of both religion and mythology should be to make us more civilized, not less."

Greta blushed. "I repeat what I was taught. Just like in America."

James only nodded.

James wondered about Ameele. His life at the college seemed ridiculously removed from him now. Those torments and pleasures seemed another universe, one ruled by laws which were as removed from his present life as traffic ordinances or rules of etiquette were from life within a prison. James wondered if Ameele really cared about that painting. He could not attach any importance to the question as Ameele seemed no more than a living toy taking its own toy pleasure.

The night was warm, too warm for spring. James could not sleep. He tried to read. The floor creaked. Greta was standing over him. She wore a long, white gown. Gently, nervously, she asked, "Am I disturbing you?"

"I haven't been able to sleep tonight."

She said, "I want to show you something."

James nodded and Greta sat beside him. She held a colorful magazine, an unusual sight in this drab house and setting, like a butterfly in a dust storm. She opened the magazine to an article about Quakers in Pennsylvania. She pointed to the images embedded in the article and asked, "Where this?"

"A few states north of here," James said. "They're originally from Germany, I think. Good people. They housed runaway slaves before emancipation."

Greta pressed her hands together tightly on her lap. "I want to go there."

"Why," James asked.

She looked ahead to nothing, as if she waited for something unknown to help her. Finally, she said, "I like way you talk to Frank. You know Buck. Buck not love Frank. I know Buck not bad but that not does me any good to know."

"Frank seems happy." James said, and he knew her words before she spoke.

"It's you. I see difference. Buck not care, not littlest bit. I know even a boy like Frank needs man in his life."

"I think I understand," James said. "Do you feel guilty because you don't care enough about Frank?"

Greta stood and frowned down at him. "No! I love my son. Why you say that? You come here for job. You have choice. What choice I have? No country, no family. Only Buck. I am woman. Woman have no choice. I am alone with sick boy needing help. Why you say I feel guilty. Why? Just to hurt me? What I do wrong? What? I do not start war. I do not want to marry American. I have no choice. You should feel guilty for saying such thing."

"I'm sorry," James said.

Greta clutched the magazine to her chest. "There is much I need to say. I wish, but who listen? Buck? Frank? Happy? I need what I never have."

"What? Security?"

"Home. I need home with my own people." She pointed to the pictures of the Quakers. "I need this."

James reclined easily against the back of the sofa. "Will you do something if I ask you?"

"Maybe."

James patted the sofa. "Sit down beside me again." She sat and he put his hands on her shoulders. He urged her to sit back and relax against him. Her body remained stiff and unyielding. "Can you make pictures in your mind?" he asked.

"No, I not," she said with confusion.

"I believe you can. Try. Do what I tell you." James spoke softly, as if he were talking to a child.

"I try."

"Make a picture of yourself as you are now, sitting with me."

She scrunched up her face like a worried hound dog, "I not like picture so much," she said.

"See the woman in the picture. Let her feel whatever you want to feel. Let her do as she wants. Let her have your feelings."

"No, I cannot."

"She can't feel if you're tight inside, so don't talk. Relax and let her feel for you." He drew her near and placed his hands on her shoulders. This time Greta didn't resist. "She's sitting on the couch," James said. "I can see her. She's here with me. I feel her head against my chest."

Greta moaned almost inaudibly, yet her body remained rigid.

"Do you see her at all?" James asked.

"A little. I am trying."

"Watch her very closely. Don't let her fade away. Let her have your feelings."

James very slowly, as if her were touching an object of great fragility, covered her breast with his hand. Her body grew soundlessly tight, then she breathed deeply through her mouth, and her body vibrated. James held her more tightly. By degrees she became flaccid. Her small weight pressed against James. He did not move at all, and she breathed evenly, as if she was sleeping.

They were so a long while. She whispered, "I hate living here."

James lifted his hand from her body; she whimpered deeply and her body quivered as from cold, as if she were remembering a fear. "Please. You hold me again. I make picture like you say."

James again covered her breast. "Is it hard for you?"

"I see picture. She ist listening and talking words, and I am here listening peaceful to her. Except when you take your hand away."

"Does it seem that my hand connects you and her?"

"Ja, you really do know," she said. "Will you do something for me, James?"

"Maybe. Depends."

"Will you help me help Frank?"

James released her and said, "I would like some water."

"You stay. I get you a glass."

As Greta went to the kitchen, James felt pleasant, cool emptiness on his hand which had held her. When she returned, he took the glass and she watched him drink. She took the empty glass from James and placed it on the floor. She took the place beside him. "You help me und Frank leave here and I let you hold my, um," she indicated her breast, "hold mine frauenbrust, ja?"

James pushed her away and stood up. "Go back to your bed," he said and she obeyed without objection.

Tanner returned smelling of whisky and complaining about a headache. He sent James to Nabal to pick up paint and supplies from the general store where James was inundated by the same group of men as he'd met when he first arrived. "Say, you never heard about Zeke Tripp, did you?" asked the man in the blue coveralls.

"No," James said as he wandered the store. "Never heard of him."

"There used to be an old man, can't remember his name, but I remember him by his face clear as day, and he'd got his legs mangled up somehow, so he couldn't hardly walk."

"I remember him," Mapp chimed in. "Name was MacSomething. MacNeill or MacDonald."

"Yep," said the man in the blue coveralls. "He'd hurt all the time, so he used to drink to get to sleep. Many the day I used to see him under somebody's porch, sleeping and curled up. Well, Zeke Tripp used to torture that old man. Zeke's favorite fun was kicking the old man's legs to get him awake and then pissing on the old man's face. But Zeke got it all turned on him when he started his hard drinking. Buck Tanner was the one gave it to him."

James stopped wandering and looked up at the man telling the tale.

"Listen," the man said. "They found Zeke stripped naked and dead behind old lady Dotson's henhouse. It was about this time of year. Word was that he'd caught pneumonia. You'll never tell me it won't Buck that done it to him."

James placed the paint and sundries for the Tanners on the counter. He asked the store keeper for a box of quinine tablets for himself. "Lots of 'skeeters out there," the store keeper said. James nodded and left the store. He walked to the bus station and asked the stationmaster about routes and costs. He wrote the bus numbers and times to Philadelphia on his forearm in permanent ink and thought it looked disconcertingly like the tattoos the Nazis put on the Jews.

The next day James was sitting on the front porch watching Frank dig at the dirt with a long stick. The boy's movements were less stiff and awkward than inside the house. He was flinging dirt to one side and grinning with satisfaction. Greta was sitting on the steps peeling and cutting white potatoes.

Tanner stormed out. "Thems enough potatoes Greta. You come on in now."

"Einen moment."

"You come in NOW!"

Greta shifted her eyes to James before she obediently followed Tanner into the house.

James knew he had committed himself irrevocably and he could not remain here much longer. This made him afraid. But as much as fear of having to leave without accomplishing what he wished, he knew the pleasant, terrible emptiness of simple egotism.

Twenty minutes later Greta returned to the porch and returned to peeling potatoes as if nothing had happened when Buck had her in the bedroom. Buck followed her out and went to the shed. He came out with a jar of moonshine and took it inside the house. James waited until Tanner was inside before he spoke. "I can't stay much longer," he said.

Greta stopped peeling potatoes. "But you are not leaving soon?"

"In a few days."

Greta's breath quickened. "Before last night I not care if you go or stay. But now we are friends. My only friend. This morning I fix you breakfast, I want eggs to be just right. I looked at eggs long time before I broke them. And now you tell me you are going away in few days. Where will you go?"

James wanted to tell her a convenient lie. "I'm not sure where I will go."

"So stay here."

James knew no way to answer her, and he did not try.

"Listen," Greta whispered, "I had thought. What if I go with you. Me und Frank, we go where you go."

"I told you I don't know where I'm going," James said.

"Then why not go to Quakers in Pennsylvania? Ja? You and me live there together. Und Frank. That good plan?"

"No," James said. "That's not a good plan."

Greta groaned and gathered her potatoes hurriedly and she went into the house.

Frank continued digging in the ground with the long stick, which stirred up the mosquitoes. James reached into his pocket for the quinine tables and took one, just in case. Finally, Frank tired and dropped the stick. His walk was flat-footed. He looked up to James, his mouth open, his arms limp at his sides. James smiled to the boy, and he rubbed the palm of his hand with his fingertips. Frank grinned. James took him to the shed, and they each sanded a piece of wood.

Tanner staggered out of the house, still carrying the jar of moonshine. James could smell the whisky on Tanner, yet Tanner yelled for more. "Greta, get me a beer!" James sat with him on the front porch. It has been weeks since they'd finished Mr. Lawrence's paint job and James knew that soon Tanner's money and good will would run out.

They sat together on the front porch. "I was fourteen then," Tanner said. "He was maybe eighteen. I called him a goddarn liar. He was big, lots bigger'n me. So when he come at me, I won't about to fight him straight. Just as pretty, I turned around for that can of gasoline, and I flung it straight in his face. Tell you one thing, he was dammed lucky I didn't have matches. I'd lit him for sure."

Greta came out with a bottle of beer for Tanner. She lowered her gaze as James looked at her.

Tanner alternated between drinking the from the moonshine jar and the bottle of beer. "You and the kid, Greta, you don't know how good you got it." To James he added, "That's right, ain't it?" James did not answer, and Tanner laughed. "Tell him where I found you, Greta."

"He ist drunk," Greta said to James. "He does not know what he is saying."

Tanner laughed.

"Greta," said James, "maybe this isn't a good time to talk that way to Buck."

"I will say as I want," Greta said.

Tanner got up, throwing the chair around. "I found her in the barracks under half dozen infantry men. She was all torn up and balling. Hell, could be Frank's one of thems kid, not mine. But she was fawning all over me after I got those men off of her. Begged me to take her to America. Her and her momma. Ain't that right? Here I thought you'd been kidnapped by those knuckleheads and all the while you weren't nothing but a whore."

Greta stood, as if to offer a challenge. "I not whore, Buck."

James covered his ears against the ruckus and begged, "Greta, sit down!"

She didn't sit. She looked her husband in the eye. "You took me to America because of what you did in Frankfurt. Dishonorable discharge!" she spit on the ground. "Why you kill that dog Happy gave you?"

"I told you about that dog, he was sick. Now, don't ask me again."

"Happy dog not sick, Buck. He just a puppy and you know he not sick. You kill him because you like to kill. Wish you were back in war so you could kill more German boys instead of Happy dog."

Tanner slapped her across the face, hard. She fell to the ground. Frank started crying and rocking back and forth. Tanner loomed over Greta. "The dog was sick!"

James didn't move.

Tanner told Frank to "shut yer squalling," then belched loudly and grinned. "Wish old Happy was here now. I had Hap right now, we'd drink some beers, and we'd be cheek and cheek moaning like a couple of front-up kids."

Greta slowly stood and wiped blood from her mouth. She went to Frank and held him in her arms. "You should move in with Happy. Leave me and Frank alone. Everyone better that way."

"Greta. Greta. Take a little sip of beer." Tanner offered her the bottle. "Well, it's all gone. You can have a little sip of my next beer."

"Nicht, danka, I not want something that smell like dirty toilet. I wish I had every dollar you waste on beer."

"So, Greta, and tell me what'd you buy with all that money."

"Something beautiful. Ja, something you could never take away."

Tanner laughed like a donkey. "Nope, Greta. My sweat and my money. You learn that good. I want beer, I'll buy beer. Wish old Hap was here."

Tanner told James, "You been mighty lucky here. 'Cause you're always so easy. Some reason you don't get mad. Most work for me start mouthing me, so I more than not end beating all hell out of them."

Frank started moaning

"I must to put Frank to bed," Greta said.

Tanner told her to bring another beer. She refused, "I must to put Frank to bed then take bath to wash this," she said, indicating the blood on her face.

"I don't give a damn what you do, Greta," said Tanner. "Just get me a beer before you does it."

With Frank in bed and Greta in her bath, Tanner went inside and fell asleep on the floor by the sofa. James went in after him and stretched out on the sofa but he could not sleep. The image of Greta was in James' mind as if she were the only other person living anywhere. He knew that she would not sleep tonight just as he knew that she would come to him.

James sat up, and he looked at the quiet, motionless room, at the window, at the furniture, at the stove. But his mind did not see these things. His mind saw Greta in her bed, her eyes open, her body twitching as she waited. James heard Tanner breathing, but he did not see him in his mind.

A silent, serpentine fear passed through James' body. He needed and he tried to think of other things. He could not. The images in his mind were of their own nature, and he was not able to control them.

When James heard the sound of the door, he sat quietly, and in his mind he saw Greta opening the door as if he were watching her. Greta tiptoed in and sat beside him. She was stiff, proper, formal. "Did you think I would come?" she whispered.

"Yes. I knew you would."

"I waited upstairs for you but you not come so I come here. I want to be with you." She glanced at her husband asleep on the floor. They both knew an earthquake wouldn't wake him.

James allowed his body to rest against the back of the couch. Greta did the same, her arm and shoulder and hip touching James'. She said, "I want to hear you speak. Won't you talk to me?"

Words were naked in James' mind like many naked old men and women standing together, ashamed. He imagined Greta touching him, but he would not tell her the image in his mind, and his will had little strength to push his imagination or to translate his vision into words. James chose among the most inconsequential of words. "I don't know what to say."

She held his hand to her face. "You have power. You help me, Ja? I will never be happy again if you not help me."

James did not want to touch her, and he tried, not strongly, to pull his hand away. But she pressed his hand more firmly to her face. She was trembling.

In James' mind she was an image and a voice and a body which was beside his own body, but, more, she was a vast and bottomless emptiness, a darkness, a sucking pit, a weakness drawing all his strength into itself while it remains weak.

James was passive as Greta turned her back to him, pressed her back against his chest, drew his arm over her shoulder, and pressed his hand to her breast.

She demanded and she begged, "I go with you!" James made a small effort to move his arm. Greta grasped his wrist tightly and pressed his hand harder against her breast.

Tanner shifted in his sleep and James and Greta froze until he settled back into his usual breathing.

"Get dressed," James said. "And get Frank."

"Why?"

James rolled up his sleeve and showed her the bus schedule he had written on his forearm. "The next bus leaves Nabal in forty minutes. You can leave, if you really want, but you must do it now because I am leaving tonight. With or without you."

Greta quietly scurried upstairs.

James' mind was easy darkness. A new awareness, a new energy filled his eyes, to which his body was altogether passive. This was awareness grown from that sucking darkness, from that time of nothing.

There can be only two living ways of life, the pursuit of power and the pursuit of excellence.

Freedom, not innocence, freedom and the pursuit of excellence. All power moving in the direction toward which it was least inclined, toward excellence, because only excellence can answer power. James rested his head on the back of the couch. He raised his eyes, and it seemed he saw two eyes over him, watching him. And, in his mind, he heard a voice which was like a living voice, saying: "All power was made to serve excellence."

Epilogue
Seventeen Years Later, as told by Elizabeth Brewer Williams.

I didn't ask James to return with me to Washington. I spent another six months with Professor Henderson, researching and writing. In the summer of 1954, I met the man who would become my husband. He was a Korean War veteran by the name of Sam Williams. My life proceeded as expected from there: house, children, dog, occasionally a career. I kept in touch with Gloria via letters. She became a mathematician for NASA when it was still called the National Advisory Committee for Aeronautics (NACA). She never married, never had children, and as far as I know, never had a dog. She did buy a house all on her own, which was something for a woman in the 1950's.

Ameele achieved a modicum of fame, as we all know, mostly for her portraits and her philosophy of art. She was attributed with saying, "The artist and the intellectual are as different as a man who was awakened while he was dreaming differs from a man who awakens naturally and doesn't remember his dream," which, of course, was something that James Campbell actually told me after we went to see his play. He must have taken Ameele to see his play, or read it to her, and discussed it with her as well. Now she is credited as being the genius and only I know the truth.

As for James Campbell, he stayed in Philadelphia and died there, as you should have guessed by now. I like to think he found what   he   was   searching   for.

Acknowledgements

I wrote this book in 1975 on a 1927 Underwood typewriter while holding my newborn son. That would not have been possible without the emotional, physical, and financial support of my lifelong soulmate, Carolyn Jones. She has endured my mood swings and tantrums and somehow stayed my best friend for over fifty years.

I would also like to thank my editor, Carolyn O'Neal of 22 August Press. She encouraged me to take my manuscript out of the box under my bed and share it with her, and with the world.

About the Author
Milton Jones is a US Army veteran. He currently lives in Virginia
with his family.

Above photo: Milton Jones in 1967 with his little sister, courtesy
of the author.

i

www.ingramcontent.com/pod-product-compliance
Lightning Source LLC
Chambersburg PA
CBHW022011170626
46808CB00001B/360

* 9 780099 668783 6 *